THE STREET OF THE
FISHING CAT

ALL-NATIONS
PRIZE
NOVEL
COMPETITION

★

INTERNATIONAL · PRIZE WINNER

THE
STREET OF THE
FISHING CAT

BY

JOLÁN FÖLDES

TRANSLATED FROM THE HUNGARIAN
BY ELIZABETH JACOBI

FARRAR & RINEHART
INCORPORATED

NEW YORK   TORONTO

THE STREET OF THE
FISHING CAT

I

IN VIENNA they had to get out of the train and travel a long way by tram from the Ostbahnhof to the Westbahnhof.

Three years ago, during the war, Father had been lying in a Vienna hospital for a fortnight. He had a bullet in the leg, he couldn't move from his bed, and then they transported him home to Hungary; still, he had spent two weeks in Vienna, and now he was explaining everything with the assurance of an expert.

"Vienna," he said to the three children, with a broad gesture taking in the view from the tramcar window. "Take a good look at it: who knows whether we'll ever get back here again. This is a big street . . . I've forgotten the name. . . . Soon we're coming to the Danube. But they've got only a narrow, mingy little Danube here, not as big as ours at home. There, you see!"

The tramcar clattered over the Danube Canal. The children brightened up at the word Danube, at the sight of the gray water of the canal; they knelt on the seat as they used to do at home. Mother worried about the luggage, kept pushing the packages under the seat. Father explained:

"The train for Paris starts from this side. Not before eleven though."

It was 1920; trains were running about like the sheep of a scattered flock that can't find each other. The Barabás family started from Budapest at dawn, and arrived in Vienna early in the afternoon. They spent the afternoon hanging around the station, all except Mrs. Barabás who would not move away from their things, sitting on one of the trunks, quiet, pensive, patient. Then, at about ten o'clock, they were able to get into the long, dark train. The children were already nodding, especially the two little ones; they slept where their mother placed them. Annuska, the twelve-year-old, did not sleep; she sat by the dark window and stared at the dimly lighted station platform with its hurrying crowds. Figures appeared out of the twilight, their faces lit by yellow flashes from the rare lamplight, then were lost in shadow again. In the carriage, the thin wire of a bulb flared up; the two children's round heads moved when the light fell on them. Klári pressed her face closer into her mother's lap, Jani into his father's greatcoat; then they went on sleeping. The bulb also showed the strange woman whom they had found in the carriage. She sat by the window, opposite Annuska, with a child on her arm.

"Get to sleep, Annuska dear," Mrs. Barabás coaxed her elder daughter.

"I'm going to wait till the train starts," Annuska replied stubbornly; and she waited. When the steel lines were sobbing and singing, when every vestige of the moving box was athrob so that even the face

of the woman opposite trembled gently, rhythmically with it, when the winking lantern-rows of
suburban stations had drawn past them, when they
had clattered across bridges and the darkness outside had become dull and monotonous, Annuska
went to sleep. Mrs. Barabás told her husband to
cover the girl up; she dared not move because Klári's
head was in her lap. Then she spoke no more to the
sleepy man. They had discussed the Paris plan for
months; there was nothing more to be argued about
now, when the train was hurrying away with them.
Gyula was industrious, a good worker; he knew
his job thoroughly. Only there was no demand for
his job at home: who wanted furs in a ruined
country? And Mr. Brüll, who'd been home on a
visit a few months ago, said that skilled furriers were
in demand in Paris. The hourly wages were two-fifty
to three francs, and in some places you could work
as much as ten hours a day. But even if it was only
eight hours, that was a lot of money.

Gyula wanted to get away at once, but Mrs.
Barabás could not make up her mind so easily.
Heavens, three children . . . and to sell every humble
treasure of the little flat. Besides, at home, if her
husband couldn't earn a penny, she was able to
help a little. Mrs. Barabás was a trained midwife.

It was hard to make up her mind, but at last she
did. Now the train rushed along with them through
the strange night. They will be in Paris at dawn
after tomorrow. Meanwhile worry is suspended for
a bit; there is no need to go after work, no cooking,

no marketing to do, nothing but to sit still and brood about things.

The bulb grows dim, the tired wire inside glows red, then it fades out. Mrs. Barabás thinks it has been extinguished on purpose, because there's no light due at night. But she wouldn't complain if she knew that the bulb had burnt out. It is night, the threatening night of a strange country; her children —the big man and the three little ones—are asleep; the train rumbles on toward Paris. She sighs a little, settles the coat over Jani, and closes her eyes.

In the morning the sleeping world is roused to motion. Barabás stretches himself and tries to talk to the strange woman. Barabás has fought on the Russian front and declares that the woman is a Pole. She, too, is on her way to France; not to Paris, but to some mine or other where her husband is working. This is as much as Barabás can make out from her talk, and he tells his wife about it. Mrs. Barabás pays no attention. The knife with which she has been cutting bread and cold goose for her son stops in mid-air. The child on the Polish woman's arm has started to whimper. He's quite big, he might be two, or at least a year and a half. And the Polish woman suckles him! The trained midwife is aroused in Mrs. Barabás; she starts arguing with signs and grimaces. The Polish woman smiles foolishly and looks with gentle misgivings at the knife that flashes with Mrs. Barabás's gestures, but she does not remove the child from her breast.

The girls clamor for food. Mrs. Barabás must cease in her efforts to spread culture. It leaves her no peace though; every time the woman suckles her child during the day, she breaks out in rapid and disapproving protest. The Polish woman only smiles sheepishly.

The children push and crowd at the windows. Great mountains, and yet greater mountains, with little white villages between, and flashes of steel-blue lakes. Then the Austrian frontier. They must get out and stand in a queue in front of a wooden hut, as they did yesterday at Királyhida—was it yesterday? They all feel that it was a thousand years ago. They must open packages at the command of the customs officer, and go into the little shed where a toothless old woman fingers Mrs. Barabás and her two daughters from top to toe. Klári is afraid of her.

They may get back into their compartment; the train starts at a foot's pace and soon stops again.

"Buchs, Switzerland," announces Barabás. The Swiss customs people enter, but they don't expect you to get out; they look through the luggage in the train, and they aren't very thorough about it. Barabás finds out from them that the train is stopping for another hour; they have plenty of time to walk about.

Of course, Mrs. Barabás won't leave the things again, but the three children clatter out of the carriage happily and almost fall over each other on the steps. On the platform, big jugs of thick, sweet milk, of cream-topped, deliciously smelling coffee, are for sale. In another moment the three children's noses are deep inside milk jugs. In Budapest that sort of thing is a rare treat these days, and the milk is thin and bluish and watery.

So intent are they on their jugs that the two small ones do not even notice the little girl moving toward them from the direction of the sleeping car. Anna, however, sees her from a corner of her eye. The little girl is about her age, all charm and distinction, a real little lady. Her white dress is uncreased as if it had just been washed and ironed, her shoes are white too, and she has a little beaded bag. She carries herself straight, holding her head in a way that is light and proud; there is something gay and defiant, graceful and arrogant in her poise. Her hair is fair, with lots of little golden ringlets; perhaps they've been curled by that fine-faced, distinguished lady who walks beside her and talks to her softly in some unknown language. The little girl's glance skims over the three children and their jugs; then she walks into the restaurant with her mother. If Anna did not feel rich people to be as distant from her as the planets, if she could imagine that their fate might be of any interest to her and linked to her own by some common bond, or if she were a naughtier, more fidgety or more inquisitive child, or merely if the milk wasn't quite so thick and sweet, she would perhaps try to find out who the fairy child might be. If she could speak German, she might ask the gold-buttoned conductor and find out from him that the little girl is the daughter of an Italian cabinet minister. She has been in Vienna with her mother, and is on her way to Geneva now.

Perhaps she would also find out that the little

girl's name is Pia Monica, and that her father's name is often mentioned in the newspapers. But Anna is interested only in her milk now, she has forgotten all about the little girl, and the little girl about her.

The hour is past, the train starts off. The children gallop from the compartment window to the corridor and back again. They don't know what they should look at first. They call each other and Father in loud and strident tones, and Mother can just manage to pull in her feet far enough so they shouldn't stumble over them. Yet it's only mountains they can see, mountains all the time. A mountain—what a simple word to say; one thinks of something high and peaked and pointed, and how this simple conception fades out when the mystic and brotherly world of stone and snow and pine is opened up before one. Stone is stone, primeval and inhuman, unalterable material; snow comes from above, in tiny, floating flakes from heaven, and is turned into unapproachable purity; a pine is a plant, it has roots and many precisely placed prickles—and stone, snow and pine together are miracle and beauty. There are such mysterious unions: sea and cloud, sky and wheatfield, sunshine and crimson flowers, and man has been endeavoring for thousands of years to approach and absorb their secret. On canvas and on paper, with words and with music, men have been attempting it; the three children try to do it simply with their eyes, and the result is more or less the same: sweet, tormented, agitated fatigue.

Jani and Klári cuddle up on the seats of the carriage; Klári falls asleep muttering to herself with little birdlike noises. It's as though she were arguing with someone. Perhaps she's arguing that it isn't fair, isn't just, to take a small child out into the strange night, into an alien world, into the solitude of snowy peaks, to hurl miracles and journeys and oppressive, suffocating beauty at her like this. Klári is seven; so the woman she is going to be is already complete within her, warlike and swaggering, scenting injustice and demanding her rights everywhere, always ready to fight and protest, a stubborn little heroine.

Jani is nine. If we let our imagination run riot, we could discover in him the fundamental inclinations of his future profession. For Jani, worn out and half asleep, is worrying about the boring of tunnels and the blowing up of caves: were we to judge lightly, we might triumphantly point out the technician of the future. However, robbers escape and hide in Jani's tunnels and caves, and the secret flying field that he has just built, in his thoughts, on a hidden plateau between high peaks serves the wicked aims of a master kidnaper. We do not pretend that Jani identifies himself entirely with the robber chief, and is himself seated in the plane that shoots forth for loot. Undeniably, however, the great chief bears a slight resemblance to him. His sleep-numbed brain is now busy with cutting a bridle path in the forest and, simultaneously, the gangsters have been transformed into Red Indians . . . no, he has finally decided that the dynamited cave should be the lair of a famous master spy, whose plane, ready for departure, is waiting for the king's orders. . . . War!

the tidings come, and the master spy flies away into enemy land to spy out its secrets and help the great king win the war. Jani quickly flings a bomb upon the capital, just for his private pleasure since flinging bombs does not belong to a spy's duties, then he goes to sleep.

Anna has not gone into the compartment. She is crouching in the corridor—crouching, because that makes her able to see higher up, right to the mountaintops; crouching with aching knees and a stiff neck, her eyes full of tears at the sight of the sparkling snow. The little girl's heart is aching, her breath comes and goes in spasms. She looks up to the heights, looks at the straight pines, at the white glow of the snow—at this hard and infallible world that needs no help. It is all so perfect, so lonely, so distant. Majesty. The little girl cowers on the dirty floor of the corridor and does not know that this is what she will seek all her life, this silence, this haughty grandeur, this majesty. She will probe her own soul for it, hunger for it in alien souls, unconsciously thirst for it as long as she lives.

II

RUE DU CHAT-QUI-PÊCHE ... the Street of the Fishing Cat. It seems mockery to call it a street, for it is only two paces wide, and no more than thirty paces long, but in Paris there are such improbable streets, short as a rabbit's tail, not only in the suburbs, but in the center of town near busy thoroughfares. The Street of the Fishing Cat juts out onto the Seine, connecting the embankment—Quai Saint-Michel—with the small but lively Rue de la Huchette. If you come out to the embankment, there are the two blunt towers and the grinning monsters of Notre-Dame on your right and the side wall of the police headquarters building opposite. That goes to show that the street is in a decent, honest neighborhood, in the heart of the city.

Of course, one couldn't dream of a pavement or a drive in a street two paces wide; there are merely six or eight worn cobblestones in a row, from house to house. At both ends of the street two iron poles have been rammed down to show that no driving is allowed—but that is pure impudence. There is no cart narrow enough to squeeze into the lane, even if the poles weren't in the way.

Two rows, of four houses each, but those at both
ends have their entrance either from the embankment or from the Rue de la Huchette, so all that is
left is two houses on each side . . . Are they old? No
one can tell. They are ageless houses, they might
have five hundred years behind them or merely fifty.
Their gateways are improbably narrow, improbably
dark. Wooden stairs wind upward into a pitch-
black void. The void presently turns out to be a
story, with another pitch-black void yawning beyond
. . . four stories to each house. People's washing hangs
in the windows.

The Street of the Fishing Cat. When Anna was
young, she often wove fancies about its name. Before
going to sleep she would conjure up a picture behind
her closed eyelids, play with it, ornament it. An old,
fat tomcat, with a big mustache like those of the
other anglers who sit at two paces from each other
on the square stones of the Seine banks, their legs
hanging down and reflected in the river. There the
old tomcat sits, with his big mustache and a pair of
spectacles on his nose, a cap on his head, holding
the rod gravely and dipping the line into the water.

Anna was not afraid of the tomcat—she was a big
girl of twelve, she only thought about him a good
deal. When had he lived, when had he stalked along
the street which bore his name? Sometimes he walked
with the fishing rod over his shoulder, then again he
would carry it under his arm. When had he lived . . .
or was he still alive? Anna would have liked to see
him and to ask the old men in the street whether
they had ever met him. She never asked because she

was not on friendly enough terms with them; they were gruff, grumbly old men. She asked no one, but at night, before going to sleep, she thought of the cat who went fishing, and somehow this was the first friendly, homelike vision in the alarming life of the strange city. One could understand the cat far better than the people who talked rapidly and made faces and were different and funny. A cat was a cat here too.

At that time they were not yet living in the Street of the Fishing Cat, but in the little hotel of the Rue de la Huchette. Their window, however, looked out straight upon the entrance of the little lane, and when they ran down to the river or returned from their shy wanderings into the city they had to cross it.

It was Uncle Bardichinov who translated the name of the street for them. He was their first acquaintance in Paris; or, to be precise, the second. But Uncle Liiv, the very first, had preceded him by only a few moments. What had happened was that Klári had tumbled on the stairs and was howling, and Uncle Liiv, whose room opened from the staircase, rushed out and helped her to get up. Anna ran out too when she heard the infernal noise, and she and the strange uncle together tried to comfort Klári. When the little girl's sobs had subsided to quiet sniffles, the gentleman asked her kindly and in French:

"What's your name?"

Klári stared furiously and with contempt, then snapped at him in Hungarian:

"Speak decently to me! I don't understand!"

Anna was shocked. The gentleman knew no Hungarian, but the expression on Klári's face was clear enough.

When Anna was shocked her feelings rarely remained platonic. This time she took hold of the little girl's shoulders and shook them until she had no breath left.

"You horrible child! Is that the way to answer when you're asked a polite question?"

Uncle Liiv stood helpless in the midst of the family tempest. He was fond of all children, passionately and heartbrokenly fond, for his own blue-eyed, black-haired little darling had died during the flight. Uncle Liiv was a Lithuanian and a socialist, and for a short time after the war it seemed as though Uncle Liiv and his friends were going to arrange things in the way they considered best. Uncle Liiv, professor of mathematics, was the chief dictator of food supplies for a few days—they said he could add up accounts, so it was the right kind of job for him. Then they had to flee, for the counterrevolutionaries were after Uncle Liiv, and that was when his little girl and his wife died—it was impossible to tell which one of them caught typhoid fever from the other. And now Uncle Liiv was hanging around in Paris and didn't know what to do with his lonely life. He was fond of all children and he would have liked to make friends with Klári, but the little girl dumbly suffered herself to be shaken, and glared at the gentleman with unaltered fury. Suddenly, however, someone caught hold of Anna's arm from behind.

"My dear young lady! Whatever has this charming child done that makes sisterly chastisement appear necessary?"

Anna started at the sound of this long, smooth speech. She understood a few words of French by now, but this polished sentence might have been Chinese for aught she knew. In her astonishment she loosened her hold on Klári, who slipped into their room like a rabbit. And there the three remained, the Lithuanian professor, the Russian banker and the little Hungarian girl. Anna felt that she ought to make up for deficiencies in Klári's manners, so she dared not move.

Uncle Liiv recounted the preceding events. Anna could understand him, for Uncle Liiv's French was far from perfect.

"The little girl had a fall on the stairs and I picked her up. Then I asked her name and that made her angry."

"And was that why the dear young lady punished her? I see, I quite see. Please accept my humble apology, mademoiselle, for interfering in a purely family affair."

This was Chinese again. All that Anna understood was that the nice old gentleman with a white goatee called her mademoiselle, and she thoroughly approved of that. So she smiled at him and said, "Merci bien," although she had no notion what she was thanking him for. That was how the friendship started; for that evening, when Barabás went down to the bar of the little hotel, Uncle Bardichinov spoke to him. In enthusiastic and complicated sentences he praised the two girls with whom he had been happy enough to get acquainted and asked for permission to converse with them occasionally, as it might be of advantage to them to obtain some exercise in the French language.

Barabás muttered something rather doubtfully; he thought that the loquacious, goat-bearded gentleman was offering to give lessons to his daughters, a thing for which he had no money at present. Had Uncle Bardichinov guessed the trend of his thoughts, he would have protested indignantly. For the year was 1920, Russian refugees still got fairly adequate support, and they imagined that their exile would last only a few months longer at the most. It would not have entered Bardichinov's head to accept money from the workman. It was boredom, solitude and simple goodwill that attracted him toward the children, and it was mere chance that later Bardichinov's sole means of support developed out of these few language lessons—one of those melancholy accidents of fate. For, when the funds of international support had run dry and the vision of a happy return faded into ever-hazier distance, Bardichinov gave French lessons to the foreign workmen who came to Paris. Jani distributed his little advertisements, offering French lessons at a moderate cost, in the Hungarian, Italian, Czech and Greek restaurants . . . but that was not until years later. Bardichinov felt that it was thousands of years later.

Now in a friendly manner, he just took the glass of beer which the barman had poured out for Barabás and carried it over to the table at which he was sitting with Uncle Liiv.

"Come, cher monsieur, give us the pleasure of your company at our table. After all, we are neighbors. May I present my friend Liiv—I might as well say my enemy, my dearest enemy. We were in the midst of a discussion—a discussion analyzing the trend of human development. Would not Monsieur care to give us the benefit of his opinion?"

Barabás sat down. He had been startled for a moment when the Russian got hold of his beer, thinking he was going to drink it. But Bardichinov, with a charming gesture, placed the glass before him and even drew back the chair for him to sit down. He was exactly like a very distinguished old waiter now.

To talk to strangers over a drink in a tavern is an ancient and venerable custom the world over. And they were neighbors after all. Besides, Barabás had a curiosity for life; he had always been a flexible-brained, reflective sort of man—he wouldn't be here today if he weren't. He would never have got as far as Budapest, and certainly not to Paris, in those days when he was newly married. His distrust appeased, he gulped down his beer and replied:

"I don't think I can say much—my French is very bad." He did not speak fluently, but the other two understood. Uncle Liiv nodded sympathetically, Bardichinov protested.

"Courage, my dear friend, do not exaggerate the difficulties. Learning languages is essentially a matter of self-confidence. And the chivalrous Hungarian nation, famous for its cavalierly courage . . ."

Barabás smiled. Bardichinov had used the word

chivalrous—chevaleresque—before, when he had
been leaning on the bar. Barabás enjoys the praise
bestowed upon his country, particularly since the
goat-bearded little man is the first who seems to have
a notion about what and where Hungary is. The
French, when he tells them that he is a Hungarian,
look at him askance:

"Did you fight with us or with the boches?"

They don't even know that Hungary was an
enemy country, that they had fought on the other
side.

"That's a good thing," the shoemaker from Sza-
badka, who lived in the Rue Monsieur-le-Prince,
had explained to Barabás. "You must say we've
fought with them; then their faces clear up and they
get as friendly as anything. I'm well out of it. I've
got a Jugoslav passport, and they like the Jugoslavs."

Barabás had shaken his head gravely. He wouldn't
say he'd been fighting on their side. There might
be an intelligent person among them who knew
France's former enemies, and then he'd be caught
lying. Barabás told the truth, and thereupon people's
faces turned grim. They got rude, deprecating, disagreeable. That is why Bardichinov's praise was
pleasant . . . but chivalrous? Barabás considers himself a good workman, an honest sensible man, but
he doesn't feel that he has any great claims on chiv-
alry. The sense of the word is rather dim too, but
undoubtedly "chevaleresque" has something to do
with horses, although no fighting on horseback was
done in the war. Never mind, Bardichinov had said
it with great approval, although he, too, had been an

enemy. The word rises out of Barabás's reflections. He remembers just having heard it, and points to Liiv:

"Why an enemy?"

"Oh—" Bardichinov stretches out his arms with a wide gesture—"that is what he should be, should he not? He is a socialist, I am a capitalist . . . at least, I was. A banker. Do you want me to tell you about all I possessed—houses, an estate, a car? I will not speak of them—it would sound like the recollections of an aged prima donna. And I have not lost them forever. A few months more—a year at the most." He raises his glass. "Let us drink, my friends! To the pleasure of receiving you as my guests in my palace in Petrograd a year hence."

Liiv, angular, awkward, with his high forehead, reaches for his glass wearily. Bardichinov grows depressed.

"At present the Office of Public Sanitation resides in my Petrograd house. I am told that this office of public cleanliness is so unutterably filthy that it will take years to clear away the dirt."

A gesture from Liiv.

"I beg your pardon, my honored friend, but this does not seem likely. The Office of Public Sanitation is obviously in possession of the means . . ."

Bardichinov interrupts him, turning to Barabás with a sweeping gesture.

"There, you see? He is stubborn, like all socialists, arguing about the most undeniable facts. Never mind. The red brigands are destroying each other, Denikin and Kolchak are advancing triumphantly

. . . a year hence we shall drink our beer at home, in my house."

Liiv reaches for his glass mechanically, accustomed on such occasions to drink to the realization of this dream. Bardichinov affectionately places his hand on Liiv's.

"I am more fortunate than my friend Liiv inasmuch as I have not been bereaved of anyone closely belonging to me. I am a bachelor. He, poor fellow—Show our Hungarian friend the photograph, Liiv."

Uncle Liiv grows crimson and so does Barabás. They are both more reticent than the charming and loquacious Russian. Liiv possesses one single photograph which he has once shown to Bardichinov on an overcast and unhappy night. Now he looks at the Hungarian workman, who turns his flaming face away. They are in Paris, at a distance of thousands of miles from the double grave, thousands of miles from everything that had been their life, their country, their home. Liiv pulls out his pocketbook and hands the Hungarian man the picture.

A dark-haired woman, a dark-haired, smiling, five-year-old little girl. And Professor Liiv, with his shirt open at the neck, his back against a tree trunk, with the sunlight filtering through the leaves, lighting up his face. Bardichinov says:

"Men who shared *my* convictions sent them to their death. Men who shared *his* convictions robbed me of all I had. Now here we are, vagabonds both, and sometimes we argue about which of us has been ruined for the sake of better ideals."

Liiv puts away the photograph and looks up.

"I have not been ruined for the sake of an ideal. Capitalism has no ideals. Capitalism, in the interests of self-support and natural expansion . . ."

Barabás listens amazed and does not understand. He does not understand the words, and still less the fact that Liiv is now lecturing dryly, with unmoved calm, although he stumbled over his French words before. How could he know that the professor is now launched on his job, the ever-identical lingo which he has learnt out of innumerable French books and practiced in the course of lengthy disputes? How could he know that the terms of sociology are just as unchanging as those of the furrier's trade, which he, too, had already learned from his colleagues at the workshop? Sociology and the furrier's trade—no, Barabás would never think of connecting the two. He sits and listens to the discussion that grows increasingly heated, but he does not understand it, and is not interested. Enemies, he thinks, vagabonds both. The photograph was life, the palace at Petrograd was life, and they are lost. Now they argue about socialism and capitalism. Barabás sighs, swallows the last drops of the beer that has grown lukewarm, and runs upstairs to the little room on the third floor, where Klári is energetically boxing Jani, because Jani has allegedly kicked her, against which accusation Jani protests, howling, and Anna, stopping her ears, yells for silence, while Mrs. Barabás ponders how she could possibly slap three children simultaneously with only two hands.

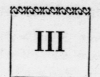

III

Uncle BARDICHINOV holds Klári by one hand, and Anna holds her by the other on their way to school. At all other times Klári would protest against such double guardianship, she would announce with a strident declaration of independence that she is a grown-up and self-reliant person; but now she wanders along tamed, firmly clutching both hands. Klári is not afraid of school. A year ago, when her mother first took her to the board school in Hernád Street, she looked around the classroom with supercilious and condescending calm, benevolently allowed teacher to stroke her hair and show her to her seat, and then waited with polite indifference to see what they would all do to amuse her. As time went on she felt still more at home, she bragged and fought, spoke back to teacher, grabbed rich Magda Marer's lunch and was the first to write on the blackboard with nice round letters, the legend of the cat on the mat, and later the story of the sheep and the wolf. Her little book was always full of good marks, except under the heading "Conduct," where teacher sometimes wrote melancholy remarks, such as: "She always wants to have the last word."

This time, however, Klári wanders along slightly dejected, the outward sign of which is the defiant tilt of her little chin. After all, a French school is different. She enters the classroom in a warlike and malignant mood, is vexed with Uncle Bardichinov who, hat in hand, explains something at great length to teacher, and she stares at the other children with hostility. Teacher calls one of the little girls, the gentlest, friendliest, pleasantest-looking one.

"Her name is Claire, too." She points to the little Hungarian girl. "Make her sit next to you, and help her in everything. Try to make her feel at home. Ginette, give up your seat to the strange little girl and go and sit by Francine."

French Claire smiles at Hungarian Claire, and puts an arm round her shoulder. She gives her a gentle shove to direct her toward the desk from which Ginette is about to remove her things. Klári, with flashing eyes, turns to Claire:

"Don't push!"

Claire looks startled. Ginette laughs:

"Take care or she'll bite you! You've got a little wild beast instead of me!"

Something dreadful happens. Klári turns on her heel, and, in the presence of the entire class, of teacher, Anna and Uncle Bardichinov, she hits Ginette a blow on the chest. The little French girl's things are scattered, but her hands are freed, and she hits back with lightning rapidity. Gentle Claire shrieks and grabs at the falling pencils, Klári, retreating, steps on her hand, Claire howls, Klári and Ginette are at each other again, energetic Maryse comes to Ginette's aid, wise Jeanne tries to separate them, the class yells, the ink is upset. Teacher and Anna reach the fighting group at the same moment, Anna's interference being more efficacious, since teacher gabbles fast and in alarm, while Anna clutches Klári's hair. Gradually peace is restored. Claire still sobs, Klári sniffles, Ginette grumbles, Uncle Bardichinov apologizes eloquently, and teacher looks at her new protégée with faint misgivings.

Uncle Bardichinov and Anna back out and Klári remains. The children henceforward call her "sauvage," wild beast, or cannibal; nevertheless—children are funny that way—her fighting has secured for her a sort of citizenship, the freedom of the school. They know that Klári is a little girl like they are, she can put out her tongue just like they do, she can howl and shout with the best of them. Anna is going to give her a thorough hiding in the afternoon, but that is purely to ease her own pedagogical conscience and has no effect whatever. Klári will remain exacting and impudent and fight till she obtains a distinguished place for herself in the miniature French society which respects courage and flamboyant self-assertion.

Jani's first schoolday is less rough but more bitter. He, too, trots along the Rue Dante between Anna and Uncle Bardichinov, anguish latent within him, but it makes him hang his head instead of throwing it back in Klári's bellicose manner. His thoughts are simple and sane. Last year, at school, they had the geography of the county of Pest; the children here surely had had the county of Paris. That would make trouble. One ought to get hold of their last year's geography book and study it with Uncle Bardichinov. Uncle Bardichinov, however, says he is not to worry for the present, teacher will tell him if he must read up anything. Still, Jani is worrying. Last year he was top boy in class 3/13 in Hernád Street—or shall we say almost top boy, because, unfortunately, there was trouble over the singing. Jani loves to sing, but he has no ear. He sings with closed eyes, in blessed and self-effacing oblivion, but hopelessly out of tune. Never mind, everybody was very fond of him in Hernád Street. There was not even any trouble over his conduct. Of course, he was wild and fought like the others, but within the usual limits. He did not go in for boxing—which teacher abhorred because it made the children's noses bleed —only for wrestling. Catch-as-catch-can. That was permissible.

They enter the classroom and Jani whips off his cap. Teacher receives him kindly, recommends him to the friendship of his future companions, takes him by the hand and conducts him to his desk. Uncle Bardichinov and Anna depart, relieved; Jani will be all right, Jani is bright and sensible, not a wildcat like Klári. They stop for a moment in the passage, Uncle Bardichinov puts on his hat; no alarming sounds are to be heard from inside.

Nothing alarming does happen. Jani sits in his class, the others glance at him surreptitiously, the lesson proceeds peacefully. Teacher explains what they are going to learn this year. Then the lesson is over, the children crowd into the passage; Jani stands alone, leaning against the wall. A little group approaches him suddenly. One boy steps forward, the others crowd behind.

"Why aren't you black?" the spokesman demands with energy.

Jani starts.

"What do you mean?"

"Why aren't you black? All niggers are black."

Jani blushes to the top of his square peasant skull.

"I'm not a nigger."

The spokesman turns to his companions.

"He says he's not a nigger." He examines Jani again suspiciously. "Nothing but niggers live in Africa."

"I don't come from Africa. I come from Hungary."

"He says he comes from Hungary," the spokesman communicates to his followers.

"Isn't that Africa?" one of the boys asks, amazed.

"Of course not, it's America!" another declares.

"No, Australia!" The little group starts quarreling.

Jani tries to make himself heard, to recall their attention.

"Let me tell you! I know! It's where I live. Hungary, Europe!"

"Europe?" One of the boys stares at him incredulously. "Europe's here . . ."

"Last year we had a Zulu boy in class," another explains. "But he was black all right."

And then suddenly they all run away because

another group is shouting to them. One of the boys is showing them something; Jani cranes his neck but can't see what it is. He is left alone. He takes two faltering steps to follow the others, then he leans against the wall again. His eyes are burning, and he feels funny when he tries to swallow. He is not crying. He is just craning his neck to hide his grief, pretending to be interested in the thing the other boys are looking at, but he isn't interested at all. He isn't interested in anything. He would like to go home, to hide, to go to sleep, never to wake up.

Uncle Bardichinov and Anna are on their way home along the embankment; they turn into the Street of the Fishing Cat.

"And you?" Uncle Bardichinov asks suddenly. "Don't you want to study?"

Anna shrugs her shoulders.

"I don't know." Anna was never very good at school, like the two little ones. She wasn't bad either, only middling. She'd had four years at board school and two at grammar school, and now she can't go on. For the present she does not even know whether she minds. She feels the dumb anguish that oppresses Jani and Klári and is glad to escape it. On the other hand, one sometimes dreams of studying and being a great lady one day. "I must cook and clean," she replies uncertainly.

Uncle Bardichinov nods and does not insist. He has taken upon himself a share in the little Hungarian family's fortune, for he has no share in any other family's. He would like to play providence for them, start them off on the road to success and triumph, that one day they may say: "Yes, old Bardichinov, the banker . . . If it hadn't been for him . . ." He couldn't tell exactly what sort of success and triumph he has in mind. So he teaches them French and takes them to school.

At present he ponders what he could do for Anna. Not much. She must cook and clean, because her mother is working too. Barabás has got a job; he got work at once as Mr. Brüll had predicted, but the part of the prophecy referring to the wages hadn't quite come true. There had been no mistake about it: the French furriers get two-fifty or three francs an hour, but people take advantage of the Hungarian workman, the foreigner. He does the same kind of fine work that the others do, but he is paid only one-fifty; they say his not speaking the language properly gives a lot of trouble, and the French way of manipulating furs is different, he has to learn that first. It isn't true, but what can one do?

Thus it comes to pass that Mrs. Barabás also has to look for work. Of course, she cannot practice midwifery; it would be too difficult and complicated in this foreign country whose language she does not understand very well and where they might insist upon her passing an examination. Mrs. Barabás had, in fact, already given up midwifery at home in Budapest; she had only practiced in Mezötur when she was a young woman. She is not like her husband. He will venture upon anything, undertake almost anything. Funny—Barabás was just a young fellow from the country; he began to learn his trade with a village furrier in Kenderes, yet it was he who wanted to go to Budapest at all costs, even Mezötur oppressed him. Mrs. Barabás was a tradesman's daughter, not a peasant girl; she came from a small town, not from the village—yet she would gladly have remained in Mezötur, her native town. But Barabás yearned for Budapest, and, wonder of wonders: on the very day of their arrival he walked along the streets of the metropolis as if he had never lived anywhere else. His wife remained provincial even in Budapest—there are such eternally provincial people. The metropolis terrified her; she dared not even practice her profession. As if children in the big city would come to world differently. They were at that time, however, hardly in need of it, Barabás made enough money; then, too, one child came after the other—the two little ones were born in Budapest—in short, Mrs. Barabás had given up her practice as a trained midwife ten years ago.

Now she must earn money. What can a poor man's wife, the world over, do when she stands face to face with this necessity? Oh, there is a profession—more international than soldiering and more ancient than fire kindling; the service of another, friendlier element—washing. The setting is familiar and everlasting. Water gushes, white mist and the vapors of boiling soap are in the air, linen rises in blisters from the caldron. The setting is everlasting and the properties immutable: trough and lather, caldron and brush, and a woman's two arms, naked to the elbow, soaked and softened and pitted. The tips of their fingers are honeycombed, the water sucks them and wrinkles them, pearls of sweat glisten on their foreheads. No troupe of chorus girls can be so accurately drilled as these women bending over the trough: from Bombay to Montreal, from the equator to the poles, they wring and rub and rinse and blue and hang other people's linen with the selfsame motions.

An ancient and honorable profession, with its own traditions and ethics. Chlorine should not be used. Soda should not be used either, but it may pass. It is a disgrace to employ a brush, yet it is useful. There are many other laws and interdictions, known only to members of the caste, to the soldiers of that international army of women, mysteriously handed down by word of mouth from mother to daughter. Common secrets and common tricks in the midst of the moistly circulating white steam, and a common lot beneath the blue cotton overalls with upturned sleeves.

Mrs. Barabás works in a laundry near by, at the corner of the Rue de la Huchette and the Street of the Fishing Cat. She leaves home early, earlier even than her husband and the children who go to school. Anna provides breakfast for the family, Anna drives and worries obstinate Klári, Anna supervises Jani's scantily washed ears. She does up Father's lunch in a parcel, prepares the children's. Lunch? Mrs. Barabás has not yet recovered from her indignation and shock. On the third schoolday both children confronted her and unanimously claimed the "quart de rouge," a quarter liter of red wine, the regular and indispensable constituent of a French child's "ten-o'clock lunch." Mrs. Barabás spluttered and gasped. In her mind's eye rose the vision of well-known posters in her home country: "Alcohol kills, alcohol stupefies, alcohol ruins you . . ." Mrs. Barabás boxed the children's ears, wept and lamented, abused school, country, government, but her husband only laughed:

"If it doesn't hurt the French children it won't kill ours either."

Klári, to everybody's astonishment, took the box on the ear silently. She sat down coolly:

"All right. It's all the same to me. I get my share from the girls. They all give me some to drink; they pity us so much because we are so very poor and cannot even take wine to school. I had at least half a liter today."

"Same here," nodded Jani. "They are sorry for me too."

Mrs. Barabás stared at them, aghast.

"Breathe on me," she ordered Klári.

Klári breathed on her; Jani breathed too. Barabás roared with laughter. The two children smelt unmistakably of wine. Mrs. Barabás did not speak a word to any of her family that day, and sometimes there were tears in her eyes. "They are ruining my children," she muttered in despair. But next morning she gave Anna money for half a liter of red wine, to be duly halved between the two children.

"Be sure to get the lightest," she explained. "Perhaps you could get three deciliters only and mix it with water. I only let it pass because I don't want them to be sneered at for being poor, and to be made drunk out of sheer pity."

Since then a little bottle dangles from Klári's and

Jani's satchels, just as from their schoolfellows'. Anna does not mix water with it, not because she is a convinced alcoholic, but because she has the bottles filled when they go to school, down at the bar where, at that hour, Bardichinov and Uncle Liiv drink their breakfast black coffee. The three children rush in from behind, from the staircase side, noisily and hurriedly, strapping satchels and straightening their caps. Anna gives her order with energy; Klári, if she happens to be in the mood, graciously kisses the two uncles.

"What's going to happen in school today?" Bardichinov inquires.

"Nothing much." Klári waves. "We will just talk and write a little. La pomme, la femme . . . Do give me a drop of black coffee, Uncle Liiv."

"You do beg from everybody," scolds Anna, busily tying the full bottles to their satchels. But Uncle Liiv gladly offers Klári a drink from his glass. Uncle Bardichinov meanwhile cross-questions Jani:

"And what are *you* going to do in school?"

"We are going into a big garden to look at the flowers. We shall also go to the market hall one day, where we shall see all sorts of fruit."

"Don't you want some coffee too, Jani?"

"No, thank you," Jani says modestly. He would certainly beg for a puff of the cigar if Anna were not standing behind him.

Anna shoves them toward the door, it is getting late. Once in the street where the school is, the children start running, the satchels bounce on their backs, the wine splashes in the bottles. They merely call a good-bye to Anna, who is behind them, and dash off. Anna peacefully trots behind them until they disappear through the two adjoining school gates. Then she changes her direction, turning toward the other side of the river, to the cheap market of the Saint-Antoine quarter. Anna carries a basket; she goes marketing.

At noon she wanders back to the school again, to fetch the children. In the afternoon she takes them for their walk, to the Luxembourg Gardens or to the other side of the Seine, to the Boulevard de Sébastopol. Toward evening she runs down again to the shops in the neighborhood to buy the things she forgot to get or could not find at the market, or any odd things her mother happens to think of.

Anna spends much of her time on the streets of Paris, and the street is a good educator. By now she understands the idiom of taxi drivers and market women, the jests and curses, the crude and merry, blatant and frank life of Paris pavements. She stands about in front of the carts laden with vegetables and flowers, she admires the tremendous amount of goods displayed in front of shops without anyone watching them, and most of all she admires the open sacks full of snails and mussels. She would love to buy some, but her mother would certainly throw them at her head. In one corner of the Saint-Antoine market place there is an empty space where now and again a singer or a dumbbell acrobat spreads a bit of carpet and entertains the assembled specta-tors. Anna watches the artist and listens to the audience. Their remarks are perhaps not entirely fit for the ears of a twelve-year-old girl, but—is life itself fit for a child, this queerly concocted, iridescent, muddy stream that rolls along highways, trenches and streets and splashes its scum upon the house walls?

Maybe he who stays at home need not step into the filthy flood. But Anna is not protected, not sheltered from every storm. She flounders at random in the stream, sometimes with pleasure, sometimes against her will. When she is contented and proud because she has managed to bargain for the Brussels sprouts down to a price of three sous, she swings her basket gaily, and with her free left hand now and then punches the horn of a vacant taxi parked by the sidewalk. The taxi drivers do not mind. They crack jokes; one of them has even driven Anna home once with her basket. The policeman in the Rue Saint-Jacques is also a friend of hers. When Anna comes with her basket or with the two children, the policeman stops traffic—not that traffic is so overwhelming, just for fun—and stands at attention while Anna runs across with a laugh. On the Boulevard de Sébastopol, the postman is her great friend. It began when, one day, Anna, agape, watched the postman pin a letter to the back of one of the benches on the pavement. The postman noticed the amazed little girl, and obligingly explained to her that the same old vagabond had been sleeping on this very bench every night for decades, so this is where his mail is delivered.

"No fooling?" Anna says, flabbergasted.

"No fooling!" The postman was not jesting.

But Anna also has less pleasant memories. Market women who cheated her because she could not understand the torrent of their jargon, men who treated her roughly when they found out she was a foreigner. Once her purse disappeared at the market. Whether it got lost or had been stolen she never knew. Anna very much suspected a fair-haired youth with dreamy eyes, who leaned with nonchalant elegance against the wall of a booth. The youth merely smiled and uttered a few indescribably vulgar words in a low voice. Anna did not understand, yet the blood rushed to her face. People laughed maliciously; Anna remonstrated. In the end they very nearly beat her, the foreigner.

Anna fled with burning eyes and wished she was dead. She did not cry—it was not in her nature to cry, and the family needed lunch. She stopped in front of the air vent of the laundry cellar and asked her mother for money. Her mother scolded her. Still Anna did not cry. She bought the victuals in the neighborhood and returned home to cook. She hated the country, the street, all life. The spirit lamp smelt strongly and was rather smutty. She had to kneel down in front of it, because it had been put on a tin plate on the floor, so that it would not burn the table or chairs. Anna chopped some onions, and breathed in the strong smell of the lamp; that made the tears come to her eyes. But she did not cry, she just hated the world.

Toward evening Mrs. Barabás came home. She was a good woman and a good mother, according to her own modest, harassed lights. Her two smaller children were playing down in the Street of the Fishing Cat.

"Don't grieve," Mrs. Barabás told her white-faced, tense-lipped elder daughter.

"I'm not grieving," said Anna obstinately. Suddenly she threw back her head. "I'm not going to the market again."

Her mother looked at her with pity. The child does not know, she is not yet broken in, she still thinks poverty may rebel.

"Everything is much more expensive in the shops," she said quietly.

Anna nodded. She knew. It had only been an attempt to break out of the circle, to defy necessity. Her mother moved nearer to her.

"Did they hurt you?"

Anna turned away and nodded.

"Do you think they don't hurt me?" Mrs. Barabás asked in a low voice. "They always do. Because I don't understand their funny lingo, because I cannot be funny with them, because I was born elsewhere. . . . Look at my hands. They make me do all the rough work. Do you see? This is from sulphuric acid. Before dyeing the clothes we must bleach them. And yesterday they scalded my feet."

Anna stares at her mother and grows very quiet. She has heard her father's outbreaks, for Barabás comes home fuming nearly every night, shaking his fists, swearing at his fellow workers, the chief cutter, the boss—they call him "patron" here. And Klári too. She comes home day by day full of complaints, sometimes marked by scratches. But Mrs. Barabás has never yet complained. If asked, she always gave the same answer:

"They treat me decently. They appreciate my work."

Now she has to call the two children from the window. They knock about in the streets with negro children, with Algerians, with French boys and girls. Anna suddenly remembers that she has never yet heard Jani complaining. Sometimes the boy is rather silent, clenches his teeth, declines to go to the Luxembourg Gardens—that is all. Anna is ashamed, and resigns herself to poverty. On the next day she picks up her basket without a word, takes the children to school and from there proceeds to the market.

And the market welcomes her. The street has forgotten its malice of the day before. Anna knocks a sou or two off the price of spinach, the market woman even gives her full measure. The curly blond commissionnaire gives her a friendly nod, maybe he is bowing to the courage which prompted the little girl to venture back here in spite of mockery and humiliations. In a corner of the market a man and girl, clad in sparkling nakedness, display their art to the crowd. The girl climbs upon the man's shoulders, grasps his outstretched hand and swings high up into the air. The muscles on his arms bulge, the girl balances, her head down, her body taut, the audience admires and criticizes. Anna makes a getaway before the little boy-assistant reaches her with his cap held out; contentedly she wanders homeward. Her friend the taxi driver calls out to her

from afar: he has just been ordered to the Boulevard
Saint-Germain; if she hurries, he might run along
the Rue de la Huchette and give her and her basket
a lift.

Thus Anna and the street jog along, sometimes in
hostility, again on friendly terms. In winter there
are little coke stoves on the unrailed terraces of the
cafés; Anna can warm her fingers when they have
grown stiff from carrying the basket. In summer
heat, in the Luxembourg Gardens, the man with
the hose lets her have a shower if she asks for one.
Children in Paris may do anything.

It would be too much to say that Anna now loves
the street. She does not love it, but she no longer
fears it. She grows and grows wise in it, she absorbs
useful and not always quite harmless knowledge,
sanity and judgment of human character, and
acquires a sound and somewhat bitter familiarity
with life.

IV

Homesickness? The feeling which grew upon the Barabás family toward the end of the second year could not quite be called that. It was rather a sort of dim uneasiness, discontent, general restiveness.

Yet, on the whole, they were getting along fairly well, and their life grew more ordered as the days went by. Barabás's wages increased, he has pretty nearly caught up with his French fellow workers. Mrs. Barabás works too, and from their double earnings they can live almost in plenty. The first hundred francs have already found their way into the savings bank.

The children have long since ceased to cause them worry. About the middle of the first term Jani came home one day and asked his mother to call on his teacher. Mrs. Barabás gave her husband an anxious glance. Barabás knit his brows.

"What have you been up to, you rascal?"

"Nothing," said Jani with self-assurance. "I can't have been up to anything because teacher patted my cheek when she sent word to Mother. Do you ever pat my cheek when I'm naughty?"

Barabás defers to the argument. But the woman's anxiety is not so easily appeased. She goes out into the passage, knocks at Uncle Bardichinov's door. Would he go along to Jani's school with her to-morrow?

Of course, Uncle Bardichinov will accompany her. Uncle Bardichinov is grateful if they give him something to do . . . As a rule there is nothing for him to do, only to go to the Russian restaurant toward lunchtime. He eats borsch and listens to the news of Denikin and Kolchak's triumphant progress. Then he has a game of chess that lasts until the late afternoon. He knocks down the pawns and bishops of M. l'Attaché Kalinin as if they were soldiers in the Red Army, he discusses the foreign political situation and the legality of Grand Duke Michael's claims to the throne, as well as the promises made by the French government. Then, with Kalinin, he fixes the date of their real revenge on the chess-board, to take place a year hence, but really and truly no later than a year hence, in his palace in Petrograd. Then, at about six o'clock, he saunters home to the Rue de la Huchette. M. Kalinin takes the opposite direction, as he lives on Montmartre. Formerly he was attached to the Stockholm embassy. He was fond of his last station, and now he says one ought to go back to Stockholm, it would be easier to induce the Scandinavian states to intervene. But traveling expenses are high, and money trickles in sparsely from the Emigrants Relief Fund. It is just sufficient to pay the rent of one's modest flat, to feed at the Russian restaurant, to pay for breakfast and supper at home and for a glass of beer in the evenings.

So Uncle Bardichinov readily accompanies Mrs. Barabás to school. Later in the evening, they try to repeat to Barabás what they were told, the one in Hungarian, the other in French. In the end the poor man doesn't know which way to turn.

"She says he can get his meals in school."

"You need only write a petition, my friend. I shall be delighted to draw it up for you. Jani's very kind teacher also offered to do so."

"Some scholarships provide ready money. Anyway, he will have books, pencils, copybooks gratis."

"In the petition one applies for French citizenship for the child and it is granted in every case—the wise population policy of the French government. But don't you believe, my friend, that they force a young man whose judgment is not yet mature into a national community he could not fuse with."

"And she says she has heard that they are pleased with Klári too, so we ought to apply for her as well."

"No, as soon as a young man comes of age, his right to self-determination is unrestrained. He may freely decide whether he wants to keep his transitory French citizenship or wishes to return to his native nationality. As I told you, the political judgment of the government . . ."

"They are given cocoa for breakfast, bread and butter and bananas . . ."

"Silence!" Barabás commands. "I don't understand one word. You are speaking about the children becoming French?"

"Yes, then they need not pay any school fees, nothing."

"You tell me, M. Bardichinov."

M. Bardichinov explains. The whole thing is not so very complicated. He emphasizes the fact that the children by no means lose their Hungarian citizenship when they come of age; when they are twenty-one they may decide for themselves whether they wish to remain French or adopt their old citizenship. There is no risk whatever, whereas the advantage they gain by it is immeasurable: they need never again pay a single sou for school fees; they will get every assistance, and if they are gifted they will be sent on with further scholarships to higher schools.

"And, no doubt my friend, they are gifted. Isn't that the reason why that charming teacher sent for Mrs. Barabás? Isn't that the reason why she is endeavoring to smooth the way for them? Already she told us that the boy will move on into a lower form."

(This is one of the things that Barabás has not been able to grasp from the beginning. School begins with the eleventh form, then comes the tenth, ninth . . . numbers decrease, and the good scholar may even, during the term, move on—backwards.)

Barabás hems and haws and thinks it over. As a rule he is the more sensible and the more adaptable of the two, and Mrs. Barabás is the one who cannot so easily adapt herself to new circumstances. But this time Mrs. Barabás is all for the petition—the teacher has convinced her. But in her husband strange emotions are aroused. To begin with, he hates the idea of his children not remaining Hun-

garians. And then, does the French state think that
he, Barabás, is unable to bring them up without
outside help?

"We don't want charity," he says.

Uncle Bardichinov won't leave it at that. He sings
the praises of the French education policy. How
many cabinet ministers were barefooted farm children whose parents could not possibly have afforded
to send them to school! And Mrs. Barabás enumer-
ates for the third time what the children will have
for breakfast and ten-o'clock lunch, and at midday.
Barabás suddenly brightens, his eyes flash.

"And is it quite sure that they can be Hungarians
again when they are twenty-one?"

"Absolutely."

"All right then." Barabás's features are lighted
by the arch smile of the Hungarian peasant. "Draw
up that petition, M. Bardichinov. We are going to
cheat France."

He has become reconciled to the idea. Yes, let the
foreign state educate his children, let it stuff any
amount of money into them; when they are of age
the children will go home and be good Hungarian
citizens. He chuckles contentedly and Bardichinov
has to go down to the bar with him; he wants to
stand him a drink.

Thus everything seems to turn out for the best, in
the grownups' life as well as the children's. They
have even started a savings account. Then suddenly
there is an outbreak of strange restiveness, an uneasy
sense of agitation; perhaps it is homesickness, after
all.

The disease is contagious. Uncle Bardichinov has caught it, also Uncle Liiv and the Algerian workman who lives in the attic with his invisible wife and six children.

It affects them in different ways, yet the owners of the hotel—M. Gaston and the two women—infallibly recognize the symptoms. They met with the same ailment before the war, when they had Turkish students staying in the hotel, and in wartime, when Belgian refugees were quartered there. They know what it means when Barabás nowadays does not come down to the bar at night, but goes across to the Rue du Levant to talk about happenings at home with the Hungarian carpenter. Bardichinov also goes to a strange café. There he sits at night, with a large group of Russians, and conspires. Liiv stays at home, broods in his room and stares at the wall. The Algerian gets drunk in negro taverns, wobbles up the stairs and beats his wife.

The symptoms vary, but the ailment is identical. M. Gaston and the women know it only too well. The hotel actually belongs to the older woman, Mme. Germaine. She inherited it from her husband, but she could not cope with it alone; the bar especially needed a man in it, so her younger sister, Hélène, with her husband, M. Gaston, came to help. Gaston used to be a good-for-nothing, idle fellow; meek Hélène could do nothing with him, but Mme. Germaine is a determined woman, she makes him work hard. Husband and wife cannot forget for one minute that she is the "patronne." She even keeps an eye on Gaston's conjugal fidelity, and if

Gaston pinches the cheek of some servant girl running to fetch wine—just because he feels it is a part of his job—it is Germaine who makes the row, not Hélène.

Now the three of them discuss this sudden restiveness, this aimless agitation. What really matters is that the bar is deserted every night. The council of three decides, after mature deliberation, that the room of the Barabás family should be scrubbed and Bardichinov's painted.

For the present they will not take any more far-reaching measures. There is no need. If the fidgety ones decide to move out, to another country or to another hotel (sometimes this is the solution), new lodgers will take their place. Nowadays, at the beginning of the twenties, politics are propitious to Paris hotel owners. Victorious revolutions, defeated revolutions. The result is always the same. A smaller or larger group of men takes flight like scattered rabbits. The majority of the rabbits, as a rule, find their way to Paris. Yesterday a Spanish anarchist put up at the hotel, today a Greek refugee from Asia Minor. In Italy, too, something seems to be happening: in the Hotel Quai-Saint-Michel, near by, Italian socialists have taken up quarters.

Gaston's is a political mind, and late at night, when Mme. Germaine is in bed, he is apt to enter into violent arguments with the French guests at the bar. Not with foreigners though, since he considers them politically immature; besides, one never knows when their sensibilities are hurt. Gaston approves of the policy of the firm hand.

"Dictatorship!" he says, his eyes flashing. "People need a strong lead. We Frenchmen get on without it, we are a people used to liberty, we are a nation capable of independent reasoning. But the others . . . cette canaille . . ."

He makes a sweeping and disdainful gesture, and there is no doubt but that the whole of Europe is included in this insulting expression. His mind, however, is capable of subtle distinctions. According to his feelings and convictions Gaston belongs to the extreme right, but it would be a mistake to surmise that he hates the communists most of all. Gaston's real antagonists are the socialists and the lukewarm bourgeois parties.

"I'd rather have communists," he explains to Francis, the son of a neighboring concierge who drinks his vermouth leaning against the bar. "I'd rather have the communists; they at least know what they want. Over there in Germany—Bavaria, I think—when they had the Commune, hotels were crammed with white refugees. Then the socialists came and defeated the communists and everybody went home."

Francis ventures the reply that a government may be good even if it produces no emigrants. "In a decent state there is room for all sorts of convictions. Democracy . . ."

"No," says Gaston severely. "Great statesmen do not put up with opposition. Opposition hampers them in their creative work. Et, vois-tu—" he pokes Francis in the chest—"statesmen begin to realize this. This M. Lenin, for instance, I respect him. For decades he has been living in Paris hotels. And now he has sent us the Russian aristocracy."

"I thought Lenin used to live in Switzerland, not in Paris," Francis modestly interjects.

"In Switzerland?" M. Gaston, taken aback, no longer respects Lenin as much. In Switzerland . . . is that so! Somehow, up till now he had never thought of hotels existing in Switzerland.

"Has the little Russian with the goatee gone?" asks Francis, and points to Bardichinov's forsaken table.

"Oh no. He has just gone crazy and keeps running after his countrymen. I am having his room repainted."

It is still problematic whether Mme. Germaine's willingness to make sacrifices could have herded the scattered flock back into the fold. It never came to sacrifices at all. A bigger event intervened, or a smaller one perhaps—certainly something more simple, more painful, something linked more directly with life. Mrs. Barabás fell ill.

The trouble had actually started weeks ago and Mrs. Barabás had begun wasting away. Husband and children do not notice such changes; for them the face they see every day remains the same. A hand cuts bread at dinnertime, ladles out stew with its golden juice—who would notice if that hand trembles? After dinner Barabás runs across to the Hungarian carpenter, the children beg for an extra half hour of play in the streets, even Anna notices only that her mother goes to bed immediately.

"Will you wash up alone, darling?"

"Certainly." Anna nods. It is nothing much; Mother has been standing all day, no wonder she is tired.

Then, one day, Mrs. Barabás does not get up and when the perplexed family stands around her bed she merely says she is rather run down, she wants to take a day's rest.

"I will not let you go to work again," says Barabás angrily. "We can manage quite well with what I earn."

"We must save," says the woman quietly. "I shall only stay in bed a day."

But when the family disperses, when Barabás has gone to work, the children to school and Anna to the market, she gets up. She dresses with great difficulty, and painfully gropes her way to the corridor. She knocks at Bardichinov's door.

"Dear neighbor, you have always been so kind to us. Would you mind going to a hospital with me? In the laundry they spoke of the Hôtel-Dieu. I think I must have a tumor . . ."

Bardichinov jumps up, and in spite of the woman's remonstrances, he calls a taxi and takes her to the hospital. The examination does not run quite smoothly. When they ask Mrs. Barabás as to her nationality, Bardichinov tells a lie. He says she is Rumanian, hoping they will deal with her more gently. One of the doctor's assistants addresses her in Rumanian, and of course she does not understand him.

"You see?" sneers the assistant. "They are all boches, Hungarians, enemies. In the war they fought

against us. Of course, now they would be pleased to
be taken for Rumanians."

Mrs. Barabás flushes crimson, she feels like jump-
ing down from the high table. Bardichinov makes
excuses, shows his own papers: *he* made the mistake,
he never asked the woman about her nationality,
they are neighbors in the hotel, he took it for granted
that she was a Rumanian. She is a kind, good woman.

"And anyway, she is a woman!" he winds up with
a disarming smile. "A woman and born to suffer.
Who would not respect the enemy's womenfolk?"

Mrs. Barabás is kept in the hospital and, to tell
the truth, they would have kept her there even if
Bardichinov had not pleaded for her, for human in-
tercourse and medical treatment are not the same
thing. Mrs. Barabás will be dealt with harshly, but
she will be treated excellently.

To begin with, she must be operated on; this is the
news that Bardichinov takes home. Anna has meanwhile returned, but she is not at all astonished to
find her mother out. Mother was feeling better, so
she got up and went to work. What could be simpler?
Her face grows white as she listens to Bardichinov.
Barabás only comes home at night, so Bardichinov
does not go to his Russian restaurant, he has lunch
with the three cowed children. After lunch, he takes
them to the hospital. Mrs. Barabás's bed is in a long
ward, the three children nearly stumble in sheer en-
deavor to walk silently. They sit at the bedside,
afraid of the nuns, although the nuns always have a
smile for them as they glide along. Mrs. Barabás
says she is going to be operated on in three days'

time, because there are all sorts of examinations to be made first. Bardichinov is wondering why they kept her there at once if that is the case? Because of the examinations, the woman says, and she sends word to her husband that he must by no means stay away from work on her account. She expects him on Saturday when his afternoon is free. The children say nothing, they look around, their hearts contract.

Barabás does not go to the carpenter after supper, and Bardichinov gives up conspiracy. They settle down in the bar and fetch Uncle Liiv who is sitting in his room staring at the wall. They get acquainted with the Spanish anarchist who saunters about aimlessly, and gladly introduces himself when Bardichinov accosts him with a smile. His name is Alvarez; he was shot at when he crossed the frontier, that is why he wears his right arm in a sling.

"What a regrettable accident!" says Uncle Bardichinov politely, and the Lithuanian professor suppresses a smile. What delightful times we are having in Europe, he thinks; men are shot at on the frontier, and it is just a "regrettable accident," it could easily happen to anyone.

M. Alvarez orders raspberry juice, since M. Alvarez is an antialcoholist and a vegetarian. Barabás watches him respectfully; he always believed anarchists kept bombs in their waistcoat pockets and ate raw human flesh. Alvarez does no such thing, Alvarez is an elderly gentleman with graying temples and a ruddy tan, and he speaks sententiously. Within ten minutes he has imparted the whole of his creed to the company, and the four-year-old discussion, enriched by fresh material for debating, goes on in full swing.

"On what grounds, sir, do you assume that anarchy is the natural state of human society?" Bardichinov puts the rhetorical question. "Even in beings of a lower degree, we can observe the beginnings of social order and organization, sometimes very highly developed. Think of the bees, of ants, sir . . ."

Alvarez replies eagerly and volubly. Liiv smiles wearily. He is the only man in the company who has studied economics; all these others are nothing but schoolboys, greenhorns compared with him. He duly looks down upon them, and listens to the simpleminded debate with friendly condescension. But soon he will no longer be able to put up with this total lack of specialized knowledge, and will take part in the discussion. Not that these people could appreciate or even so much as notice greater authority—not they! Nevertheless, Uncle Liiv *must* speak, rather like a prophet in his own country where no one heeds him, where no one even notices that he does not belong to them. Perhaps only Barabás, the least schooled, the most ignorant of them all, feels that Liiv knows the things he knows in a different way.

But today Barabás pays no attention, he is thinking of the woman lying in the hospital. She did not say one word about being sick, and there it was . . . in three days' time she will be operated on. She has sent him the message that he must not ask for the day off, but he is going to do so nevertheless. It may be just a mere trifle, they do sometimes operate for minor complaints—however, he is going to see her tomorrow.

Having thus settled the matter to his own satisfaction, his attention again returns to the talkers. He listens to Alvarez's flamboyant declarations of liberty, to the cool data of Liiv, to the smooth, comprehensive philosophy of Bardichinov, and he puts a word in modestly but with the self-assurance of an equal.

"To my opinion, gentlemen, M. Alvarez is correct. There is no need for a government. Of course, a certain authority is wanted to stand above the people, but that's what a king is for. Where they have a king, what is the use of all the cabinets? They only suck the people's blood. I vote for M. Alvarez."

M. Alvarez is slightly taken aback, this is not quite what he meant. He enters into a quick and voluble explanation to which Barabás keeps nodding as if every one of the words justified his own. There is no denying that each of these four speaks mostly for his own ears, but this has been the case ever since the world began and political debates were invented.

On the following day Barabás comes home at two and sets out for the hospital with the three children. Anna carries a kilo of oranges. They cross the Seine bridge, and Anna looks down upon the quai where a row of anglers sit at a distance of two steps from one another. She thinks of the fishing cat, not seriously, just in playful fancy, wondering what it would be like if one day the cat were crouching there among the others, his big mustache reflected in the river.

Then they step softly along the passage and silently, cautiously, open the door of the ward. The

nun quickly runs to meet them and with her finger
on her lips leads them to the bedside. They do not
know why cold shudders creep into their hearts, why
there is a sudden hush over all the world.

Then they know. On the bed where Mrs. Barabás
was lying yesterday an unconscious woman lies pros-
trate with a yellow face and deep-sunk eyes. She
seems almost a stranger. Her breath rattles, her lungs
whistle.

"The operation has been very successful," the nun
says comfortingly.

They stare at her uncomprehendingly. Barabás at
last finds his voice.

"She said she would be operated on in three
days . . ."

"Did she say that?" The nun smiles. "Perhaps she
did not want you to be anxious about her. The operation could not be put off, not for a single day; in
fact, it ought to have been done weeks ago."

The nun walks on, the four of them remain standing there. Barabás and Jani are fingering their caps,
Anna her parcel of oranges. Barabás's face twitches,
his lips shape the word "Boriska." It would be difficult to put his thoughts into words. He has a vision
of long past days in Mezötur, sunny Sunday mornings, churchgoings, patches of garden with the scent
of sweet basil. At that time there was a great difference between them: he was a peasant, Boriska a
tradesman's daughter. He was able to marry her
after all, for Boriska's father was not so proud as her
mother. Then came Budapest, the war, the children
—what became of the difference? They have seen

good and bad days, they have had their stormy days
—who has not? But they always belonged to each
other. Now here lies a strange woman, she pants,
her breath rattles and she seems to be no longer of
this world.

The three children stand there mutely. They have
not known Mezötur, except perhaps Anna, but she
was too small to remember. Yet there is something
they have known. It was only two steps from Nefelejts Street to the Eastern Station. They used to loaf
about on the edge of the pavement looking at the
soldiers being carried out on stretchers. There they
had seen such yellow faces, such sunken eyes, such
panting chests. But that was something different.
Those were soldiers, wounded heroes, not quite human, so to speak. Klári silently starts crying.

They stand there for two hours; then Anna puts
down the oranges on the night table and quietly they
go out again. They cross the bridge, they walk along
the Street of the Fishing Cat, they are at home again.
On other days, at this hour, Barabás is at work, Anna
is taking the children for a walk. Today they stay at
home and lounge about in their room and in the
gray passage. Barabás knocks at Uncle Bardichinov's
door, but Bardichinov is still having his game of
chess with Kalinin. He knocks at Liiv's door; Liiv,
however, is out. The Lithuanian professor has hardly
any fellow conspirators, yet he often goes for long,
melancholy walks.

So Barabás loafs about, waiting for the night to
bring him company. He even hurries supper. At
seven they are sitting at the table. Just then Bar-

dichinov arrives. He has come home and wants to hear about Mrs. Barabás. Barabás asks him to stay to supper. When they have swallowed the last mouthful, they go down to the bar, calling for Liiv on their way. Alvarez is already waiting and joins them at once.

M. Gaston meanwhile informs Mme. Germaine that Bardichinov's room need not be painted, but that she had better have the room of the Barabás family scrubbed. Mrs. Barabás will look upon it as a kindness when she comes home from the hospital— women are grateful for such things. Germaine takes a look at the assembled company, her eye catches Alvarez's raspberry juice. She says she is going to think the matter over.

Tonight their number is increased by a new member, although the member is a wayward and unreliable character, or, according to Bardichinov's reproachful criticism, a shirker. The new visitor has also been attracted by Klári, who does not feel like knocking about the streets today but has sneaked into the bar. Her dim object, unadmitted even to herself, is to nestle up to her father's coat sleeve, to borrow strength and warmth from him. An unusual procedure for Klári. But when she steals through the door, a dark man with dreamily soft eyes—the Greek refugee whom few people have seen yet, who just happened to drift here, homeless and brooding— jumps up with a confused, hoarse cry. He seizes Klári, lifts her up in the air, presses her to his face, hugs her and talks to her incoherently.

Pray do not forget that Klári is nine, a self-conscious, grown-up young lady, who even in youthful years could hardly tolerate manifestations of physical tenderness. Any offense to her dignity she avenges with an act of violence. To strangers she is positively rude; Uncle Liiv has tried in vain to win her favor for the last two years. What happens now is not quite clear. Perhaps she is shaken by the afternoon in the hospital, perhaps she feels instinctive sympathy toward this dark man with the weary eyes. Although she blinks in slight alarm, she does not kick, and suffers herself to be petted.

She lets the stranger carry her to her father's table, and she remains in his lap when the others ask him to sit down. Uncle Papadakis breaks into a torrent of words. Feverishly and tremblingly he tells his story, relates how Kondylis raided Asia Minor, describes Kemal's raging guerilla warfare and the night when the Turks massacred his wife and set fire to his house where his three black-eyed little ones were burnt to death. He fled from Kondylis homeward, through the line of Turkish outposts, because news had trickled through that Kemal was taking that direction. He fled, only to find smoldering walls.

"My eldest was as big as this one," and he hugs Klári.

This is history, Liiv thinks, giving Papadakis a jealous look because Klári does not object to sitting on his lap. Klári rests her head on the Greek's shoulder and listens to his words as if he were telling a fairy tale. Fairy tales in Europe in 1922 were like that.

Henceforward Papadakis is a member of the company, although a disorderly, rambling one. Bardichinov sometimes threatens him with his finger—shirking lessons, are you? Once or twice a week he spends an evening in the bar; on the other nights he goes to the Greek restaurant in the Rue du Levant. He talks about the same things in both places: he talks about the horrors of Asia Minor every night, and in the daytime too if he can find an audience. For a whole year he will tell the same story, indignantly and tremblingly, with a shrill break or a catch in his voice. For a year he will tell the story, then one day he will tell it no more. Thenceforward, Papadakis will be a silent man. He will go after his business quietly, look on life's changing pictures with unconcern. He will be rather like Liiv—Liiv in the shape of a Greek merchant.

However, this is far ahead. Papadakis is not yet aware of it. He strokes Klári's hair and begs to be allowed to carry her upstairs when she goes to sleep on his lap. And the company gathers in the bar every night with Papadakis or without him; they discuss anarchism, capitalism, socialism. Barabás takes an afternoon off from the workshop every second day; on the alternate days Bardichinov takes the children to the hospital. Mrs. Barabás's wound takes a long time to heal; weeks, perhaps months, may elapse before she is allowed to leave the hospital. She lies on her bed reflecting upon life; the four men sit in the bar and talk politics.

Germaine decides not to have Bardichinov's room painted. Homesickness has been lulled to sleep.

V

Has homesickness really gone to sleep? Homesickness never goes to sleep. It may subside, grow calm, move down into the lower currents of the soul, but there it ripples and murmurs like an underground stream. Did you ever live near a brook? Did you ever stay in a house where a dynamo is at work? Then you know that your ears get used to the murmur, get used to the house oscillating to the rhythm. You get so hardened to it that in the end you do not hear it at all. You just go on living your everyday life, you do your work, get up and lie down, follow the paltry routine of the day and do not sense the low and inexorable throbbing in your heart. Yet you would start up stunned and amazed if suddenly the murmur were to cease, if the source of the din should run dry.

Such is nostalgia. Barabás only grumbles because the wine here smells of varnish. Mrs. Barabás only complains about money and weights being so difficult to understand—sou and livre, who ever heard of such things? Anna only says it is a nuisance that it is so difficult to get lard, you must go right to the

other end of the Saint-Antoine quarter to get it.
They use nothing but butter and oil here.

Nothing else is said, only once in a while, very
rarely. One day Barabás, sitting at his wife's bedside
in the hospital, tells her that the wife of the Hungarian carpenter wants to leave her husband. The
woman weeps all day long, she says she cannot bear
this life any longer. She is fond of her husband, but
she does not care. She wants to go home to Hungary.

"Couldn't we go home?" asks Mrs. Barabás
timidly. "I have thought about it too. Mrs. Koppány
writes things have improved since we left. Business
is looking up."

"We have not even saved enough for the traveling
expenses," Barabás replies gruffly, but not at all surprised, which proves that he has been considering
the matter himself. "We sold our furniture when we
came away. Go home with three children and empty
hands? And we want to save some money, don't we?"

"We do." His wife nods. "I was just wondering.
But, Gyula dear, we ought to take lodgings. It would
not cost more than the hotel . . . and they let one pay
for the furniture in installments."

It's out. For a long time the thought has obsessed
her. A flat is no remedy against homesickness, still it
is a home. A Hungarian workingwoman in a French
hotel—there is something very pathetic about that.

Barabás sits brooding.

"We will," he says hesitatingly, "in time." He does
not want to contradict the sick woman, yet he is
afraid of taking a flat. To him it would mean settling
down, something definite, resignation. Barabás

would prefer to wander on, he has often thought of
South America lately.

It is the same with the others. Their restlessness
has calmed down, the superficial observer does not
hear the rumbling inside. Only at times some unexpected emotion breaks out from underneath.

Bardichinov tells them that a great friend of his
has arrived in Paris, an Italian ex-cabinet minister.
Bardichinov had met him and his beautiful wife before the war, here in France at the most fashionable
seaside resort, Biarritz. He also remembered their
dear little girl; she was five then, she must be as old
as Anna by now. Since that time his friend had risen
to the rank of cabinet minister—under the bygone
liberal government, of course. Now he had had to
decamp in the face of the victorious fascist revolution. However, he was able to save a small part of
his fortune, and they are living on Montparnasse in
a good hotel.

Liiv is ill-humored today.

"Yes," he nods bitterly. "That is always the way.
The leaders escape and enjoy life in the security of a
foreign country, while the poor people—the tortured
proletariat—stay on and atone for all that the new
government charges up to the old. The proletarian is
tortured, thrown into prison, the leaders succeed in
'saving their fortune.'"

"Is that so?" Bardichinov bends forward, and his
gentle, watery blue eyes flash, a phenomenon Barabás has never witnessed during the three years of
their friendship. "Is that so? Well, I am going to tell
you another story, my friend. I know only one thing

for certain. The proletarians that elected you as their cabinet minister are sitting at home in the cozy corner by the fire, applauding their dictator. Here you are, perishing from hunger and loneliness; the proletarians are feeding on your porridge at home. It is always the elite that must fly, the better men, the ones who matter. They have to tramp the world like stray dogs, while your beloved proletarians stay peacefully at home and cheer every government. Proletarians! Worms, that's what they are!"

Bardichinov wipes his forehead, the others are still. Everybody has been shaken by this outburst. Bardichinov, who has always spoken in smooth phrases, whose tone was paternal superiority itself . . . Bardichinov choking, beside himself, his soul stripped naked.

Even Liiv has nothing to say. At last Barabás begins to speak:

"Maybe this is the case in wealthy countries," he says quietly. "Perhaps in rich countries the proletarians can stay in their cozy corner no matter what change takes place in the government above them. But my country is a poor little country. From *my* country there has been emigration even in times of peace. And it was not the *rich* who had to go and find new homes, you may believe me, gentlemen. It was the poor people who chiefly found their way to America. And it is absolutely indifferent to the poor whether they are driven from their homes by politics or by destitution."

"Spanish peasants emigrate to the Argentine," nods Alvarez. "All this has happened because society's natural distribution, healthy, organic evolution, has been frustrated by artificial direction, by force. Whereas anarchism . . ."

Here we are on the selfsame spot. The debate flows along its old tracks. The subterranean stream which burst forth for a second has ebbed away again. It is once more tamely hidden beneath the smooth sand and round pebbles of the river bed. True, it continues to murmur down there at the bottom of the soul, but the ear grows accustomed to it, no longer takes any notice. Other voices, those of work, of weekdays, of sickness and of money are so much more blatant.

Then Vassily appears, and suddenly everybody feels a shade more at home in this alien world. Even in your own country you would feel more at home with the knowledge that Vassily was near.

As a matter of fact, Vassily has not come alone. Fedor Jarossev-Pelczinski is with him, but Jarossev-Pelczinski has an unheard-of elegance and wears a monocle—of course, only at night. In the daytime he wears blue overalls just like Vassily. Next day they both have jobs, and needless to say it was Vassily who found them both—Vassja, as he is called within twenty-four hours by everybody in the house. This is the name that Anna whispers to herself every night, little Anna who encounters love for the first time.

Vassja and Fedor have not come from Russia recently; Fedor escaped in 1917, and no one knows when Vassja got away. Two years ago they got acquainted in Hamburg; since then they have been living together. Vassja taught Fedor his trade. Fedor used to be an officer in the Guards; Vassja calls himself a mechanic. Anna does not believe a word of it, she is convinced that he must be a grand duke.

Vassja is wonderfully good-looking. Anna could not possibly describe him, certainly not by the modest words of coherent speech. Perhaps by music, or with the rays of the sun, or in rainbow colors. He is so tall, his eyes are so blue, his laughter is so sweet, so good to hear.

Vassja arrives on the day when Mrs. Barabás is allowed to leave the hospital. But she must remain in bed for two or three weeks at least. It is characteristic of Vassja that he knocks at their door on the first evening and brings Mrs. Barabás some strawberries, although it is only May and strawberries are very expensive. Vassja enters, looks about him with a smile:

"I am staying in this hotel too . . . I heard you are ill. Allow me, madame . . . this little gift. I am your neighbor. What was the matter, madame?"

Before Mrs. Barabás can think twice she has told Vassja the whole story of her operation, all about the anesthetic, about the nuns and the woman who had cancer and died in the bed next to hers— everything.

"What you want now, madame, is a thorough rest. We shall take mighty good care that you don't get up, shan't we, my boy?" With his strong arm he pulls Jani to him. "Have you got a radio yet?"

"A radio?" says Jani, astonished. "What is it?"

Vassja tries to explain to him. He explains it in

such a way that not only Barabás, who is a jack of all trades, and Klári, who takes a great interest in such technical matters, but even Anna and Mrs. Barabás can understand.

"We are going to make a radio for sure," he promises Jani. "One gets lovely concerts sometimes from the Eiffel Tower, only we must find out when. It will surely be in the newspapers. I have just arrived, so I am rather out of things."

"Make one for me too," Klári begs.

"We are going to get enough earpieces for everybody," Vassja replies gravely. "And we three are going to make the radio between us. What is your trade, M. Barabás?"

They discuss the furrier's trade with professional understanding.

"And the young lady? Has she got a job yet?"

Anna, the young lady, is terribly ashamed of having no job, of only cooking, sweeping, washing, sewing and not being a blacksmith at the same time.

So there is a kind word and henceforth a little present for everybody when Vassja comes home at night. A cigar for Bardichinov, a newspaper for Alvarez, the picture of a saint for Papadakis, a loaf of bread for Liiv who by now is almost starving. Mrs. Barabás gets a fruit cake, Klári some marbles, Jani new parts for the radio. And Anna? Anna sometimes gets flowers. And yet Anna knows that Vassja does not care for her; at the most he regards her with friendly indifference, just like the others. He does not notice that she is a girl at all, and he would certainly not believe it if he were told that she adores him. He would simply laugh, sweetly, roguishly, as he always does when he sneaks through the door in the evening, quickly puts his presents on the table and runs off with a laugh, glad that his little joke has come off successfully, seeming to say gleefully: you see how I've tricked you.

This is Vassja. He even makes friends with the Bulgarian student who lives in the attic next to the Algerians and whom no one ever sees. The Bulgarian student creeps out of his den once a week, and probably eats only on these occasions too. But Vassja bursts in upon him and drags him away to dine.

Anna's heart is breaking. Vassja cares more for everybody else than for her. Most of all she is jealous of Jani, because Jani is Vassja's most intimate friend. It is evident that Jani is Vassja's favorite, just as evident as the fact that Anna is Bardichinov's, and Klári Papadakis' and Liiv's, although for Liiv there is no hope at all. Vassja and Jani sometimes put their heads together for hours and talk in whispers. Anna once tried to get information from Jani. He put her off with lordly nonchalance:

"Men's affairs, young lady!"

Whether it is the example set by Vassja, or his still more practical assistance, one thing is certain: everybody seems to start moving, everybody grows more lively and active. It is high time too, for aid from relief funds and charity institutions trickles in more thinly every day. More than the rest, the Russians are able to keep alive an interest in their fate; they still get some sort of help, the others are forgotten. Uncle Papadakis is the first to find a job: he presses caps.

Presses caps. It sounds an odd kind of profession. But heaven knows and the hosts of foreigners who have lived in Paris are witness—those foreigners who were not skilled carpenters, locksmiths, furriers or ironmongers, that is to say, those who were students, would-be artists, ex-officials—they are witness that this profession is a special and flourishing trade in Paris, and its absorbing capacity is boundless. Everybody in Paris who did not know a blessed thing took to pressing caps; at least a hundred Hungarian students were at it, and sometimes in their bad dreams, legions of Paris caps marched past them, millions and millions of caps, enough to dam the ocean and sufficient for many generations. If the French citizens did nothing all day long but buy caps, then, perhaps . . . Certainly there are the colonies . . . perhaps the colonies swallow this tremendous amount of caps, maybe the Zulus . . . In short, Uncle Papadakis also took up pressing caps, because he used to import choice kinds of wood from Persia to Europe, and he did not know any other trade. It is not a bad job. On the first two days you scorch about eight or ten caps, the price is deducted from your wages, then you learn how to do it properly.

Bardichinov is not quite so confident now concerning the imminent victory of the White Armies. He has posted a bill on the wall of the bar saying that foreigners may have cheap French lessons here. Bardichinov has an innate knowledge of such things. In the last two years he has given Anna all sorts of lessons, not only French, but geography, history, all the branches of education down to proper table manners. Anna handles a knife and fork like a born lady. Alvarez paints Spanish dancers in lace mantillas on glass, then he goes and hawks them . . .

The general commotion takes hold of Barabás too. He finds a new job, his knowledge of French secures him higher wages.

Things don't go so well with poor Liiv. Liiv is an unlucky person, all thumbs. Vassja advises him to take up bookbinding, that being a proper job for such a learned man. He can say that bookbinding has been his trade in his own country, Lithuania. Never mind if he doesn't know the trade; if the worse comes to the worst, he'll get the sack at the end of the first day, but during that day he will have learnt something. Perhaps it will help so that in his next job they sack him only on the second day. When he has passed through a dozen bookbinding shops he will be an expert at the trade.

Liiv is horrified. He refuses to swindle, he does not want work under false pretenses. Yet starvation is a mighty boss, and Liiv gives in. Faithfully he walks the track that Vassja has foretold. There is just the slight difference, that after each working day it takes him a week to have his wounds attended to. The poor fellow is terribly clumsy, he either gets his knees bruised or his fingers caught in the press. So many days, so many casualties—Anna says it is a miracle he has not yet cut off his head.

Speaking of Anna—well, Anna has declared that she wants to work. For weeks now she has worried

her father, worried Bardichinov, she absolutely
wants to learn a trade.

"But you are needed at home," Bardichinov tries
to appease the girl.

"I'm not," Anna says, shaking her head. "Mother
mustn't go to work anyway, not for a long time. She
can easily do the housekeeping."

"Well, and what would you like to learn, Anna?"

"I don't know," Anna says thoughtfully. "Dressmaking perhaps . . . Vassja says it is a fine profession.
Vassja says it is so touching. Deft white hands stitch-
ing silk material and creating something very beautiful for other people to wear." Anna looks down upon
her hands which are not particularly white.

"H'm. Did Vassja say that?" meditates Bardichinov. "I wanted you to become something
better than a dressmaker, Anna."

"Vassja says it is very fine to be a dressmaker."

"Does he? Well, maybe he is right . . . Anyway it
is all the same now, since you could not go to school.
I hoped I could teach you to be a lady."

"Vassja says you are a lady if your soul is refined."

"Well—yes. But going to school is no drawback
either. A dressmaker . . . well, I suppose you have a
certain gift for it, you have mended my shirts very
nicely indeed."

"Uncle Bardichinov!" Anna breaks out at last.
"What is Vassja? Surely he must have told you,
since you are a Russian too."

Uncle Bardichinov looks up, astonished. He, at
any rate, does not think that Vassja is a grand duke.

"He told me he was a mechanic. He used to be

a locksmith, and then he learned all about cars."

"And he has passed his exam as a taxi driver too. The taxi company has engaged him, he starts tomorrow." Anna conveys the great news, then returns to the question that is preying on her mind. "But, Uncle Bardichinov, how *can* he be a mechanic? It isn't logical." Anna boldly uses words like logical, not only because they sound quite natural in French, but also because Uncle Bardichinov has taught her so many things. "A mechanic is a workman. And workmen could remain in Russia, only gentlemen and rich people had to escape. Why did Vassja come away if he is not a gentleman?"

Indeed, Bardichinov himself has already considered this problem, though not so often as Anna.

"Your father has emigrated too," he says with a shrug.

"That's different. There was no work in Hungary. But Vassja . . . And Vassja is so *good*. Vassja is quite divine, Uncle Bardichinov."

Uncle Bardichinov is lost in thought for a while. Then he tells Anna that Russians, particularly simple folk, poor people, have something Christlike in their nature. He mentions Dostoevsky, one of whose works he once let Anna read. The Russian people's soul is like a child's and there are men among them like messiahs, around whom the atmosphere grows luminous.

Later Anna has a talk with Liiv, and almost literally tells him what she has heard from Bardichinov. Of course, she repeats it as a result of her own reflections, or rather as an incontestable fact, as an eternal, fundamental truth. Liiv just wears his usual weary smile.

"There is something of Christ in every people, Anna. In yours and in mine also . . . and as for messiah-like apostles . . . One must try to be good, Anna, that is all."

Since that day Anna mistrusts Liiv. She hates the idea of other nations being put on the same level with Vassja and the Russians.

While Anna is discussing the future with Bardichinov, Klári has a talk with Papadakis.

"Tell me about your big boy," Klári demands. "The one who was about my age."

And Papadakis tells the story.

"Now tell me about the attack," orders Klári.

"The Turks assaulted the village from the north," Papadakis begins obediently. (Pray do not forget that only a few years have passed since the World War. Official reports and war correspondents have left their mark on everybody's way of speaking. We say things like: the Turks assaulted the village from the north.)

"Were they regular troops or just roving freebooters?"

Klári knows the answer as well as Papadakis does. Their conversation is rather like a teacher hearing her pupil recite; Klári wants to find out whether Papadakis knows his lesson.

"Just roving bands. But the regulars who came three days later were no better. They were the ones I fled from."

"Why did the Allies let them? Didn't you say the

English fleet was stationed in the Dardanelles?"

Klári knows more about the history and foreign affairs of our times than a dozen other pupils of the Hernád Street board school put together.

"It *was* stationed in the Dardanelles, but it was not moving. They did not want to pick a quarrel with Kemal. You know that sort of thing—" Klári nods—"home affairs, diplomatic complications, provocation must be avoided. Soon after that, the fleet was commanded home."

"Of course," says Klári shrewdly, "they wanted to see who would win, Kemal or the Sultan. If Vassja had been there, he would not have let your wife be hurt."

"Vassja? What could Vassja have done?"

"Vassja is awfully strong. I saw him carrying Fedor upstairs."

"Why did he do that?"

"Don't you know? Something fell on Fedor's feet, a machine or something. Vassja brought him home in a taxi, then took him in his arms and carried him upstairs. They live right above us; I opened the door for them. Tomorrow Vassja is going to have a taxi of his own."

"Is he?"

"Yes, and then he will often give me rides. Surely Vassja would have taken care of your children. Although, if those freebooters had big guns . . . a cannonball can carry away even Vassja's head, can't it? And do tell me, Uncle Papadakis, if you were such a great tradesman, why did you live in a small village?"

"It was not a very small village. Just there the road of the Persian caravans ran into the Baghdad railway track. There we loaded into wagons the wood that had been brought on camels' backs."

"Oh . . . and do you think a cannonball could carry away Vassja's head?"

This is the kind of conversation Klári has with Papadakis. If we remembered to look for Jani, we should certainly find him in some quiet corner with Vassja. They are building the radio: they wind wires on reels, fit crystals in their places with great care, and betweentimes they are secretive and talk in whispers. Fedor is in the room sometimes but takes no notice of them. Fedor is the coolest, the most taciturn man in the world. As soon as he gets home from work he washes himself without a word, dons his dinner jacket, adjusts his monocle and hurries to meet distinguished Russians. His bearing is erect, his features are cold and hard, his monocle flashes, he does not speak to anyone. If Vassja makes a joke, he answers curtly. Liiv is the only one he sometimes speaks to when he wants to be enlightened on some mathematical problem, for mathematics is the only subject that interests Fedor. Even on such rare occasions he remains aloof and tremendously aristocratic. Fedor is the type that can look elegant even in overalls.

Nevertheless, it isn't Fedor whom Anna loves, it is Vassja. Sometimes she cries at night, sometimes she kisses the door handle Vassja has touched. She begs Papadakis to give her the saints' pictures which Vassja gave him, although they are only pictures of

Greek Church saints, not real ones. Once she implores Vassja to let her sew on the buttons that have come off his uniform, but Vassja laughs and shakes his head: he would deserve to be hanged by the neck if he did not even know how to sew on buttons.

Then one day Vassja brings home an advertisement. A young lady wishing to learn dressmaking would be taken on as an apprentice. Anna goes out to apply for the post; she declines even Bardichinov's company, and she is accepted. Anna learns what it means to work as a foreigner. Anna has to run about, Anna has to work hard; still, she carries the advertisement in her heart; Anna sinks into bed tired to death, yet sometimes she dreams of snow-clad mountains in Switzerland on whose peaks dwells majesty.

VI

"Boriska," Barabás calls out to his wife one night when the children are fast asleep. Mrs. Barabás knows the little sounds of each child's slumber: Klári breathes heavily, then with pouting lips says "pheu" —one breath, one blow, one breath, one blow. Jani breathes very deeply, and his regular breathing is not even interrupted when he throws himself about. Anna sleeps almost soundlessly, very rarely do her lips let out a minute, tremulous murmur. For countless nights Mrs. Barabás has listened to these little sounds; without them the stillness would not be complete and home would not be snug.

"What is it, Gyula?" she says, turning towards him.

"I did not want to mention it before," her husband begins. "Why did you send me word that they would only operate on you in three days? Didn't you know it would be on the next day?"

"I did . . ." The French doctors had not been so considerate as all that. They had even made her sign a paper saying that the operation *might* end lethally, but that without it she would certainly die. "I did not want you to worry."

"Operations are sometimes fatal. Didn't you think of that? Didn't you wish to say good-bye to me?"

Indeed, Mrs. Barabás had *not* wished to say good-bye. That was just what she had wanted to avoid, that last pathetic and awkward meeting. She did not want to leave a dramatic memory. Perhaps it was because she had been a midwife and had had to deal with the feeble flame of life that, to her, simple and fundamental things like death seemed more natural. She wanted to die making those she loved believe that she was not afraid, that she had gone to sleep full of hope. How could she explain this to Barabás?

"I never thought of it," she replies. "I didn't know it was going to be such a serious operation."

Barabás believes her.

"You ought not to have done it. If I had known, I should have called in the evening before the operation; they would certainly have let me see you."

"Maybe I was wrong, but it doesn't matter now since I am alive."

Barabás laughs. That is quite true. She is alive, and slowly she is regaining strength. The present year promises to be more peaceful than the past ones. Barabás is happier in his new job, the children move automatically into grammar school, first Jani and soon Klári also; they will be gentry-folk. Anna is learning her trade. Mrs. Barabás stays at home, which is the right place for her. Life in the hotel is peaceful and quiet, there are no new boarders except, now and then, visitors putting up for a day or two—these do not count.

Homesickness, of course, sometimes rears its head. When this happens, Bardichinov vanishes for a few nights, Barabás frequents the Hungarian restaurant in the Rue François-Miron, Liiv shuts himself up in his room, while Alvarez rambles about alone like a damned soul.

The owner of the Hungarian restaurant in the Rue François-Miron is an emigrant, and so are most of his guests. At that time, Hungarians in Paris could be divided into three groups. To the first group belong those who had nothing whatsoever to do with communism or politics. They have come of their own accord, because work was scarce and they could not make a living at home. The second group, the emigrants, can again be subdivided into two groups: socialist and communist. These two are no more friendly for emigration. The third group is the dregs. Suspicious individuals, loafing adventurers, petty mountebanks, in short—and according to the word that has been created in Paris at the time—the "grabbers." The grabber sucks the blood of the other two groups and of the charity institutions. Some came here because, at home, things had grown too hot for them, they had embezzled, or swindled, or cheated at cards. The others came only because, in a rich country, it is easier to live on the good faith of one's neighbors.

Between the emigrants and the workers who have emigrated of their own accord there is no link, no contact whatever. For years they may be living in the same alien town and hardly even see each other. There is one exception though: when one of them dies. To an emigrant's funeral the whole colony of workingmen will come; when a workingman is buried, all the emigrants draw up in rank and file. How the other group finds out about the death remains a mystery. Newspapers do not mention it, and no one sends an obituary notice. How do they get to know about it all the same? When, at what time, at which cemetery? They know. These are the unfathomable secrets of the homeless. Everybody is assembled around the coffin of the deceased Hungarian, journeymen from the Renault works in Billancourt, laborers from Vincennes, film supers from Joinville-sur-Marne, emigrants from the quartier and from Montmartre. They stand around the coffin hat in hand, the cemetery is black with them. It is very sad to die far away from home— they all know that.

The Rue François-Miron is chiefly the home of communists. Barabás does not like to mix with them, partly because he is just a little afraid of them and partly because he always feels discontented when he comes away. He does not know why he still goes there from time to time.

Of the company in the bar, Bardichinov had been a banker, Liiv a professor, and Alvarez a painter—a very bad one, by the way, and Barabás feels honored to belong to their circle. In the Hungarian restaurant he often sits among professors, bank clerks and artists, yet he does not feel honored. There it is *he* who feels superior, because he can go home any day,

whenever he has the desire and the money. The
others cannot go home.

Barabás feels the waves of envy surging around
him. He considers this loud, lamenting nostalgia
an immodest thing.

"I wish I could once more sit in the Café New
York and drink my coffee!" Barabás's neighbor
sighs and drops his head on his fists. Barabás fidgets
awkwardly. He is not pained because he has never
had black coffee at the Café New York—when you
have been torn away from your country for four
years, you have come to understand all the varieties
of homesickness; he is pained because he thinks it
unmanly to speak about such things without restraint, to wail like women. Not as though his wife
would wail. No, thank God, Boriska isn't that sort,
she only keeps worrying about the flat that she has
found in the Street of the Fishing Cat, three tiny
rooms, kitchen and shower . . . does not cost more
than the hotel rent . . .

"Let us play!" Radnai, the chemical engineer
moves. "Who knows the biggest number of cafés in
Budapest?"

They take pencil and paper and become busy
scribbling. Barabás's mood darkens as he watches
them. He thinks these games are childish—how
many cafés do you know, and who can tell where a
certain tram line stops and such like—pastimes,
they ought to be ashamed of themselves. Barabás
goes home, he is upset and irritated, and will not go
near them again for weeks to come.

One night he has just come home from the Rue

François-Miron; he is angry and sleepy; it is about eleven. He finds the house alive and buzzing: Mrs. Barabás, in their room, is weeping in torrents; the children are out. The other boarders clutter in in great agitation. The Hungarian carpenter in the neighboring Rue du Levant has murdered his wife.

Barabás runs across to drive the children home. The hotel in the Rue du Levant stands with its back to the back wall of Barabás's hotel; they might be twins. If one night the two hotels were to change places, the neighbors would never notice it.

In front of the hotel there is a great crowd and the bar is teeming with people. The Hungarian carpenter has gone. After having killed his wife he took the hatchet dripping with blood and rushed to the police to give himself up. The police are upstairs now. Barabás forces his way through the crowd and finds his children. It appears that Jani has seen the body with René, son of the patron of the Rue du Levant hotel. They stole into the next room. They have a kind of French window here, just like in the Rue de la Huchette, with a bit of balcony in front. The two boys climbed out, and then—three stories aboveground—across onto the other bit of balcony belonging to the next room . . . Barabás shudders when his offspring boasts of his acrobatic feat, cuffs the boy's ears hurriedly, and drives the flock home.

In their room, Vassja is already sitting up with Mrs. Barabás—Vassja, who always knows where he can be of use. He has soothed her somewhat, she is weeping quietly now; then, suddenly, Anna starts howling. God knows why, perhaps only to increase the confusion, or perhaps to be comforted by Vassja too. Vassja does comfort her, and it will be Anna's most cherished memory, this night, when Vassja hugged her, caressed her and spoke gentle and wise words to her.

"Do help me, Anna. Let us put the little ones to bed," says Vassja. Anna instantly forgets her grief. Barabás has hurried back to the Rue du Levant, the two put the children to bed and then have a long talk with Mrs. Barabás. Barabás is somber when he returns. They have just carried the body away over there. Barabás sits down in the bar, Liiv and Alvarez join him. Bardichinov also comes home after midnight; he hears the news, sits down for a while, but Bardichinov is not young any more, he cannot sit up late at night. He soon says good night and goes up to bed. Papadakis puts in an appearance instead, and, soon after, Fedor. Fedor, in his evening clothes and monocle, sits down at their table, a thing he has never done yet. He drinks quantities of absinthe, does not say a word, and sits up with the Barabás family until dawn.

Next day neither Barabás nor Anna goes to work. The newspapers tell them exactly what happened. M. Alphonse, the M. Gaston of the twin hotel, attests that the carpenter had consented to his wife's going home. For years they had been wrangling about it, but now he was acquiescent. He did not want to go yet, he was saving money, he wanted to have a workshop of his own when he got home. But he told the woman to go since she was so terribly anxious to. Then, when she had packed her things, when she was ready to leave by the nine-o'clock train, all of a sudden the carpenter went crazy and seized the hatchet . . .

That was what had happened. For a few days longer the hotel will be swarming, and it will swarm again when the carpenter stands before the Court of Assizes. The carpenter will be sent to jail for many years, he will hardly be able to save money for the little workshop now.

Meanwhile life calms down again: Anna goes to work, she grows quieter and wiser. Until now she had thought hers was the harder lot—feeding the family and keeping everything in order, rushing to the market, into shops and offices. She knows now that there is nothing so hard as working among strangers. But hers is a wise and resigned knowledge, without anger and without resistance, because she has learned two great things. First: the sin does not lie in the fact that Hungary was France's enemy in the World War—the little seamstresses know very little about that—nor in that Anna is the enemy, but in the fact that she is a foreigner. And the other thing is: it is her own fault. She is different. That is the cause of a long string of humiliations, of torment; that is the cause of contempt.

"You are different, and no wonder," says Bardichinov. "They were not dragged out of their country when they were twelve and taken into a foreign land. Besides, I have taught you a lot, you are better educated, more than all the others put together."

"Vassja knows how to adapt himself to anything," Anna declares.

"Indeed. Vassja has a very lucky disposition."

Anna shakes her head.

"He is a great man. That makes all the difference, Uncle Bardichinov, that Vassja is a great man. An apostle. Everybody is happier when he is near."

Excepting me, Anna admits to herself, for Anna is in love. Otherwise she is almost right. For truly all faces light up when Vassja comes home at night and runs through every little room.

"Ça va?" he asks smilingly everywhere, and his tone conveys: Isn't everything all right and life delightful? And everybody smiles back at him and says "Merci, ça va." Vassja lays his little present on the table and rushes on. He does not stay long anywhere except where there is trouble. He takes the Bulgarian student out to dinner sometimes, he brings Liiv a pigeon with a broken wing, for Liiv is the loneliest of them all. But only with Jani does he have long talks, and Jani is prouder of that fact than of being top boy in his class. Jean Barabas—the name does sound somewhat strange; still Jani is a regular French citizen, fairly gobbles knowledge and is determined to be a pilot.

Claire Barabas would be at the top too if there were less trouble about her conduct. Even so, she rises easily from grade to grade. She is a very determined character, she knows for certain what career she is going to take up: she is going to be a doctor. Yet Claire Barabas's parents, her sister and

brother, who know only the determined and energetic traits of her character, would indeed be amazed
if they saw her with Aline, her best friend.

Aline is the frailest and the most backward
scholar in the class. Not that she is stupid; if you
once looked into her intelligent, sad eyes, the sad,
intelligent eyes of a delicate child, you know that she
can't be stupid. She has one great failing: a bad
memory. What she has grasped well today, and
repeated word for word, will be gone out of her
head tomorrow, lost, vanished. Her father, a rich
merchant, had her coached by a long string of
tutors; they knew no remedy. Klári is the only one
who can help her a little, Klári with her infinite
patience and tenderness.

Infinite patience and tenderness? Well, she does
get wild sometimes and pinches Aline's thin little
arm so that the blue spots show for two weeks. But
this is an exception. Klári, the invincible, the
haughty little soul, loves Aline; she loves only the
weak and helpless.

"You can't have forgotten it," she says for the
hundredth time. "Just think. Remember, we had
such a good laugh at one of Turenne's sayings.
What was it?"

"Wait!" Aline's eyes light up. "I have an idea . . .
No, I can't remember," she ends dejectedly.

Klári is indefatigable. Nice tea is not the reason
she goes to Aline, although this is the fib she invents
at home. She coaches Aline and tells Aline her day-
dreams.

"The physician alleviates the sufferings of mankind," she utters the new and original idea. Aline gazes at her in admiration.

"What sort of doctor are you going to be? My uncle is a specialist for ear diseases."

Klári makes a disdainful gesture.

"I might go among lepers," she says pensively. "Do you remember when we read about the Dominican fathers who spent their lives in the leper colonies?"

Aline does not remember. Klári is annoyed, but she conscientiously repeats the pretty story from their reader about the heroic and saintly life of the missionary doctors.

"That's where I am going myself," Klári winds up. If the Barabás family could hear her, they would not believe their ears, particularly Anna, who maintains that Klári is a heartless monster.

That is because Klári giggles maliciously when Anna, at night, even when she has come home tired to death, spends hours target-shooting with the catapult Vassja has carved for Jani.

"Off the mark, off the mark," Klári jeers and makes faces at her. "And you think that will make him fall in love with you! Vassja is going to marry the daughter of the Czar!"

Before Anna can smack her, Klári has escaped from the room and run to Papadakis.

Anna, poor thing, is indeed passing through a difficult period of her life. She is no longer a child, and is not yet a woman. She tries to win Vassja's favor by catapulting and by bruising her knee in assiduously trying to ride the bicycle Vassja gave

Jani, but she can suffer as deeply as any adult and unhappy woman. Her love is mute and devoted. If Vassja fell ill and she could nurse him . . . or if there was a fire and she could carry Vassja out of the burning house in her arms . . .

Then comes the horrible, murderous night when there is no sickness, no fire, but something a thousand times worse and heartbreakingly final—death.

VII

Mrs. Barabás wakes first. She sits up in bed and grasps her husband's arm. By that time Gyula Barabás has stirred also.

"Yes," he whispers, "I can hear it." For one second he listens, holding his breath; there are drops of sweat on his forehead. Then he jumps out of bed and pulls on his trousers.

The room is suddenly alive. Anna is sitting up too, and listens. Jani dresses with trembling hands. Only Klári sleeps on peacefully: she hasn't heard anything.

"You go to bed," the father bids Jani, but does not notice the boy's disobedience. And Anna puts on her clothes too, deadly white, her teeth chattering. No one heeds her. The sound that reached them in the night and tore them out of their dreams is not human. It is a plaintive howl that makes one shudder, a howl louder . . . louder than anything. It fills the room, it fills the house; it is like the howl of a wolf or of a man being dissected alive. In the lamplight four pale faces stare at each other. The howl keeps swelling, it is not human, it is not animal, it is gruesome.

Barabás wrenches open the door, flies up the stairs three at a time because there is a light on the fourth floor, and that is where the sounds come from. The two children follow close on his heels, their mother shouts after them in vain.

Vassja and Fedor's room is right above them, the door is ajar, the light streams out from it. Barabás stops dead on the threshold, the room is so strange. A policeman stands in the middle of the floor, and with him a man in plain clothes and M. Gaston, who has pulled his trousers over his nightshirt. And Fedor . . . Fedor is crouching in front of the bed in his dress coat and he knocks his head rhythmically against the hard edge of the board and howls and howls and howls. . . .

"What has happened?" asks Barabás, but can scarcely utter the words. Someone stirs beside him; it is the Bulgarian student who has reached the threshold first.

"Vassja . . ." the student whispers. "Vassja has had an accident."

Anna, who stands behind her father, presses her hands to her heart; Jani squeezes his fist into his mouth. Liiv staggers in from the corridor, behind him Alvarez, then the Algerian workman and Mme. Germaine. She does not stop on the threshold; with her sinewy arms she energetically makes a way for herself and enters. Fedor goes on knocking his head against the bed, the monocle hanging from a thin string from his buttonhole dangles at every move. The howl does not swell and does not decrease; the howl remains the same, and it is ghastly.

"Mon cher ami," the man in plain clothes accosts Fedor. Gaston also bends over the crouching figure and touches his shoulder.

"M. Jarossev-Pelczinski . . ."

Fedor does not see them, he does not hear them, he does not feel Gaston's hand on his shoulder.

"What has happened?" asks Mme. Germaine impatiently.

They have given up trying to stop Fedor. The man in plain clothes raises his voice, and he and Gaston begin to explain.

"He ran into a lorry . . . Maybe it was the lorry driver's fault, the inquest will clear that up. The collision hurled him off his seat, directly under the wheels of a tramcar."

"Is he dead?" Germaine screams.

The man in plain clothes nods. Anna presses her hand upon her heart. Jani's tears begin to flow. The Bulgarian student steps forward.

"He spoke to me. He said he must deliver his car at midnight in front of the Madeleine. He asked me to go along with him, we could walk home afterward and have a bit of supper on the way. I didn't go, I had a headache."

They all know that the Bulgarian student did not have a headache—he had not wanted to accept another supper. Uncle Bardichinov appears, quite dressed, then two transitory visitors, Mrs. Barabás, Mme. Hélène and four Algerian children who hold each other's hands and tremble. They are all here by now except Papadakis, whose slumber is deep and drugged, and Klári, whose slumber is deep and peaceful. Alvarez comments upon what has happened in whispers. Mrs. Barabás begins to weep silently.

"We were able to establish his identity from his license, and we telephoned through to the taxi company," the man in plain clothes says. "They gave us the address. So he has no relatives staying here?"

All eyes look at Fedor, but Fedor is like a stone. He knocks his head against the bed, his howl, long drawn out, unremitting, is terrifying and monotonous.

"They were merely friends; they lived together," Gaston explains.

Bardichinov leaves the group huddled at the door and goes up to the man in plain clothes. His small figure seems very old now, his steps are faltering. He introduces himself. His French sentences are not quite so smooth and polished as usual. He is a Russian and he was an almost paternal friend of the unfortunate young man, could he be of any service to the police? No, he knows nothing about Vassja's family affairs.

The man in plain clothes speaks to the policeman and together they go up to the chest of drawers which Gaston says belonged to Vassja. They pull out a drawer, and in the next moment their faces reflect grave astonishment. Bardichinov is taken aback. Germaine clasps her hands.

"I don't understand!"

The crowd in the doorway stirs and pushes forward. Anna can look into the drawer now. There

are Vassja's old overalls, his stockings, his few
changes of linen, everything in perfect order. And
in the other half of the drawer there lie, folded with
meticulous care, a woman's silk dress, underwear,
a pair of silk stockings. In the middle, a pair of
woman's brand-new shoes.

"I can't understand it." Gaston shakes his head.
"He has lived here for nearly a year and a half, and
not once has a woman been to see him."

"I don't understand," Germaine repeats, and
holds up the light blue silk dress.

In the crowd on the threshold there is a sudden
commotion. Two little brown fists beat about wildly
among the standing figures; a child, his face grubby
with tears, forces its way through. It is Jani, choking,
sobbing, wailing:

"I know! He told me . . . he was expecting his
fiancée! He was expecting her next week!"

Anna leans against the door, her face white, and
the world quietly revolves around her. She will
never remember what happened next. Dimly she
sees Jani's face with the tears streaming down it, sees
the man in plain clothes stroking his hair, comfort-
ing and questioning him. Jani replies, sobbing and
choking spasmodically.

"His fiancée was a Russian girl, a seamstress. Her
photograph must be here . . . no, not there, under
the radio. Vassja has not seen her for six years. He
saved money, because he wanted her to come out
here, and that costs a lot for the girl had to flee—
through Finland. Her name is Dinotchka."

The policeman finds the photograph under the

radio. Germaine looks at it with some disappointment. On the faded, much-worn picture, the girl's features are scarcely discernible.

"Was he expecting his fiancée next week?" the man in plain clothes asks.

"Yes. Two months ago he had saved all the money . . . a thousand five hundred francs . . . he sent it to Finland, to a friend of his. I was at the post office with him. And yesterday he had a letter from the girl saying she had boarded a ship, a Finnish steamer. She will be here next week."

The little group at the door moves.

They look at each other, and now their heads droop. The policeman noisily shuts the drawer. The man in plain clothes sits scribbling something. Jani does not know that he is the hero of the hour, that everybody hung on his lips, that he alone was able to answer when the others were silent. He stands in the middle of the room, forsaken now and immersed in boundless woe.

Bardichinov goes up to the man in plain clothes.

"Where is he now?" he asks in a low voice.

"At the morgue," the man in plain clothes says, looking up.

"We are Russians," Bardichinov says simply. Now his sentences are neither polished nor elegant. "We conduct our dead to the cemetery from the home where they lived. Could we have the body brought here?"

The man in plain clothes explains, his features showing benevolence; the policeman also puts in a word or two. The man in plain clothes collects his

notes, the policeman salutes, the group in the doorway separates to let them pass, they are gone. It is
three o'clock in the morning. Outside, the February
fog is drifting. Vassja's car skidded on the rainy
street, or maybe it was the lorry that skidded. The
cold in the city and in the house is damp and pene-
trating.

They begin to disperse now. Liiv and Alvarez go
to Barabás's room. Mrs. Barabás makes tea. Bardichinov stays with Fedor. Anna takes his cup up for
him. She puts one in front of Fedor too, but next
morning she will find it untouched. Fedor is unapproachable, even more than he was in his haughty
seclusion. He knocks his head against the bed and
howls . . . until he suddenly falls asleep, crouching
on the floor. Those downstairs shudder at the silence
that has suddenly descended upon them.

All next day Bardichinov runs about, and in his
small face the wrinkles multiply. He runs to offices,
to the police, to the more influential members of the
Russian colony. M. l'Attaché Kalinin faithfully
follows him. They are successful: on the third day
they may bring Vassja's body home.

By the time the black hearse reaches the door,
the Russian colony is already gathering. They, too,
know when there is a funeral. They have come in
white blouses. Kalinin has pulled his over his worn
frock coat, the waiters—the numerous Russian emigrants who work as waiters—wear theirs over their
dress coats. Tuchachevski is a professional dancer
in the smartest night club on the Champs-Elysées;
he has been working till seven in the morning, and

has probably just had time to run home somewhere behind the Rue de Rochechouart to change into his white silk blouse. Now he stands with drooping red eyelids, his patent leather pumps out of shape from dancing, and he helps to lift the smooth black coffin from the hearse.

The boarders see Fedor for the first time since that night. Above his white blouse his face is cold and rigid. He is the first to take hold of the coffin and move with it toward the door. The little old room is four stories up, and the winding staircase terribly narrow. Four men are carrying the coffin, although there is hardly room for two on the narrow stairs . . . but it would be the same at home in Russia: the dead man starts upon his last journey from the place where he lived.

The Russian priest arrives and goes upstairs to consecrate the coffin. The Russians in their white blouses stand in file on two sides of the staircase and light their long candles. A tiny child could scarcely pass between these two rows and here the coffin must be carried down! From the ground floor to the fourth story the double file of white blouses stands, the candles flare, and the heavy melancholy Russian psalm rises into the air.

The procession starts from above: the priest is in front, behind him four men in white blouses with the black coffin. It is terribly hard work; all must help with the hand which is not holding the long candle with its yellow flame. The men help and cry. They cry and sing. The coffin wavers above the sea of white blouses, a heavy black coffin that bears no

name. Where it has passed, the surging crowd closes
in behind it.

It takes a whole hour to get to the ground floor.
There Bardichinov takes the place of Tuchachevski.
The two other men are also replaced by others, only
Fedor stubbornly holds onto the corner of the coffin.
He is singing and shakes his head when someone
offers help.

So Vassja's coffin threads its way along the streets
of Paris, and the French stop at the edge of the pavement, because they have not seen many Russian
funerals. There is a hearse in the procession, the
taxi company has provided it, but it remains empty;
the four men will not give up their load, they carry
the coffin on their shoulders. Behind them the white
blouses crowd in the light of the candles, after them
follow the others, the boarders, the strangers.
Bardichinov, after a hundred yards, is panting and
stumbling, he cannot hold out any longer. Barabás
takes his place. The singing does not cease, the
psalm soars and is wafted over the everyday streets
of Paris.

Then they come home from the cemetery, and
now the house is weary and silent. It is lunchtime.
Mrs. Barabás quickly concocts something, and asks
Bardichinov to eat with them. Luckily Klári is
lunching at school; Jani also would be there, had he
not missed school on account of the funeral. Silently
they sit at table, Anna staring ahead of her with her
hands in her lap. She has wept for Vassja during a
year and a half; since that night she has no tears.
After lunch, when Bardichinov has taken leave,

Barabás goes to the window and for a long time stands there looking out . . . There is not much to see from this height. The Rue de la Huchette is narrow and the wall obstructs the view of the pavement on the other side and of the lower stories. Straight opposite, the Street of the Fishing Cat begins, but unless you bend out far, you see only the farther end of the street.

"Boriska!" Barabás suddenly turns around. "Is that flat over there in the Street of the Fishing Cat still to let? If it is, you might take it."

VIII

Mme. germaine and M. Gaston look at each other aghast. Fedor began it. The morning after the funeral he appeared, more cool and distinguished than ever, paid the rent for the obligatory three days, and ten minutes later had moved out with all his belongings.

"But, dear M. Jarossev-Pelczinski . . ." M. Gaston tried to remonstrate. "I hope we have done nothing to make you angry."

Fedor gave him a look through his monocle, cool and remote, like a supercilious aristocrat glancing at an importunate beggar.

"Certainly not," he said stiffly. "Good day, M. Gaston."

Then he disappeared. Next, Liiv gave notice, then Papadakis, then the Bulgarian student, then Alvarez, then Bardichinov. Barabás met Bardichinov coming out of the tiny office, the size of a mousehole, behind the bar where these important announcements had to be made.

"You, too, M. Barabás? You have taken a flat? Accept my sincere congratulations. You are perfectly right, dear friend. A hotel is not the right kind of place for a family man, particularly for the father of high-spirited children in the prime of their youth."

Gaston booked the notices mechanically.

"M. Fedor has already moved out," he announced in a sepulchral voice.

Bardichinov suddenly went pale and clutched at Gaston's narrow desk for support.

"Fedor has moved out? But then . . . who will stay? That girl arrives next week . . . I . . . I wanted to be gone before she . . ."

"So do I," Barabás nodded. "I don't want to be here when she comes."

Bardichinov stood still and reflected.

"Cher M. Gaston, please consider my notice canceled. I am going to stay."

No one ever asked him whether Vassja's fiancée arrived. No one, not even Anna.

So they were all scattered. Fedor, Papadakis and the Bulgarian student disappeared in the bottomless pit of the great city. Liiv and Alvarez moved into another, similar little hotel at the corner of the Rue Saint-Jacques and the Quai Saint-Michel, and the Barabás family to the Street of the Fishing Cat. Even the company that used to meet every night changed its headquarters. Now they meet in a little bistro in the Rue Saint-Jacques, discuss sociology, anarchy and capitalism, and sometimes they talk about Vassja, whose death has left every one of them rather lonely.

"My daughter Klári always used to tease my daughter Anna about him," Barabás says with a smile. "She used to kid her by saying that Vassja would marry the Czar's daughter."

"The Czar's daughter . . ." Bardichinov crosses himself in silence. The emigrants have long ceased to have any doubts about the fate of the Czar and his family. "My friend Barabás's daughter Annuska, however, may have guessed aright," he says. "The young lady, whose intellect is extremely keen, always declared that Vassja could not be a simple workman. Dear Annuska argued that workmen did not need to flee from their homes in Russia since at present they rule the country."

"Political convictions are not always decided by social standing," Alvarez interrupted eagerly. "Often entire strata of the population fail to recognize their most vital interests and support a form of government that aims at their own suppression. For instance, they may be royalists . . ."

Liiv turns away and does not listen. He guesses the truth. Vassja's secret is a simple and humble one. He took part in the socialist movement, he fought with enthusiasm for the revolution, and then, when they had triumphed, he suddenly realized that it was not what he had imagined. It happens sometimes. Liiv, too, had felt time and again that it wasn't quite what he had expected. Yet he held out, thinking that perhaps, after all, goodwill and human dignity would blossom forth from all the bloodshed. Vassja had turned against his party, fled from the country where his revolution had triumphed. What does it matter? Liiv reflects bitterly. Here they have met in Paris in a little hotel that is no home for either, and here both will be buried.

Liiv's guess was close enough to the truth. Vassja was no grand duke. He was a mechanic. He had never spoken of his past. No honest man is proud of being a renegade, even if it is his convictions that separate him from his old comrades.

The others still think of Vassja sometimes, but there are two who never utter his name, two children who have grown up in a single night, the night of death: Anna and Jani.

They did not both grow up in the same way. Anna hides herself behind a smooth and polite surface; she seems to be more communicative than before, but life, for her, is at some remote distance, she could hardly say where. Jani, who used to be the most cheerful of the three, the easiest to handle, has grown gruff and irritable. Both retire within their shells and have little in common with the world around them.

Sometimes they have curious conversations with each other, at the end of which they unfailingly start to quarrel.

"Anna," Jani queries, "do you think life has any sense?"

"I don't know," Anna ponders. "It's sure to have some sort of sense."

"It hasn't." Jani shakes his head. "Do you remember Gilbert—that thin dark boy who was in the Luxembourg Gardens on Thursday? Do you know how his father died? He had very bad toothache, he'd been having it for days; at last he made up his mind to have the tooth out. He went to the dentist, he had awful pains when the tooth was being pulled out, and then, on his way home from the dentist, he was run over by a car. Well, if he was to die, why did he need to have his tooth out first? Why wasn't he run over on his way to the dentist? I think it's terribly unfair."

"A trial," Anna ventures. "Life is full of trials. They purify the soul."

"That's just like a girl—such silly resignation. Everything's good enough for women, they don't revolt at anything. It's because women can't suffer."

"Women can't suffer!" Anna can scarcely speak for indignation. "Women have much finer perception, only they hide their grief and don't whine about it for all the world to hear."

"You drive me crazy," Jani growls. "Women howl all the time, although the real troubles always come to men. It's they who get the dangerous jobs: now I, for instance, am going to be a pilot. Women sit at home at their sewing machines and keep whimpering all the time. I'm sure to be killed in an accident," he adds darkly.

"You're being pretty sorry for yourself in advance," Anna says deprecatingly. "For the moment you aren't even a pilot."

"Silly goose!" Jani turns his back on her. "We discuss philosophical questions and she gets personal. How like a girl!"

Anna shrugs her shoulders and discusses the point no further. This is how their theoretical conversations nearly always end. Both continue to live their queer and secluded grown-up lives. Jani goes to school and experiments with chemicals at home, while Mrs. Barabás watches him with profound awe, partly because she fears for the glossy parquet floor of the new flat and partly because she expects him to blow up the entire family at any moment.

This year Jani is just a shade worse at school than he used to be. Instead of being first, he is second or, at worst, third in his class. Scholarships, books, prizes fall to his lot as they did before, there is scarcely any difference; still there's this behind it: Jani no longer cares for his comrades, his studies, his teachers; he cares for no one. When he has a bad fall in the gymnasium and his arm is fractured, he is almost pleased after the first alarm is over: he won't be able to go to school for a few weeks. Next day, however, it appears that his arm has only to be securely bandaged to his chest; he can't write, but he can do everything else. Jani is resigned: it doesn't really matter; and in time he fights his way to the top of the class again merely for the fun of the thing, merely out of contempt for the strange boys, for the teachers and for life in general.

Anna goes to the workshop and is no more an apprentice. She is a proper seamstress now, and since she has learned the secret of easy, meaningless politeness, she gets on very well at the shop. She knows how to please everybody without so much as giving it a thought. The manageress says she has taste— Uncle Bardichinov proudly believes that it is his instruction that brought it to the surface—and persuades her to learn tailoring. So Anna attends a night course for tailoring, and once mentions that it wouldn't be a bad idea to study fashion designing. Alvarez almost shouts with joy when he finds he can be of some use in life, and starts with feverish enthusiasm to give Anna drawing lessons. This causes strained relations between Alvarez and Bardichinov for some months, but Anna has so completely grown up that she even knows how to pacify both.

"What you've told me about the Empire period is tremendously interesting, Uncle Bardichinov. Taking drawing lessons would be no use whatever if you didn't teach me art history. It's the basis of everything."

And to Alvarez:

"You know, M. Alvarez, theory is no use whatever without practice. Uncle Bardichinov always tried to explain to me how rich and elaborate the Renaissance was, and the things at the Czar's court; but one can't really understand it except from drawings and pictures."

Yes, Anna has grown false and deceitful. Or, if you like, she has grown up and become wise. There is only a clash sometimes on Sunday mornings when both want to take her to a museum simultaneously. Anna gets over this difficulty too; she cajoles them until they believe that she gets the greatest pleasure out of a joint lecture from them both.

And in the meantime joy and sorrow have disappeared from Anna's life. It would be no use for a girl of seventeen to confess such a thing: no one would believe her. Anna does not confess it. Sometimes she feels her mother's eyes upon her, but she does not see the anguish in them. No more does

Jani. Yet secretly, Jani had always been his mother's favorite, even though she never showed it. Jani resembles her most, mentally and physically. Jani is the gentlest of them all, although the other two are girls. There was a time when Jani used to run to his mother with all his little worries and troubles. Mrs. Barabás could remember his sweet, despondent little voice:

"Mother darling, I can't lace up my boots . . . there's a knot in the bootlace. . . . Mother darling, don't thrash me . . . I've knocked my knee and it's bleeding."

All that is over now. It is not so surprising in the case of Anna and Klári. Klári is exactly like her father, which is why she is his particular pet. She always was a little savage, she always got on by herself, she never liked to be petted. And Anna had always been quiet and odd. She never asked for kisses and tenderness, but her eyes sparkled when she got them. Jani always wanted petting, he would nestle up to you like a kitten. Now one is more alien than the other.

Yet, as things go, Mrs. Barabás ought to be very contented. Her husband is a good man and gets good wages, two of her children will rise in life, the third is learning a trade and getting on nicely, the new flat gives her much pleasure and a great deal of happy work. Still, life is cold and lonely. Barabás is a good man, it's just that he's different, that he's a man. His worries are a man's worries. Any mother could be proud of three such children. It's just that they're drifting away from her, that their life is carrying them in a different direction, that she can't look into their souls.

They're good children, hard-working children. But all their mother's share in them is when Jani breaks his arm and the zealous school doctor sends him home in an ambulance, or when Klári catches the measles and doesn't say she is ill, says nothing until she slips off her chair with a temperature of 104°. Nothing much, nothing to make a fuss about: three weeks later the children have forgotten all about it. But when the ambulance stopped on the Quai Saint-Michel, near the narrow entrance of the Street of the Fishing Cat, and Jani was lifted out of it, when Klári suddenly lay in a heap on the floor . . . those are the things that wear one out, that mix gray hairs with the brown. Mrs. Barabás thinks everything would be different, would be better, at home. Maybe she is mistaken. Children are children everywhere, and mothers are left alone the world over. But Mrs. Barabás sometimes leans out the window, gazes across the yellow Seine, over the two blunt towers of Notre-Dame, and longs for home. Anna is studying some sort of French tailoring book; Jani, when she asks him a question, answers gruffly that he is "dissolving water into its constituent elements"; Klári recites *mezza voce*, "N'y touchez pas, il est brisé"; Gyula is discussing things with the gentlemen at the bistro—the world is an empty place.

Then gradually the world grows populated again, so far as it can in this alien country. It is István who recalls Anna to life, although he does not know it and Anna would not believe it if she were told.

Who is István? We have said that Hungarians in Paris may be subdivided into three groups. The third group is that of the idlers, the wastrels, the good-for-nothings, the grabbers. Well, István is one of them. He was a bank clerk at home, but somehow work didn't seem to agree with him, perhaps he had even done something that wasn't quite regular. Now he lives in Paris, has done so for the last three years. He knows very well that the Protestant Church distributes small sums of support on Mondays, that you can get a free meal at the Theosophists' on Tuesday; on Wednesdays, the Rothschild office gives five or ten francs to anyone who asks for it; on Thursdays there is supper at the vegetarians', only you must first listen to the lecture; on Fridays alms are distributed by the Jewish Community; on Saturdays, a package of gifts by the Freemasons—true, only for political refugees, but anyone who's clever enough can mingle with them; on Sundays there is a festive dinner at the Roman Catholic vicarages. István knows all this, he changes his religion and his nationality every day, he has in his pocket a dozen kinds of papers that qualify him to receive aid from various sources. Occasionally he works: as an extra in pictures or as a model in an art school. With all this, István has an engagingly frank countenance and melancholy dark eyes; also he feels that he was born to be an artist.

He makes the acquaintance of Barabás at the Hungarian restaurant of the Rue François-Miron, at which he calls to get a few francs out of the emi-

grants there. István at once senses the aristocrat in
Barabás—for a skilled worker with regular wages
counts as an aristocrat in the Hungarian colony—
and promptly joins him, tells him savory stories
about the other emigrants whose money he has just
borrowed and sketches the story of his own life with
a few well-chosen, emotional words. The strange
part of it is that Barabás, the suspicious, shrewd
peasant, should believe him. Yet he does. He is
sincerely sorry for the unfortunate, yet ever cheerful
young man, and when István shyly asks whether
he may call on Mr. Barabás's family someday
because the company of such an estimable man is
most encouraging and he yearns for the intimacy of
a family circle, Barabás is conquered and invites
him to supper next day.

Anna is not for a moment taken in by István.
Afterward she states with bitter satisfaction that she
instantly recognized what a shallow good-for-nothing, what a bad character he was. Of course, István
starts making love to her at once. Anna is not beautiful, but she is seventeen. Seventeen—a strange age.
It has its advantages and its drawbacks, and it is
all irretrievably and touchingly lovely. Anna's skin
is velvety and fresh, although sometimes marred
by pimples. Her movements are uncertain and awkward, but they have the clumsy charm of a bear
cub. There are aggressive freckles on the slightly
snub nose, but below it there dreams the gentle
ripeness of her mouth. Her brown eyes are faithful
and musing, even if their expression sometimes
lacks understanding. That is Anna. Some years

hence her features will grow finer, but István likes her as she is now. There are never enough women for a fellow abroad, and even a cunning scamp like István has difficulty in finding a companion to his taste: the regular wage-earning, more or less lady-like, kind.

Anna despises István and has no illusions about him; yet the fine words, the flatteries she has never heard before, please her. No one has yet discovered the girl in Anna, the awakening woman, the solitary young soul that longs for tenderness. István says "You are beautiful"; he says "I love you." At such times girls realize with a shock that they are girls.

And that is how the saddest love in all the world begins. Can any kind of love be sadder than that of which you feel ashamed?

IX

UNCLE BARDICHINOV has a lot of work these days. France knows no unemployment, workmen are constantly pouring into Paris from the east and south of Europe, and from time to time Jani visits the Hungarian, Italian, Czech and Greek restaurants and distributes the cards printed in many languages, in which Uncle Bardichinov recommends his low-priced French lessons. The newly arrived foreigners hope to get work more easily and quickly if they speak the language, and the old gentleman has regular groups of students now.

Anna calls on him every fortnight to tidy the confusion in the bachelor cupboard and to take away the shirts to be mended. Of course, she goes at a time when Uncle Bardichinov has no lessons, but this time, to her surprise, she finds a lady in the room.

"Come in, Annuska," Bardichinov cries when she draws back. "This isn't a lesson. I have a charming new neighbor . . . let me introduce her."

Anna notices with dismay that the lady has two stout sticks near at hand, and that she can rise only by leaning heavily on both.

"Don't, please," she says quickly, and the lady sits down with a grateful smile.

"Cathrina Aldhufond," she says, presenting herself. "I only arrived two days ago, and made M. Bardichinov's acquaintance today. He was kind enough to ask me to have a cup of tea with him."

"But you must make the tea, Annuska." Bardichinov laughs. "No one but you can handle this contraption."

When the Barabás family had moved to the Street of the Fishing Cat they presented Bardichinov with their old spirit lamp. The new flat has a proper kitchen.

"What if I hadn't come?" Anna teases.

"I knew you would. You promised."

Anna pours water into the kettle and lights the spirit lamp.

"Are you Russian too, madame?" she inquires politely.

The lady shakes her head. "No, I am Finnish."

"Today, dear Mlle. Aldhufond, today!" Bardichinov reminds her. "In the good old days before the war I had the good fortune of belonging, together with you, dear mademoiselle, to the great national community of my Russian fatherland."

Cathrina Aldhufond smiles.

"I cannot say I considered it such a piece of good fortune. The Czar's government exiled me to Siberia."

"To Siberia?" Anna is so interested that she moves closer. Up to now, this has merely been a word, strange and romantic, a word that one reads about in books, in Uncle Bardichinov's Russian books. And now here was someone who had really lived there, who had been exiled to Siberia.

"Yes." Cathrina nods. "Back in nineteen-twelve, as a student of eighteen. I lived through the war out there. I was only released by the communist revolution."

Anna glances involuntarily at the heavy sticks and at the oddly placed, stiff feet. Perhaps they had been frozen in Siberia, or . . .

Mlle. Aldhufond catches the glance and answers it calmly and naturally.

"No, my feet have nothing to do with it. I have been a cripple since I was a child. I had infantile paralysis."

Anna does not speak the question that is on her lips. What could this paralyzed woman with her crippled legs have done to make the Czar exile her to Siberia?

Bardichinov asks no questions either, he merely states:

"A political crime, of course."

"Of course." Cathrina nods. "I was a communist. When I returned from exile, Finland received me in triumph. Then the situation changed there too . . . I left prison only a month ago. To tell the truth, I was released conditionally, but I preferred not to wait till it was over. So I fled."

How does a crippled woman flee? Anna ponders, but Bardichinov shakes his head sympathetically, his white goatee all atremble.

"Exile, prison. . . . I am very sorry indeed, dear mademoiselle."

Dear mademoiselle moves her hand with some show of self-assertion.

"Oh, my life is a regular romance."

Anna hides a little smile as she bends over the kettle. She hasn't met a single life in Paris that wasn't a regular romance. Cathrina recounts her story eagerly, from her birth up to the present.

Bardichinov listens politely while he assiduously pours tea. After the fifth cup, the story is at an end, and Cathrina rises.

Anna springs forward. "I'll help you get to your room, if I may."

"Oh no, dear. No need at all."

No, there is no need, Anna can see that. Cathrina, with her two sticks, with her two stiff feet raised simultaneously, is more agile than anyone else.

"A very attractive lady, is she not?" Bardichinov asks when he is left alone with Anna. "How do you like her?"

"She's interesting," Anna replies, for she does not quite know how she likes her. Cathrina is lively, gay, loquacious, with no trace of the suffering she has undergone; she is determined and defiant.

"Extremely interesting." Bardichinov nods. "Now, however, I don't mind that she has gone. I want to ask you a very important question, Anna."

"Yes, Uncle Bardichinov?"

"I've told you about that acquaintance of mine, the former Italian cabinet minister who has emigrated to Paris with his wife and daughter. Do you remember?"

"Of course, Uncle Bardichinov."

"Well, the little money they brought along has all gone. The girl would like to get some work. I believe she is about your age, seventeen. Unfortunately, she has not qualified for any special work, but besides her mother tongue, she speaks French, English and German, and she is simply lovely. Her beauty is perfectly angelic, Annuska, light and ethereal like a butterfly, her hair is sparklingly golden, and yet her eyes are dark, very dark gray, or perhaps dark brown."

"Yes, Uncle Bardichinov," Anna interrupts because she is touched to the quick by other girls' beauty these days. István says she is lovely, but she often has bitter misgivings about it. "You were going to ask something. What is it?"

"Oh yes, of course. Well, as I have been saying, the little girl is simply fascinating and her manners are enchanting. She thought that perhaps, at your dressmaking establishment—as a mannequin, she might . . . Not a very pleasant profession perhaps . . ."

Anna reflects.

"Is her figure quite perfect?"

"Impeccable! A Greek goddess, a Diana—"

"What's her waist measurement?" Anna interrupts. "Because she mustn't be more than twenty-six . . ."

"As slim as a reed! And a lovely walk. I believe that is of importance."

"Well, I ought to see her first," Anna declares. "I may be able to get her the job. I think one of our mannequins is leaving on the first."

"She's the daughter of a cabinet minister, Annuska, and her manners . . ."

Anna smiles.

"One of our mannequins is a Viennese countess."

"Ah!" Bardichinov is amazed. "An emigrant too?"

"No." Anna shakes her head with a smile. "She's just poor and needs the money. She can't or she won't do it at home."

"Then maybe Pia's idea was not so bad," Bardichinov rejoices. "If aristocratic girls of other countries choose the same career . . . I confess I am prejudiced. But perhaps she is right, after all. I will speak to Pia Monica tomorrow and introduce her to you."

"Very well." Anna nods. "I'll find out in the meantime whether there's really going to be an opening."

Anna is as good as her word. Not only because she is glad to help a protégée of Bardichinov's, but also because, if she finds a good mannequin, her manageress may be grateful. Good thing the girl speaks several languages . . . there are always Americans and other foreigners at the fashion shows.

First she questions Mlle. Rose, the skinny, almost hunchbacked little Polish Jewess who is the oldest of the seamstresses. She has lived in France since she was two years old, and she only knows from her parents' recollections how they had had to flee from a pogrom. At present, Mlle. Rose is about thirty-five and a real Frenchwoman.

"A mannequin?" She shrugs her shoulders. "Yes,

we'll probably need one; I've heard Vivienne is leaving. You had better ask Mme. Andrée."

Mme. Andrée is forelady, the head of the workshop. She had married the day before war broke out, and by the time her husband first came home on leave, her eldest little boy was born. And the day before he was to come home on leave again to see his second little boy, he was killed.

"One day before." Mme. Andrée is wont to tell the story with a dramatic accent on both dates, to stress the part that Fate has played in it. Anna thinks of Cathrina, who said that her life had been a real romance; she glances at Rose, glances at Andrée, and smiles again.

Mme. Andrée is omnipotent in all that concerns the workshop only, but knows less about the business affairs and salesrooms.

"I don't know," she replies uncertainly to Anna's question. "I think someone told me that Vivienne is leaving. Ask Mme. Jacqueline."

Mme. Jacqueline is the manageress. She is very tall, her hair is snow-white; a lovely woman, with sparkling youthful eyes. The girls say that she used to be a singer. She had been a singer, traveled all over the world, made a great deal of money, and men went mad about her. With her marriages, however, Mme. Jacqueline had no luck. She had been married three times, but all her husbands died early, the first after she had been married to him four months, the second after two years, the third after four. Then Mme. Jacqueline lost her voice, and now she is the manageress of the establishment. She does not know much about the business, but she has excellent connections and knows how to deal with customers. They say Mme. Lucienne does not like her because she is so dignified and almost condescending even to her; yet she is kept on because she is very useful.

Mme. Lucienne herself is not at all dignified. She is the boss, the owner of the establishment. A small, insignificant, terribly nervous woman with a glass eye. One can't quite tell which is the glass eye; the girls always try to guess, but they can't. It happened during the war when she was getting her wounded husband from one of the field hospitals. He wasn't badly wounded, but on their way home there was a railway accident. Mme. Lucienne lost one eye, and her husband's spine was fractured. He still lay on his back, sometimes in a plaster cast, sometimes supported by all kinds of steel contraptions; and Mme. Lucienne, with one eye left, founded the dressmaking establishment. She knows her business thoroughly, she knows all about designing and color combinations, about calculations too, but she mustn't go near the more erratic kind of customer, because she is impatient, irritable and likely to offend. That is where Mme. Jacqueline comes in.

So Anna goes to the front of the shop, to the elegant sales department, to find Mme. Jacqueline.

She does not often come this way, only when she is entrusted with some quick alteration, and takes it back to the customer herself, or at the fashion shows, when she hangs around in the mannequins' room, to pull their dresses off them the moment they come in and help them put on the next.

Anna closes the workshop door behind her and looks around. It is early morning, and no customers come at such a time; the salesgirls are chatting idly.

There is no sign of Mme. Jacqueline; perhaps she hasn't come in, she seldom arrives before ten. Mme. Lucienne has locked herself up in her office; she is doing accounts or ordering materials, dictating letters, doing all the business about which one knows nothing in the workshop, yet without which there would be no work.

Anna suddenly makes up her mind to go to the mannequins' room. The simplest way is to ask them. She knocks and enters through the narrow door. Vivienne and two other girls sit at the table playing cards. Comtesse Marguerite, from Vienna, is dangling her legs from the window sill and looks dejectedly down into the narrow courtyard.

Anna does not want to disturb the card players, so she goes up to the Viennese girl.

"Comtesse Marguerite . . ."

The slender, dark-haired, blue-eyed girl suddenly turns on her, jumps down from the window sill and looks at her with vexation.

"What do you want?"

"I was only going to ask something, Comtesse Marguerite. But if I'm in the way . . ."

Comtesse Marguerite got out of bed on the wrong side this morning. She approaches Anna threateningly and glowers at her:

"I say, you're Hungarian, aren't you? My former

compatriot, or something of the kind. Can't you speak German?"

"No."

"A Hungarian girl who can't speak German! And can't you speak like a human being?"

"I beg your pardon, Comtesse Marguerite . . ."

"Comtesse Marguerite, Comtesse Marguerite! I've been living in this cursed city for the last four years, and I hear nothing else all the time. I'm like a stray dog. No one speaks like a human being to me. They keep me in this place because Comtesse Marguerite sounds well, or they'd get rid of me soon enough. I'm twenty-two, and I've been living alone for four years. My father was a diplomat, he's been a diplomat for you too, you frog! After the debacle, he adopted Jugoslav nationality, because he's a Dalmatian and he had property in Dalmatia; he thought he might save it that way. But the Serbs said he was a damned Austrian, and confiscated the estate, and he'd lost his pension by going over to Jugoslavia. Then he went down to Egypt where he was last stationed. He said he had many good friends there, they would help him build up a new existence. Poor man, he's been building it up ever since; he keeps writing me desperate letters. My mother lives at home, in Vienna, rents furnished rooms and sits waiting for the few francs which I manage to scrape together to send her. Comtesse Marguerite, Comtesse Marguerite . . . Is that all you can say, you Hungarian frog? At home they used to call me Gretl," she adds suddenly, and her eyes are full of tears.

"Don't bite my head off." Anna's smile is conciliatory. But only her lips smile, her eyes are grave. "I didn't know you were so lonely, or I should have asked you to come and see us."

"Who isn't lonely?" Marguerite says with a shrug, and wipes her eyes. "Forgive my snapping at you, but you happened to find me in a vile temper. Well, froggy, what do you want?"

"I only wanted to ask whether it's true that Mlle. Vivienne leaves on the first?"

"What does that matter to you? Do you want her place? You're too wide around the hips, and you've got freckles." However, Marguerite does not wait for an answer, but calls out to the group at the table: "Eh, Vivie! Does it still hold good that you're leaving on the first?"

"It does," Vivienne replies, without looking up from her cards. "Is it so hard to believe that I've found a man who wants to marry me?"

"He might run away before the wedding," one of the girls says almost mechanically. Vivienne does not condescend to answer but calls out:

"I'm rummy!"

"Perhaps I can recommend someone to take her place," Anna explains to Gretl. "Maybe you would make friends with her; she's a girl of good family, her father used to be a cabinet minister in Italy."

"Italian, is she?" Gretl makes a grimace. "I don't care for Italians. How old is she?"

"My age. Seventeen."

"A baby," Gretl briefly remarks. "Come along, let's speak to Jacqueline."

Anna wants to say that she'd rather take a look at the girl first, but Gretl has already opened the door leading to the salesrooms. Mme. Jacqueline has just arrived; two zealous salesgirls are helping her off with her coat.

"Mme. Jacqueline, this frog here knows of a mannequin to take Vivienne's place. The daughter of an Italian minister or something."

"H'm," says Mme. Jacqueline. "I'm not sure that Mme. Lucienne hasn't engaged someone. There was a girl here yesterday. The best thing is for you to ask her." She does not add what she thinks: that she ought to be informed of these things, and that Mme. Lucienne's absurd secretiveness is simply ridiculous. Not to mention the fact that she knows far more about choosing mannequins than Mme. Lucienne does. But that good lady wants to do everything herself, she trusts no one.

"Come in!" The answer sounds irritable when Gretl knocks on Mme. Lucienne's door. "What is it? A new mannequin? Yes, we need one. Italian? Sure to be too dark. What, you haven't seen her yet? Well, take a look at her. Daughter of a cabinet minister? That's not bad, manners are essential. Report to me afterward."

They are outside in the salesrooms again. Gretl accompanies Anna to the door of the workshop. The Hungarian girl stops on the threshold for a moment. Her glance wanders over Mme. Jacqueline's snowy hair, then to the door of the office behind which Lucienne with her glass eye is working, then it rests on Comtesse Marguerite, whom they used to call Gretl at home.

"Oh, Cathrina," she whispers as she enters the workshop. Gretl probably thinks that she has suddenly gone mad.

X

István practically lives at the Barabás'. He only goes home to sleep—he has got free quarters at an American students' home—and goes his grabbing way during the daytime; the rest of the time he spends with them.

He usually turns up sometime during the morning, to the great joy of Mrs. Barabás; helps her peel potatoes and amuses her with gay and humorous stories, with recollections of home, with his silly chatter that makes her laugh.

Strange how much surer the children's judgment is than that of their parents. The children have no confidence in István, the two grownups have fallen in love with him right away. Klári treats him with unconcealed scorn. Jani is cool and contemptuous, at any rate, in the beginning. Later Klári graciously suffers István to amuse her, and Jani involuntarily grows interested in him.

For life is undeniably more amusing since István came into it. For instance, they know nothing of Paris, that great city of many faces; they only realize now how little they know it. Their days were spent

moving between a few fixed points. Barabás goes to
the Rue du Faubourg-Saint-Honoré, to the fur shop
and back again, and at night to the Rue Saint-
Jacques; Mrs. Barabás goes to the market of the
Quartier Saint-Antoine and sometimes to the sales
of the department stores on the Rue de Rivoli;
Anna walks to the shop on the Champs-Elysées and
hardly anywhere else; the children go to school and
to the Luxembourg Gardens. Now they discover that
Paris has other aspects, interesting, strange, fascinating aspects. At night, on the Place Pigalle, a thousand signs sparkle in colored lights; in front of the
Opéra, five rows of motorcars crowd the street in a
stream that never stops roaring; near the Porte
Maillot, smart riders and amazons in bowler hats
gallop on Sunday mornings. (On weekdays too,
István says, and the family is particularly impressed
by this.)

As a matter of fact, this Paris is no newer and no
stranger to them than similar parts of Budapest
would be, which they knew just as little. Still, they
feel that they are now getting an inkling of remote,
great and mysterious Life for the first time. There is
some truth in that. Perhaps it is only that Paris is
more lighthearted than Budapest. The city is per-
vaded by an easygoing gaiety, a natural and secure,
familiar, almost idle, gaiety. Budapest is feverish
when it is gay; Paris is merely light and happy. The
air is thinner than it is at home, the war has been
over for seven years, the city has forgotten that it
ever was in danger; Budapest will not be able to forget it for decades. The Barabás family climb Mont-

martre to the Sacré-Cœur and look down upon the city, they venture into the distinguished silence of the Parc Monceau and feel they are in a place as strange as America, Mars or the Milky Way.

István takes them to the races at Longchamps, takes them to Versailles and Fontainebleau. Of course, Barabás pays for these excursions; Barabás pays all the expenses, and he does not mind at all. The expense is not so very great; they go to the cheap places, they travel third class, and, after all, one should get acquainted with the country one lives in. Not even Mrs. Barabás takes any notice of the fact that since they began to be on friendly terms with István, they haven't taken a single centime to the bank. Yet Anna, too, earns decent wages now, and the two children really cost next to nothing; they needn't even give them supper unless they want to, their schools would gladly take care of them entirely. Until lately Anna handed over all her earnings to her mother, but she keeps a few francs now; after all, she is a grown-up girl—and no one knows that István irrevocably borrows these few francs from time to time.

Anna fights tooth and nail against love, this new love which she feels is cruel and humiliating. The fight is in vain. István is a scoundrel, he knows what he wants, and it is so delightful to believe him.

"Anna, why do you always want to run across to old Uncle Bardichinov when I'm here?" Anna usually wants to, but doesn't go in the end. "Don't you care for me, Anna? You know I care for you.

Come here, look into my eyes." István's touch is dreadful, it makes one want to cry and nestle up to him. "You've such lovely, warm eyes, Annuska; no use trying to look angry, you can't."

Anna turns away and tries to withdraw her hand.

"Let me go to the kitchen, I must help Mother get supper."

"She doesn't need your help. Your father hasn't come home yet. Come and sit beside me, Anna. Your mouth is beautiful, do you know that? It's sullen and sad, but it would smile right away if you'd let me kiss it."

"No! Let me go, István. I'll call Mother."

"I could kiss you if I wanted to, Anna. I'm stronger than you are. Get away if you can. But I shan't kiss you until you want me to. Or do you want me to, only you won't say so? See, my mouth is here, near yours, only an inch from yours. Why won't you do what you're longing to do? I want you to come nearer. My mouth is waiting for you, Anna."

"The children are in the next room . . ."

"The children are doing their lessons. They won't come in, no one will come in. Just one little kiss, Anna, just a sisterly kiss, to ease your conscience. Silly little girl, why don't you give in? Your eyes are full of tears. Shall I kiss you? I see that's what you want. . . . Was it so very terrible? Come and let me put my arms around you. There! I don't think anyone has ever kissed you before, baby."

No one has ever kissed Anna. This is the first time, and it's lovely and terrible. For Anna sees István clearly now, although later her vision of him will grow dimmer; sometimes, for some moments, in the trance of passion, she will believe him to be true and noble. Today she is merely conscious of tormented agitation, hypnotic attraction and mortal terror. She fears István like fire, she fights with clenched teeth against love, and the first kiss does not break down her resistance. István must go on bargaining for every pressure of her hand, for every fleeting kiss. Undoubtedly István is the stronger of the two; he is wicked and masterful, and sometimes he plays with Anna as a cat plays with a mouse—but even in her weakness, Anna is an unhappy and determined opponent.

It is Sunday afternoon, the family is preparing to go out. István is taking them to Montmartre, to a little cabaret called Cabaret de Néant. A sign on the door says: "Admission five francs, but it isn't worth it"; another: "Think twice before you spend your money on such tomfoolery." And the ushers are dressed like undertakers, István says.

Anna hardly listens. She is not naïve enough to be amazed, and not cynical enough to smile benevolently at that sort of thing. And today, thank goodness, she must go to Uncle Bardichinov to meet the Italian girl. If not, she would join the others, irrefutably join them as she mostly does, after vain attempts to persuade István and herself that she is busy, that she must work, launder her things, draw or do some sewing. Today she must meet the Italian girl—an official duty, previously arranged and not to be put off; so she speeds István and the family on their way with a sense of relief and yet with a heavy heart.

"I don't love him," she tells herself and stubbornly repeats: "I don't love him."

She often stands before the glass now, looking squarely into her eyes, and says again and again: "I don't love him"; she often walks to the rhythm of those words along the streets, and hears them in the throbbing of the métro.

Then Anna puts on the brand-new and very pretty dress that she finished late last night—she did not put it on for István to see, just to spite herself; she resisted the temptation heroically, she did not, she did not put it on, although she knows that she made it for István, to please István. She did not really need a new dress. Anyway, she didn't put it on. Now she slips into it. "I don't love him," she repeats, "I don't love him," and goes across the street to Uncle Bardichinov's.

They sit in his room waiting for the Italian girl.

"You don't read much these days," Uncle Bardichinov says reprovingly. "Of course the drawing lessons are important, but still, education . . ."

Anna does not confess that she has lately rather neglected the drawing lessons as well. She is at the workshop till six, she could always use only the evenings for study, and now István is always with them for the evenings. When she was an apprentice, she never came home before half past seven or eight, because the workshop had to be swept or dresses delivered; yet she had found more time to read than she does now, more time to keep her things tidy.

Uncle Bardichinov's shirts too . . . Anna is ashamed, and promptly decides that she will take the mending home tonight.

"I've been making this dress," she apologizes. "How do you like it?"

Old Bardichinov looks at it with critical eyes.

"Very pretty. Quite right of you to get a few smarter dresses." Uncle Bardichinov bends closer and says in an agitated whisper: "Lenin is dead. The Soviets try to keep it a secret, but he is dead. He had cancer, just as I told you. I'll take you to Petrograd with me, Anna. I will adopt you. Will you come?"

"Of course, Uncle Bardichinov," Anna replies politely for the hundredth time. That is precisely the number of times she has heard the rumor of Lenin's death, always under the seal of strict secrecy and with the promise of adoption.

An eager and shy finger knocks at the door.

"Come in!" Uncle Bardichinov cries, and both rise. Pia Monica Meneghetti has arrived.

Of course, the two girls do not recognize each other. It is more than five years ago since they met at the station in Buchs for a few moments: nothing could be seen of Anna above the rim of the milk jug except her nut-brown eyes, and Pia Monica had been just a vision, a fairy child, fleeting beauty; her corporeal existence counted for nothing. Anna has forgotten the vision, but even were she reminded of it, she could not have recalled a single feature.

Uncle Bardichinov has not been wrong in his judgment: Pia Monica is lovely. Anna looks at her in some embarrassment, but with the eyes of an expert, and her impression is that the girl is perfect; no malevolent eye could find a flaw in her. Of course, it would be good to have a look at her back . . . although her poise shows that her figure must be lovely from the back too, a dressmaker's eyes cannot be deceived . . . still, one might as well . . . well, in a little while; one can't go for her the moment one is introduced.

They sit opposite each other, both slightly embarrassed, and Uncle Bardichinov helps them to make conversation. There is need for help, especially in the case of Anna, who gazes in fascination at the other girl's radiant fair hair, the tender golden-brown bloom on her velvety skin, and her large brown eyes, and is busy envying Pia Monica. If only she were as beautiful . . . no, Anna couldn't say what would be changed, would be turned for the better . . . Gretl, for instance . . . Gretl is nearly as beautiful, and yet—Anna breaks off her chain of thought.

Pia Monica has grown lively and is no longer shy.

"I wish I could get some work," she explains eagerly. "Not only because I need the money, really not. Until now I went to the lycée, but I didn't like it. I wasn't good at lessons, and the girls are so different from our girls at home. They aren't modest at all, and they only appreciate those who are aggressive and arrogant."

Anna nods with a smile and thinks of Klári, who is the uncontested leader of her class. She thinks Pia's remark hits the nail on the head. Bardichinov gives a subtle analysis of the French spirit, its zest for self-assertion and the prestige of the Cadets de Gascogne.

Pia Monica listens with scant attention.

"Never mind." She waves airily. "A good thing it's over. We've no more money left for schools. It's dreadful of me to say so, when my father and mother are so worried about it. Father wanted me to go to the university, Mother thought of a Swiss finishing school—both absolutely useless. Had I known we were so short of money, I shouldn't have let them send me to such an expensive school at all. We've been here for three years. If I had started to learn dancing or gone to a stage school right away, I could make a lot of money by now."

"Do you want to be an actress?" Anna asks with interest.

"I don't know," Pia Monica replies frankly. "I'll tell you how it is. . . . I don't know how to do anything properly. Other girls want to study law or chemistry or make discoveries . . . or be dress-makers," she adds quickly, with a glance at Anna to see whether she has hurt her feelings by almost omitting her modest profession.

Anna laughs.

"No, I don't think other girls particularly care to be dressmakers. And what do you mean by making discoveries?"

"Well," Pia Monica says rather uncertainly, "all sorts of discoveries. The North Pole, and unknown places in Africa, or new rays, like Mme. Curie."

Uncle Bardichinov throws himself into the breach

and explains the difference between the two kinds of discoveries.

Pia Monica hardly listens, but nods gratefully.

"That's what I meant," she says, and turns to Anna again. "Well, you see, those serious sorts of things don't attract me. It's a disgrace, but it's the truth. That's why I thought there was nothing else for it but the stage. But Mother went into fits when I so much as mentioned it. Perhaps she'd let me do it now, but it's too late now for a profession that takes years of study. I must earn money as quickly as I can. Do you think I'll do?" She looks at Anna apprehensively.

"I certainly do." Anna nods.

"And your dear father, my excellent friend, M. le Ministre," Bardichinov puts in, "would he have let you go on the stage?"

Pia Monica gazes at him reflectively.

"I think so. By his political convictions he belongs to that old school that doesn't try to make people happy against their will."

"My convictions are the same," says Bardichinov.

"You two are behind the times, M. Bardichinov," smiles Mlle. Meneghetti.

"Yes," Bardichinov agrees quietly, and he, too, smiles.

Pia Monica gently pats the old banker's carefully manicured, tremulous hands.

Anna glances at the little face with its golden-brown flush, and is a little confused. Up till now, she felt infinitely older than this communicative, gay and sweetly silly child, but she is not so sure of it now.

She has caught a momentary glimpse of a different Pia Monica, a bitter and wise adult, matured by homelessness, whose carefree laughter is nothing more than a blaring orchestra playing on a sinking ship.

It is only a fleeting impression. Anna thinks no more of it and does not guess that never in her life has she been so close to the majesty hidden in the human soul, to the secret of solitude and poise, to the strange nakedness that is impenetrable, impervious concealment itself. Since she has known István she no longer dreams of snow-covered peaks. Even when she tries to deceive herself by thinking that István's charm and his gift of quick and humorous repartee have their source in the bright purity of his spirit, even when she tries to believe that the easygoing contempt with which István regards every honest effort is a sign of his superiority, she knows that is not what she is looking for. She seeks strength, the lone and chill clarity of the soul, complete freedom from petty and shameful weaknesses, which probably does not exist at all. She knows she is yearning for something impossible, but so does everyone who seeks something beautiful and noble. Impossible is only another word for ideal. And the ideal of a girl, especially of a lonely girl, early hardened by self-command and servitude, is the same where man or where life is concerned— majesty.

Men probably do not understand this. They, too, seek an ideal in womanhood, in their future life companion or in the abstract vision of their desires, but this ideal generally tends toward the pet canary or the lap dog type. They want her to be faithful, humble and devoted, or gay, chattering and care-free, but they have no desire for the untamed freedom of the spirit, for the light that shines within itself, for the Law and for the Secret.

"Do you really think I'll do?" Pia Monica turns to Anna again, and her face is once more that of an eager child, bearing no trace of what passed over it a moment ago.

"May I ask you to get up for a moment and turn around slowly?" Anna asks, full of official zeal.

"Of course!" Pia Monica jumps to her feet, turns and struts about the room with her arms akimbo at a graceful angle; then she inquires anxiously: "Are my movements all right?"

"Rather exaggerated." Anna laughs. "You'll stop that in time. As soon as you get accustomed to a mannequin's job, your movements will be quite natural."

"Accustomed!" Bardichinov grumbles. "I hope she will have no time to get accustomed to it. I hope this senseless and terrible exile will soon come to an end for us both. And as for having to choose this unpleasant profession . . . I can't tell you, Mlle. Meneghetti, how much I sympathize with you."

Pia Monica fidgets in some embarrassment.

"I am very anxious to earn money," she falters evasively. She looks at Anna as though she expected assistance from her, but Anna does not speak. Pia Monica cannot explain to a man so much older the thing that she feels but dimly herself—that her gen-

eration was born on a volcano. When they were six,
their fathers went to war and their mothers went to
live with their parents, or sent their children to them
and nursed the wounded in field hospitals, or took
a two-room flat instead of the old eight-room one,
or moved with their children to the sordid hotel of
some little town behind the front where their husbands were in hospital, or fled from scurrying troops,
or wandered from a modest bourgeois home to the
luxury of a ministerial mansion, or into exile, or into
a refugee's railway carriage home—or went through
all these variations without transition. This generation was born and shunted about, was born and had
to flee. The ordinary changes of life which men used
to call Destiny, no more surprise them. They do not
appreciate their historical value and are not sorry
for themselves.

"I am very anxious to earn money," Pia Monica
says simply, and looks at Anna because she expects
her to understand. Anna understands only too well,
so well that she thinks no comments are necessary.
She takes the measurement of Pia Monica's waist-
line and nods with satisfaction, then launches upon
instructions as to what time she is to present herself
at the shop next day and whom she is to ask for.
Bardichinov watches them with disapproval and
feels injured as a representative of the old order of
things.

XI

NEW HUNGARIANS keep arriving these days. They are not many, yet there are two kinds, neither of which can be classed among the three old groups.

Many interesting things have been going on at home, although the Hungarians in Paris know little about it. The newcomers tell the tale of the three past years with expressive gestures: "inflation" is one of the words they use, "conjuncture" and "boom" are others—words which few people have heard before. Barabás never has. Luckily Liiv is here, and he knows all about it. Liiv explains, speaks of false prosperity, of a brief and deceptive carnival, of the mirage which valueless money displays to deluded eyes. The newcomers speak of millions: Barabás begins to understand that they are false millions, worth no more than his week's wages.

So they find out that during the past two or three years money has been flowing in streams at home, although in diluted and troubled streams. A smaller part of the newcomers are gentlemen—or perhaps ex-gentlemen—who, during the boom, promptly got rid of their landed property and founded banks, or gave up government posts to enter into partnership

with stockbrokers, for the stock exchange was the
source of the sudden money wave, and prices rose
with the precipitated sinking of currency. Then the
stream ebbed away. Some of the gentlemen were
sent to prison, because it was alleged that they had
not taken proper care of the money entrusted to
them, yet they had only grown lightheaded with
easily acquired wealth and thought it was going to
last forever. The clever ones put a bit of money
aside and went abroad to start new lives.

Barabás understands the second group of newcomers still less. They say they were just put on the
"B-list." It sounds like a military formation, but
these people are all thin, narrow-chested clerks and
officials. They say they've lost their jobs, but they
can give no explanation that sounds plausible to
Barabás, and since the majority of the group are
Jews, he concludes that a B-list must be something
specifically Jewish.

The two groups resemble each other inasmuch as
the members of both have a little cash on hand. They
are noisier and gayer than the old arrivals. They
entertain grand business projects. Some mean to
establish a gambling casino, others talk of theater
ticket agencies or of Hungarian confectioneries. All
the projects aim at something that caters to luxury
and entertainment. They had learnt this at home,
when they drifted along in the diluted stream of
unexpected wealth. There's no real chance except
in luxury stunts, they say.

Peter Hallay, for instance, intends to establish a
Hungarian night club. His impression is that the

French don't really know how to enjoy themselves. He is going to teach them. He tells István about his plans, and he could not have found anyone more suitable. István has a thousand ideas—the club is to be furnished like a Hungarian peasant cottage, with painted furniture and embroideries, with peasant pottery and garlands of paprika on the walls. Or it might represent a fishing barge on the Tisza River, and the fish stew could be cooked in a big caldron on the dance floor. It wouldn't be half bad either, to have a little Buda tavern with geranium pots in the windows and little imitation summerhouses. And a gypsy band, of course, in crimson Hussar uniforms. Hallay assents, thinks István might make a useful manager, commissions him to find a locality and advances him a little money.

As a result of the advance, István is as elegantly dressed as a duke and does not come to the Barabás' quite so often, and when he does, he speaks exclusively of the future undertaking and of his own genius. The trappings of the Hungarian night club arouse Barabás's latent patriotism; his wife is interested too because furnishing and decorating are woman's business; Klári pricks up her ears, for after a childhood spent in the sordid city neighborhood of Nefelejts Street, all this is as new to her as it is to the French.

Anna is grim and silent. This new affluence and this new importance in life only increase the distance between István and herself. They had been strangers until now, and incurably different. István, a bank clerk, a small bourgeois brought up to be a gentleman, who condescended to the dressmaker, the workman's daughter, with the superiority, the security of a higher social standing. This is the last straw. István already dreams of the dancers at the night club over whom he will be omnipotent. It isn't that he does not take Anna in his arms in the dark hall, it isn't that he does not call for her at the shop sometimes and draw her into some dark gateway on the way home—but that is not what Anna wants. It isn't what she wants, although her heart throbs suddenly at his kisses and her body flutters like a butterfly stuck on a pin. Even now, when István talks of the night club again:

"We'll have a gypsy band out from Budapest, and sell Hungarian wines: Egri, Csopaki . . ." His hand seeks Anna's under the table, and Anna grows pale at its pressure.

Jani's silence is grimmer still. Jani hates the name of Hallay. He was the first to meet with it. The others know nothing about this, only Anna, and she does not know much. Peter Hallay did not arrive alone. He brought his fourteen-year-old son with him, and probably it was István who recommended the school where Jani studies. Jani was looking forward to the Hungarian boy's arrival with feverish joy. Since the death of Vassja he has been friendless—no, not quite; there are Félicien, Gilbert and Julien, with whom he gets on rather well; there is the entire class in which Jani is popular . . . but it isn't the same thing. The Hungarian boy will be different, a friend, a real companion, more than a brother.

"Jean Barabas—Elemér Hallay," they introduce

themselves, and the two boyish faces search each other awkwardly for a moment.

"How long have you been living here?"

"I, oh, over five years."

"What's your father?"

"A furrier."

Elemér is astonished.

"Funny. They told my father this was an exclusive school."

Elemér is a good-natured boy, and as soon as he has uttered the words he is sorry, especially when he sees Jani's cheeks grow crimson. He has been here only two weeks, he cannot yet be aware of the sensitiveness born from alien surroundings, and does not know the absolute democracy of a French school, where every boy is the other's equal and a self-assertive little citizen, wherever he has come from. Elemér means well, but up till now he has attended a private school and had a valet to serve him.

"It doesn't really matter if one's father is a furrier," he says quickly and conciliatingly.

"I advise you not to come to this school," says Jani in a polite tone that bodes ill. "Some of us are the sons of peasants . . . Pierre, for instance. He's top of the class in geography, probably because he works on the land all summer. Alain's father is a lamplighter. Take care whom you speak to, you might get your hands dirty. Good day."

Jani turned his back upon the other boy and was gone. Elemér looked after him, then shrugged his shoulders. He hadn't meant to hurt Jani's feelings —apparently the fellow's crazy. Well, he'll get over it. But Jani never spoke to him again. Worse still, he started a regular campaign against Elemér, set the boys against him, made his life miserable.

Félicien didn't understand it.

"You were so pleased he was coming. You said you were the same kind of . . . Hungarian, was it? . . . of Hungarian origin. And now you're mad with him."

Jani is confused. He has an instant, fleeting recollection of a piece in his board school primer about Ferenc Rákóczi II, hero of eighteenth-century Hungary. He starts to lie glibly:

"There are Hungarians and Hungarians. A Kuruc is one thing and a Labanc is another. We, the Kuruc, fought on your side; the Labanc fought with the Germans. They betrayed us to the boches. Hallay is a Labanc, that's why I hate him."

Félicien listens, amazed. He calls Julien and Charles, then Gilbert and Camille to listen too. Jani adds new details to the pretended atrocities of the long-extinct Labanc faction.

Of course, the class believes Jani because he is Jean Barabas, a French boy even though he may be of "Kuruc" extraction; he speaks their language, he has been their comrade and friend for years. Even if Elemér were made to face the accusation, he could scarcely defend himself, for he speaks the kind of Fräuleiny French that is taught to Hungarian children by Swiss nursemaids—and that's not good enough here. But he does not know what he is accused of. He only knows that the whole class is hostile. Whenever he walks past another boy, they pretend he's tripped them up and start a fight. They smash his fountain pen. They throw down his coat from its peg. They steal his lunch. They soil his copybooks. They mock and jeer and contradict him, whatever he says. Whoever makes any mischief lays the blame at his door and the entire class is ready to swear to the truth of the calumny. If he protests, they thrash him.

Elemér stands uncomprehendingly in the midst of the storm and sometimes seeks refuge with Jani. But Jani is cool, polite and aloof. He takes no part in the man-hunt that he started, that he kindled and fed; he takes no part in it, but neither does he try to put a stop to it. He looks on silently and a bit uncomfortably like the magician's apprentice who did not expect such powerful spirits to rally to his call.

"Why do the boys go for me all the time?" Elemér queries petulantly.

"How should I know, M. Hallay?"

"Why do you call me by such a silly name? All the boys call each other by their first names here."

"Only poor boys like me, M. Hallay. I wouldn't dream of calling a fine gentleman like you by his first name."

"You did when we first met."

"That was in the beginning before I knew who it was that had kindly condescended to go to school with us. Forgive my impudence, M. Hallay."

Elemér turns away with tears in his eyes. He is dimly conscious of the fact that Jani is his greatest enemy, Jani who never says a word against him. The others seem to hurt him mechanically, almost absent-mindedly. Elemér puts up with it a few weeks longer, then he plagues his father to take him out of the school.

Jani, on the other hand, feels that he has not been acting quite correctly. His guilty conscience makes him tell the story to Anna, almost as it had happened, except for the fact that he had let his imagination run riot with some details of Hungarian history. Anna listens with limited interest, and doesn't give Jani the absolution he had secretly hoped for. She does not say that Jani is justified in hating the conceited fellow. Anna has seen a good many things, and has decided that the laws of friendship and affection are incalculable. Things always turn out different than one had expected.

For instance, Cathrina. Bardichinov introduced her triumphantly to the company at the bistro. Cathrina is a communist, so one might rightly have expected Liiv, the socialist, and particularly Alvarez, the anarchist, to receive her with enthusiasm. What happened instead? Liiv received her with rigid reticence, and Alvarez quarreled with her so violently at their first meeting that Bardichinov feared there would be bloodshed at the table that had been the scene of so many peaceful debates.

Bardichinov does not take Cathrina with him any more. Yet he, the conservative, has a frank liking and esteem for her. Stranger still, Mrs. Barabás is enamored of Cathrina. So is István. In the morning Cathrina, leaning on her two sticks, stumbles up to the fourth floor, and sits until lunchtime in Mrs.

Barabás's kitchen, sometimes helping her to shell peas. If István is there, they crack jokes and make Mrs. Barabás laugh; these last weeks, since István comes less often, Cathrina sits alone on the kitchen stool. She entertains Mrs. Barabás, telling her stories of Siberia and the revolution in Finland, and the friendship between the two women grows warmer every day.

The strangest thing, however, is the affair of Gretl and Pia Monica. Anna could have sworn that they would be inseparable, close and intimate friends. Instead, Gretl loathes Pia from the first moment, simply persecutes her and embitters her life in the thousand and one ways in which an old hand can torment an inferior.

Anna tried to intervene, but Gretl went for her.

"Your place is in the workshop. What business is it of yours? I've got to teach her if I want to turn her into a decent mannequin."

"But you're torturing her!"

"What if I am? She'd better learn what life is like."

Anna sighs and withdraws. And Pia—Pia is not so wise as Anna. She suffers, pale and silent, or she hides in the storeroom and weeps. She tries terribly hard to do her best. But it is not in her nature to disarm the enemy, neither with flattery nor with gentleness. Goodness, what an enemy Anna found in Mlle. Rose when she first came to the shop! She found fault with everything, hustled, scolded, bullied. In those days it was Anna who suffered in si-

lence and did her best, and hid away to weep. Then
Vassja died, and suddenly Anna had grown in-
sensible and wise.

"How kind of you, Mlle. Rose, to take so much
trouble with me," she would say when Mlle. Rose
threw her work back at her head. "If we had sent it
to the salesroom like that, Mme. Andrée would have
noticed and I'd have got into trouble."

Mlle. Rose was taken aback and scarcely ever
found fault with Anna's work again. Nevertheless,
Anna continued to show her everything.

"You've always been so kind to me, Mlle. Rose.
Would you mind looking whether this is all right?"

Mlle. Rose believed that she had always been
good to Anna, and after that she actually was.

Today she simply worships her. If there is some
urgent work to be finished and Anna has to stay at
the shop after hours, Mlle. Rose snatches it out of
her hand.

"Leave it to me, I'll finish it. Run along, your
boy's surely waiting."

"Dear Mlle. Rose. I really can't let you . . . You're
so infinitely kind."

"Get out!" she tells Anna energetically. "If you
are here a moment longer, I'll throw the iron at your
head."

Mlle. Rose stands up to Mme. Andrée if she wants
to keep Anna at the shop after hours.

"The little girl must go home," she blares forth.
"She goes to a tailoring course . . . Mme. Lucienne
wants her to learn tailoring. What are we to tell her
if she asks us why we don't let her go to her lesson?"

Everybody gives in to the argument. Anna takes her coat and runs along. Yet István rarely waits for her these days. István is busy with the night club.

"When we've done with the decorating, I'll have more time," István promises. "Then it'll be early enough if I look in about nine or ten."

Anna nods, but there is a lump in her throat. Formerly she always wanted István to work, to earn his daily bread like other decent people. Now that he is working, it isn't what Anna imagined it to be.

One evening Pia Monica is waiting for her in the street instead of István. Her dark eyes are radiant, her fair hair and perfect teeth are radiant too, and she asks Anna to have tea with them next day. Her father and mother would like to meet her and thank her for helping Pia to get a job.

Anna laughs, murmurs something about it all being Uncle Bardichinov's doing, she only wanted to do the firm a favor—and promises to come. Next day is Saturday, their afternoon is free.

Anna dresses carefully, but without any stage fright. A visit at the Italian cabinet minister's house holds no fears for her. After all, she knows plenty of cabinet ministers, Uncle Liiv is one, if one likes to put it that way, and Uncle Bardichinov has once taken Anna to the Café Royal when he was going to have a game of chess with Venizelos. So a cabinet minister more or less doesn't count. Meneghetti is a very dark-skinned, wiry, dry little man. His features are mobile, his black eyes beautiful. Pia has inherited his eyes, but in other ways she resembles her mother, a cool, blond, lovely woman with a delicate complexion. And there is something else that Pia has from her father, her long, narrow, nervous hands, with gestures as graceful and expressive as dancing. Under Meneghetti's rugged white eyebrows his black eyes flash, the silvery hair has thinned on his brow in the shape of two little horns: the little dark man has something of a Mephisto in every way.

He is full of flashing vivacity, of wit and humor. Anna falls in love with him at once. After five minutes they chat like old friends. Anna enjoys his quick and light temperament, his wise, melancholy mockery, and she thinks she has never met a more wonderful man than Meneghetti. The conversation skims over many subjects. Every one of his remarks is original, and tremendously amusing.

"Feminine fashions?" he says. "There was a time when men wore bright and rich clothes. At that time life was worth living. Today every man wants to dress like his neighbor. They wear black fascist shirts or black Russian blouses. And all wear the same sort of cap. Caps are more dangerous than anything, Mlle. Anne. Bear in mind what I tell you. The world will finish hanging itself when you ladies won't be able to tell your caps apart in the cloakroom, just as we stupid and unimaginative men can't."

"If women start wearing uniforms, we'll both starve, Pia Monica and I," Anna remarks.

"Very likely, and many other things will die out which have stood for beauty in this crooked world. Feminism, Mlle. Anne. Better take care of that too.

You've made a mistake, Mlle. Anne, you've chosen the wrong slogan. You've been crying 'rights for women' although what really happened was that you have voluntarily and generously relinquished all your rights. You have really given us a present, a big present in work and in taxes. You have absolved us from the duty of keeping you, marrying you off, helping you on with your coats. I don't mean that I won't help you on with yours . . . May I peel an orange for you, Mlle. Anne?"

There is coffee on the table, plenty of fine fruit and sweet red claret—an Italian tea party. The hostess, the beautiful blond woman who is half a head taller than her husband, sits cool and absent-mindedly and scarcely takes part in the conversation. Anna, who in spite of all her wisdom knows little about life, decides that she is probably very distinguished, and despises her husband as well as the humble guest. Anna thinks that Meneghetti probably was a highly gifted man of humble origin, who fought his way up into the cabinet and married a countess. She doesn't know that to be really unconstrained and to create a sense of equality without condescension is a gift that belongs only to a very distinguished few, those who are distinguished in spirit and by education alike, and that the rigidity of Mme. Meneghetti is that of the ambitious bourgeoise. Meneghetti could use the title of marquis if he chose, and his wife is the daughter of an honest shopkeeper.

Anyway, Anna feels very happy, and when she must start for home she runs lightly down the stairs of the pleasant Montparnasse hotel. Someone rises in the lounge as she passes. It is István.

"I looked in on you, and heard you were here. You mustn't hurry home. I said we were going to the pictures. But we won't. Now, at last, you'll come to me."

Anna shakes her head with a bitter smile. The proposition is not new. István has begged, entreated, insulted and threatened her for weeks now. For weeks? For months, almost ever since he has known her. But the night club and the last weeks have increased his confidence; he now insists on Anna's visit as a sort of homage that is his due.

They leave the hotel behind them, then Anna answers bitterly and dryly:

"Let's stick to the pictures. I'll pay."

"You needn't. I've got money . . . But, Annuska, my darling little ladybird . . ."

Anna sighs. She knows precisely what's coming. She could repeat every word. She has heard it a hundred times. Entreaties first, sweet, ardent and imploring words that are so difficult to resist: "I love you, Annuska, and you love me too . . . Why do you torment me? Why don't you let me take you in my arms . . . smother you with kisses . . . be good to you? Why won't you let us be happy?"

Let's get over this, Anna thinks wearily. The rest is easy, for the rest is insult, the hostile and petty abuse of bourgeois morals, of foolish prejudice, of her cowardice. It hurts, but that doesn't matter.

What is it that gives Anna the strength to hold out, to resist, to shake her head stubbornly in spite of love and awakening desire? She has drifted from her country, which, at the same time, means a moral stronghold in the way of literature, of the pulpit, of public opinion. She has outgrown parental authority. These two kind people whom she loves are different, more childish, more unsuspecting. School is far behind her. She sees no example, no reward and no ideal. Vassja is dead. There is no one to protect or to lead her, no support or source of strength anywhere.

Yet there is. Anna has been brought up by the streets of Paris, the relationship of man and woman has few aspects that she does not know. She has wandered along the pavements of Paris and observed this unequal conflict. It would be too much to say that she has learned precaution or wise judgment. She has merely learned sane skepticism, a feeling of proportion and a sense of balance, has learned to distinguish between that which has no weight and that which endures. István has no weight, and his desire is not enduring. He offers no protection from the dangers which are very unequally divided in this age-old game. Anna yearns for some sort of truth, which is merely another way of saying that she longs for a clean and honorable love. The memory of the sparkling snow on the peaks has grown dim, but a little radiance is still reflected from them, although faintly and from far away. This is not love.

If István would ask her to marry him, Anna would probably accept, although she knows that she would have to work for them both all her life. Still, she might make herself believe that this is love. But István will not ask her; István is a bank clerk and aims higher. He only desires Anna's young body, and he begs and entreats, insults and threatens.

They do not go to the pictures, they walk along the streets and quarrel. That is to say, István quarrels and Anna weeps in silence. She loves István and is ashamed of this unworthy love; she shakes her head stubbornly and goes home.

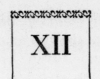
THE NIGHT CLUB is ready, and Hallay is short of money. Of course, everything has cost more and is of cheaper quality than they had planned—that is always the way.

"All we need is a few thousand francs for publicity until people get to know and like the place." István explains to Barabás and announces that Hallay is going to call on him next day.

Had Hallay not come to the Street of the Fishing Cat, Barabás might have taken his little hoard out of the bank and given it to István. For if a gentleman merely sends for your money, it may mean good business. But if he comes to get it himself, if he shakes hands with the humble workman and cajoles and flatters him . . . then either the gentleman is no gentleman, or the business is not business.

Yes, Barabás might have confided his money to István, the mountebank, but he will not give it to Hallay—Hallay, who owned an estate and a model farm until he went and founded a bank in Budapest. Yet Hallay is a pleasant and companionable Hungarian gentleman, superficial perhaps, but certainly no liar, and he does not even descend to flattery;

yet Barabás feels that the visit alone is a humiliation!

When Hallay and István have gone, a great family council begins, in which even Klári takes part. Anna and Jani veto the plan energetically. Klári says it would be great fun, Mrs. Barabás keeps anxiously silent. She fears for the little money they've put by, yet she believes implicitly in István and in the promised high rate of interest. Barabás is suspicious.

After violent speeches of protest from Anna and Jani, the family reject the plan of a loan.

István does not show up for five days. He is angry. At last, one evening, he turns up because he is hungry. Barabás is at the bistro, his wife has gone to bed.

"I thought I'd look in before going to the night club," István says. "Can I have a bite? I'll have supper at the club . . . I usually sup on lobster or oysters these days . . . just something to keep me going until supper."

Anna ransacks the storeroom, but cautiously makes Klári go along with her so that István can't follow and find her alone. Then the four of them sit around the table, István eats ravenously and relates:

"It was silly of your father not to go into partnership with Hallay. It's a gold mine. A few years more, and I'll have made myself independent. I say, children, we've got a headwaiter . . . the most original type you ever saw. I'm going to take him along. . . . Please get me a little salt, Anna." Anna gets the salt. István goes on with his story. "Do you know how easy it would be to make a wopping lot of money? I've got a wonderful idea for a huge check fraud. Shall I tell you about it?"

"Do," Klári commands.

"For a check fraud?" Jani is amazed.

"Of course, I don't intend to do it. I've just thought of it. It's the idea of a genius. Imagine a very distinguished American gentleman walking into the Crédit Lyonnais. With a nonchalant gesture he throws onto the desk a check drawn on an American bank. The check is made out for half a million francs."

"Is the check genuine?" Jani inquires.

"Of course not. The American gentleman has had the check printed in Paris. Of course, the Crédit Lyonnais does not honor such a huge check on an unknown American bank. With many apologies they say that they must first inquire whether it is covered. 'Mais naturellement,' says the gentleman with an American accent, and throws a five-dollar bill on the desk. 'For cable expenses,' he says grandly, and departs."

"Without the money?" Klári jeers. "That's easy enough. I could do that."

"Wait, silly," István silences her. "Well, he departs. The Crédit Lyonnais sends a cable. Next morning the telegraph boy arrives and brings the American bank's reply. Mr. So-and-so has a deposit of three million dollars."

"How's that possible?" Jani demands, taken aback.

"Isn't the check forged after all?" asks Klári.

"Well, what do you think? Guess if you can. Half an hour later the gentleman arrives and his check is honored without further delay."

"The check was genuine," Klári says.

"Of course, it wasn't."

"Then the cable was forged too," is Jani's guess. "But how can you forge a cable?"

"You're on the right track," István admits. "Don't rack your brains any longer. You couldn't guess anyway. It takes my own genius to do that."

"But still, how's the trick done?"

"Listen. You send two telegrams to your own address. One says: 'Mr. So-and-so has a deposit of two hundred dollars at the Crédit Lyonnais, Paris.' The signature doesn't matter. The other telegram says: 'Such-and-such a bank of New York'—you here put the name of the American bank in question —'has a capital of three million dollars.' The signature doesn't matter here either. Do you see the point? Two innocent telegrams, yet they contain the necessary words for the bank's reply, even down to the address 'Crédit Lyonnais, Paris' and the place where it is sent from, New York. All you have to do now is to get an empty telegraph form in a post office, stick the carefully cut out words on it. Your accomplice dresses up as a telegraph boy and delivers the cable at the bank. Now, what do you think of that?"

They are amazed. István swallows the last mouthful and gets up. "Well, I must be off to the night club. It's the time when guests begin to pour in. So long. See you again soon."

Peace is restored. And that's bad enough for Anna,

for when István comes again it is Saturday afternoon, and Pia Monica is just returning Anna's call at Montparnasse. "Enchantée, M. Weygand,"—she smiles when he is introduced, and her voice is music in his ears for weeks to come.

Even a mountebank may fall in love.

Incredible things happen to István that afternoon. He doesn't tell a single lie, he is simply mute. He gazes at the graceful blond girl with admiration. He is only galvanized back to life when Pia says good-bye. Then István jumps to his feet and offers to take her home.

The visit isn't quite so great a success as was Anna's at Montparnasse, where M. Meneghetti was present, small, thin, dark and enchanting. As a matter of fact, the two girls don't quite know what to say to each other. They certainly understand each other, their fate has brought them close, but there is nothing to be said about it. Beyond that, they have little in common—at most, a faint and hazy sympathy, that is all. So as soon as they have finished discussing the affairs of the shop, the conversation flags. Luckily Klári approves of Pia exceptionally, and the two of them joke together. Anna did not notice that István was overwhelmed, neither does she remark that he stays away again for a time. She believes that the night club is prospering. Whenever she does not see István, it is rather a relief and yet it hurts a bit.

It also hurts a bit, but it's all in the order of things, that István never waits for her in front of the shop now. Perhaps it is even better. Anna would have no time to loiter, say farewell at every corner with a kiss, then go on together laughing, arm in arm. Uncle Bardichinov is very ill; he has pneumonia. Anna hurries to him straight from the shop. They have organized nursing him in turns. In the morning, Cathrina sits at his bedside, in the afternoon, Mrs. Barabás, in the evenings, Anna, and of course the men, Liiv, Alvarez, Barabás, whenever they have time. Russians come too, the friends of Bardichinov: Kalinin, Tuchachevski, Countess Marnov.

Anna would gladly undertake to sit with him through the night, but Klári surprisingly interferes, although, according to general belief, she is completely heartless and cares for no one.

"I can give him cold compresses as well as anyone, perhaps better than you can," she tells Anna, "and you'd better stop treating me like a child. I'm thirteen, you might almost say fourteen."

"Mother won't let you," Anna says.

"Leave Mother to me. You sit with him until one o'clock at night—that won't give you anything to do but amuse Liiv and the other visitors. I'll go to bed at eight, sleep till one, and take my turn then. By that time, thank God, the visitors will have cleared out, and that will leave you plenty of time to sleep until morning."

The Barabás family has learned that it is of no use to contradict Klári. Klári is stubborn, thickheaded, and torments everybody until they let her have her own way. So long as she was little, Mother's slaps sometimes were of some use, but today she stands before Mrs. Barabás with an expression that is so

hard and determined that she dares not touch her,
no more does Anna. After a long argument, they
compromise on two o'clock instead of one, and nursing in relays begins.

Of course no one knows, not even Anna, that daybreak is Uncle Bardichinov's worst time. His fever
abates, he becomes conscious and is tormented by
the fear of death.

"If only I were at home, Klári dear; but to die
here, in a strange country . . ."

"Uncle Bardichinov, sick people have the privilege
of talking nonsense. I'm not going to contradict you,
but think how ashamed you'll be when you're
better."

"You're wise, Klári, wise and shrewd. But I won't
believe you. I'm afraid of death, Klári."

"You've been sleeping in the afternoon, Uncle
Bardichinov. That is why you don't know how the
weather has cleared up. That is all you need, Uncle
Bardichinov, a little sunshine. Next week we'll sit
outside in the Luxembourg Gardens, or shall we go
up to the Buttes Chaumont? There I can pick you
violets."

"Violets," mumbles Uncle Bardichinov, and drops
into a restless sleep.

Klári stays until seven in the morning when
Cathrina comes in, and Klári runs home to get ready
for school.

Toward evening Bardichinov's fever rises. He is
delirious. He holds agitated speeches, argues, quarrels. Anna at first thinks that he is in trouble with the
communists, then gradually discovers that it is a

bank meeting, and Bardichinov is arguing with the shareholders. The last ten years have dropped out of his clouded consciousness. He is at home, discussing interest, bonds and shares with his codirectors and with the investors. Sometimes he is raving; he only recovers with the light of dawn, and that is even worse.

Jani has taken over his lessons in the afternoons and evenings, running about in the workmen's hotels of the neighborhood. Fortunately, the majority of the pupils feel for the old gentleman in his trouble and do not protest against the substitute. Jani has the first volume of Berlitz under his arm, and now it is his turn to repeat twenty times a day . . . c'est le crayon, où est le crayon? . . .

Then, one night, the Russian doctor's face wears a particularly worried look. Liiv and Alvarez accompany him to the corridor where the Russian spreads out his arms with that international and identical gesture common to all doctors the world over, and which means the same thing as an army lowering its flag before the enemy.

"He is sixty-eight. I don't think he'll live through the night."

Liiv nods silently and returns no more to the sickroom. He shakes hands with the doctor, shakes hands with Alvarez, and hurries home through the Street of the Fishing Cat to the Quai Saint-Michel. In front of the Barabás' house he stops and looks up at the windows. Of course, they are alight. Mrs. Barabás has gone home a little while ago to prepare

supper for her husband. Liiv has often been in the
little flat on the fourth floor . . . now he seems to reflect whether he had better go up and tell them the
bad news . . . then he shakes his head and hurries on.

Alvarez returns to Bardichinov's room with tears
in his eyes. Anna is inside, with Kalinin and Cathrina. Alvarez wants to speak but there is no need.
Before going, the doctor said a few words in Russian
to Kalinin. They know everything.

They sit around the bed, they weep sometimes and
sometimes they talk. Do you know these strange,
stifled and pious conversations in the face of Death?

"Maybe God will send a miracle," Kalinin whispers. Alvarez, the anarchist, does not protest, no
more does Cathrina. They, too, the old enemies,
hold each other's hands. Anna wrings out the compresses with sore fingers. Her eyes are feverish with
sleeplessness, her lips are bloodless.

As the hours pass, Alvarez grows paler, his knees
are trembling, sweat glistens on his brow. At midnight he suddenly starts to his feet.

"I'm going home. I . . . I can't look on any longer.
I'm frightened."

He almost cries out in his fear. Anna and Cathrina,
alarmed, try to soothe him. Anna puts his hat on his
head. Cathrina with her crippled feet sees him to the
stairs. Alvarez escapes at a run along the Street of
the Fishing Cat, and enters his hotel panting. If only
Liiv were awake. He can't, he won't remain alone
now.

A narrow streak of light shows under Liiv's door.

Thank God! Alvarez knocks and enters. A moment later piercing screams arouse the house. Liiv is seated in his armchair, blood flowing from his wrists.

"Calm yourself, my friend," Liiv whispers and faints.

At the screams, the patron rushes upstairs and several lodgers creep from their rooms. Frantic explanations, telephone calls for an ambulance, for a doctor, for the police. Alvarez's next conscious memory is sitting in the ambulance beside Liiv, spasmodically clutching the rug that covers the unconscious body. He takes a deeper breath, and gradually approaches something like sense and sanity. At the hospital he can give connected answers and dictate Liiv's personalia.

"Perhaps . . ." The doctor shrugs. "Perhaps."

At two o'clock Klári presents herself in Bardichinov's room to take over the night watch. On the threshold she stops, raises her eyebrows and looks at Cathrina and Kalinin who have no business to be here at such an hour.

"What's this?" she asks with profound resentment. "A public meeting?"

They tell her in tears what the doctor has said.

"You can't stay here," Cathrina adds.

"*You* can't stay here," Klári replies with cool malevolence. "First of all, you're breathing all the air there is, and then, what will happen if he happens to be alive in the morning after all? If you stay up now, you'll go to sleep at seven when you ought to be nursing him." Klári's eyes wander contemptuously from one to the other. She would like to say something about always having to be prepared for life and not for death, but her thirteen years do not find the appropriate words.

"I want to stay with my friend," complains Kalinin.

"You are old and tired," Klári replies cruelly. "Do you want to make yourself ill too?"

"I'm not going home," Anna says with determination. The two sisters look into each other's eyes. They know each other, they are combatants of about equal strength.

Klári nods.

"I don't care if Aunt Cathrina stays, but you have to be at the workshop tomorrow, and Uncle Kalinin is too old, and"—Klári approaches them and lowers her voice—"he always wakes at daybreak. What shall we tell him if he sees this illustrious company? That we are all waiting for his death?"

Anna and Kalinin leave.

Half an hour later there is a gentle knock at the door. Cathrina starts. Klári rises aggressively. Alvarez has returned from the hospital. He is still upset, but madness no longer flickers in his eyes.

"What are you doing here?" Klári is furious. "Do you think this is a public passage?"

"Liiv has committed suicide," Alvarez says in a low voice.

There is silence in the room. Liiv has committed suicide. He did not want to stay here without his only friend and enemy.

Later Cathrina says:

"How weak are the ties that attach one to life!"

"What is it that attaches you?" Alvarez asks gently.

Cathrina looks up and smiles.

"I don't know. Perhaps being a cripple. I really have a thousand reasons for . . . perhaps just for spite."

"Probably I'm in the same boat."

"You? You are a man, and you've got the use of all your limbs."

"Yes . . . and I fight for something that propagates kindness and justice, and has done nothing but kill so far. Do you know what a prison one's ideals can be?"

"How shouldn't I know? It's the only place I've got to live in. Love might have made a home for you . . ."

"Perhaps it might have. People here don't know, Cathrina, but I had a wife. I left her because she did not understand my ideals."

Klári interpolates wickedly:

"Kindly keep your thoughts to yourselves. I think he's going to wake up. Anyway, by tomorrow you'll want to deny that you've said such nasty things about your creeds. As for love, that's all nonsense. I'll never fall in love. That's only for people who have no aim in life. I'm going to be a great doctor. You sit by the window behind the bed so he can't see you."

The two adults look at each other aghast and move to the window. Alvarez's teeth chatter, and he thinks that organized society has, after all, succeeded in bringing some sort of ghastly order into certain fearful eventualities. Accidents, for instance: telephone, ambulance, hospital. We might adopt this, Alvarez thinks. Dawn breaks, gray and chill. The sick man moves.

"I want to go home."

"Uncle Bardichinov, listen to me." Klári bends over him.

"Only until I can get home . . . I don't want to die here."

"Listen, Uncle Bardichinov. We kept it a great secret, but I can tell you now—you've been very ill. I can tell you now, because you're over the danger. The doctor said so. The critical day was yesterday. You're better this morning, aren't you? Today is the first day of your reconvalescence. Do you understand me, Uncle Bardichinov?"

The sick man seems to understand. There is a faint sparkle in his eyes. Klári gives him a drink, applies a fresh compress, then takes his hand into her own and speaks to him eagerly in a low voice, so low that the others near the window can't hear. Bardichinov groans once or twice, then falls asleep.

Three weeks later, on a sunny afternoon, the two old men—for in Klári's eyes sixty-eight-year-old Bardichinov and forty-five-year-old Liiv are both old—start arm in arm for the Luxembourg Gardens. Jani is carrying the rugs. Klári commandeers the party like a governess.

"Not that bench—this one. It's more sheltered. Jani, you're crazy. Don't let the rugs trail on the ground. Yes, cover up their knees. Goodness, you're giving me a lot of trouble today!"

Life is calmer these days. If István does not come to fetch Anna at the shop, he sometimes turns up in the evening, accidentally just at suppertime. He still tells gigantic lies about the overwhelming success of the night club, but rather halfheartedly. The bailiff is a daily visitor at the club. The club is dying. Yes, maybe István was right . . . If they had only had a little more capital, been able to make more publicity, hold out a few months longer . . .

"Come up to my room, Anna. I'm so worried. You can't think of all the responsibilities I have. You're the only person who could cheer me up."

But he no longer says he loves her. Be it said to István's credit, he hasn't uttered the word to Anna since he met Pia Monica. He only asks her to come to his room, because he wants her for a light and brief episode, until . . . This "until" is not quite clear. István worships Pia Monica humbly and ardently, and he knows that it will not be easy to attain this laughing little girl. István wants to make a fortune so that he may marry Pia Monica.

XIII

THE CLUB comes under the hammer, and there are a number of legal proceedings against Hallay and István for various lesser offenses. The law is as sensitive as a snail; if you touch it with a blade of grass it retires offended within its house and spits forth a flood of writs at you.

In the midst of all this trouble, Elemér is not sent to a new school. On István's advice, Hallay for a moment fosters the plan of having Jani coach his son, then, perhaps, he might adapt himself to a French school in the autumn. But Elemér protests so desperately that his father shakes his head and gives up the idea.

One evening before closing time, Anna goes in to Gretl.

"Isn't anyone waiting for you? May I walk with you part of the way?"

"Of course, froggy. Who'd be waiting? You can come up to me if you like. You haven't been for a long time. I'll give you a cup of tea."

Gretl lives near the Boulevard Saint-Germain. The girls wend their way toward the Seine.

"Speak up, froggy."

"Gretl, you're cleverer and more experienced than
I am. Can one really care for a man whom one
despises?"

Gretl stops to laugh aloud.

"You fool! One can only love a man whom one
despises. Do you think it's real love when everything
runs smoothly like a moonlight idyll, and Papa and
Mamma give their blessing? One can only love with
clenched teeth, my child, with clenched teeth, dis-
graced and humiliated. What are you standing there
for? Let's get along."

"Can't things be different?"

"Apparently they can't. You never care for some-
body *because* he is clever, good and faithful, but *in
spite* of his being wicked, nasty and faithless. Have I
ever told you about my fiancé?"

"No."

"Well, I've had one. An officer—slim, smart, out
for fun. Then the world just tumbled about our ears.
He was demobilized, and as for Father . . . you know.
My fiancé married the daughter of a rich manu-
facturer. All the time he kept swearing that he
adored me. Perhaps he did. He said he'd only done
it to put financial obstacles out of the way of our
happiness. He can take a flat for me now, he can
keep me . . . he's got plenty of free time in the
afternoons."

"And you?"

"I? I came to Paris. Much good it did me."

"Do you still care for him?"

"Of course, I do. Haven't I told you that he was

base, wicked and despicable? Sometimes he writes and asks me to come back. He's got two children now."

"Gretl, this is awful."

"It is. And since we're talking about it, Anna . . . I wasn't going to tell you, but perhaps I'd better. Your way home is toward the Rue de Rivoli. You don't know anything about it, but I always come this way toward the Trocadéro and the Boulevard Saint-Germain. Your boy, that spongy Hungarian knight, waits for Pia, your protégée, every night at the corner of the George-V—not in front of the shop, so you can't catch them."

Anna grows pale.

"That's how it is, my girl," concludes Gretl. "Perhaps I've been rather cruel, but it's better that you should know."

"We are nothing to each other," Anna stammers. "It's his good right to walk with whomever he pleases."

"Of course, you're nothing to each other, and it's precisely this nothing that's making you sick. Well, I've only told you so that you may get out of it if you can."

"Thank you, Gretl. I'll try."

Gretl looks at her pityingly. She does not believe in the possibility. She acquiesces when Anna refuses to go up to her for the promised cup of tea. Let her run home and cry her heart out, since that is the rule of the game in such cases.

Anna, however, is not the crying kind. She wanders home numbed, and thinks. She cannot be angry

with Pia Monica. Maybe the girl did not even suspect this unlucky love affair, but István . . . István,
who only three days ago had entreated her to come
to him . . . she shakes her head in an effort to get
rid of the bitterness within her.

"I shan't speak to him again," she decides, and
for a moment the tears well up in her eyes.

And, in truth, she speaks no more to István, but
that is not her doing. When she gets to the Street of
the Fishing Cat, Jani is waiting for her in front of
the house. Jani is pale, his lips are trembling.

"I've been waiting for you for over an hour. I
wanted to show you this, because we can't talk
properly upstairs. Read it."

Anna takes the paper uncomprehendingly. Slowly
she reads the item to which Jani has pointed and
gradually a chill settles around her heart. A big
check fraud has been committed at the expense of a
bank. An American gentleman, or one who spoke
with an American accent, presented a check on the
Chicago Guarantee Trust for three hundred thousand francs. The bank wanted to make inquiries,
not being acquainted with the Chicago firm. The
gentleman left money for cable expenses, and next
morning the reply came saying that he had a deposit
of a million and a half dollars. The bank accepted
the check. By that evening, the original check was
returned. It could not be delivered, because the
Chicago Guarantee Trust does not exist.

Anna and Jani gaze at each other petrified.

"Perhaps it wasn't he, after all," Jani ventures.

Anna shakes her head. She knows better.

"The police have got the description of the American gentleman," Jani says with stiff lips. "What will happen now?"

"I don't know."

"Perhaps he's got away. Who can the other man have been?"

"I don't know."

"Shall I run across to István's?"

"I don't know."

"It wouldn't have much sense. If he's here, he's seen the papers too. Pull yourself together, Anna. Don't tremble. We must go upstairs. Father hasn't read the paper yet, but even if he does, it won't mean anything to him; only be careful that Klári doesn't get hold of it."

They go upstairs, Jani holding Anna's arm tightly.

"Are you fond of István, Jani?"

"I am fond of you, Anna."

Neither of them knows what they eat for supper. After supper, Klári clamors for the paper, and Barabás, who only looks into it and merely buys it for reasons of self-respect, gives it to her without hesitation. Klári turns the pages. Anna and Jani watch her in alarm. Klári finds the article, her eyes dilate, she reads it. When she has finished, she reads it again. Then she throws down the paper, yawns and rises.

"There's nothing interesting in this. Good night."

Later, when Anna goes into their room, Klári is lying in bed with closed eyes. Anna sighs and leans against the wall for a moment. Klári raises her long lashes—her large gray eyes and her long lashes are

perhaps the best features in the childish face that is
still rather crude—and says quietly:

"If that idiotic chimpanzee ever shows his face
again, kindly kick him out of the house. If they
find out we know him, they'll deport us right off.
But if he's got away with the money"—Klári
laughs—"then he's cleverer than I thought."

Anna shivers. She can't make up her mind to
undress. Klári sits up, looks at her in calm contempt,
then she lies down again and shuts her eyes energetically.

"Howl if you like," she says pityingly. "I'm going
to sleep." And she does.

Three difficult days follow, full of suffocating
excitement. The papers bring new details of the
check fraud, describe the trick of the two telegrams.
The telegrams were addressed to Martin Brunot,
to a small hotel near the Panthéon. Martin Brunot
took rooms for two days at the hotel. His description
tallies exactly with that of the American, but—it
does not resemble István in the least. Tall, beefy,
forty, gray-haired—that is not István.

"Perhaps it wasn't he, after all," Jani sighs again.
But Anna once more shakes her head.

On the fourth day of the nightmare, she buys the
Petit Parisien as she does every day. Only a few lines
in it this morning. The police are on the track. They
have found the printers who printed the forged
check book. Anna drops the paper on the seat of the
métro and leans back. István has got away. She will
never see him again. Perhaps it is for the best, but
that is hard to believe just now. The affair of the

description is rather difficult to understand, but if he were innocent, he would have turned up since, to rage at having his idea stolen, if for nothing else. He has got away, and it is for the best, but it hurts.

At the workshop Anna spreads out the beige silk dress at which she was working last night, and tries not to think. She starts and pricks her finger when she hears her name spoken unexpectedly.

Mme. Jacqueline stands in the doorway.

"Mlle. Anne, please come with me."

Mme. Jacqueline has come for her herself instead of sending one of the salesgirls. What does it mean? The atmosphere in the salesroom is charged with electricity; the tall white-haired woman leads the way toward the mannequins' room.

She goes in, and Anna follows. The salesgirls outside crane their necks to see what is going on.

Inside, two girls lean against two opposite walls, facing each other. Gretl's face is crimson, her eyes are flashing. Pia Monica is as pale as death, but there is a flaming red mark on her right cheek.

Mme. Jacqueline closes the door and glances at the girls.

"Comtesse Marguerite and Mlle. Pia have had a slight difference of opinion which, if I understand the matter aright, concerns you, Mlle. Anne. To be precise"—Mme. Jacqueline adds dryly—"Comtesse Marguerite has boxed Mlle. Pia's ears."

Gretl darts from the wall like a rubber ball on the rebound. A crumpled newspaper is lying on the table. She picks it up and thrusts it into Anna's hand.

"There! That's what she's done. First she took him away from you, then she induced him to cheat and steal for her sake. There! You've got her to thank for it!"

"But I didn't know," Pia Monica wails. "I thought they were just acquaintances. How could I guess? I never encouraged him by a single word. All he did was to wait for me evenings and walk home with me. I did not take him seriously for a moment."

Anna does not hear a word of all this. She is looking at the *Matin*, which is better informed than the *Petit Parisien*. It contains a photograph of István. Above it, headlines in large type: the police have arrested the check forger's accomplice, Etienne Weygand, a Hungarian subject, who delivered the forged cable, disguised as a telegraph boy.

"This crazy girl was in love with him!" Gretl raves. "She was in love with him and she might have made a man of him, although . . ."

"Anne, I never knew!" Pia Monica pleads. "Had I only guessed . . . It was at your place that we first met, do you remember? He walked home with me, asked for permission to meet me now and then. I didn't mind; we just chatted, he made me laugh. Forgive me . . . Anne, you never told me . . ."

The room revolves around Anna steadily and persistently, with the picture, István's picture, revolving in faster circles.

"I had nothing to tell," she says wearily, and gives the white-haired woman a look of entreaty. "Might I go home now, Mme. Jacqueline?"

"Yes, go home." Mme. Jacqueline's voice is un-expectedly gentle. "You may stay at home for a day or two."

Anna staggers out of the room, the salegirls' whispers following her to the door of the workshop. Here, too, all is agitation; Anna is overwhelmed by a flood of inquisitive questions, but she merely shakes her head and gropes blindly for her things. Mlle. Rose starts to her feet in alarm, rushes to her, puts her arms around her.

"What is the matter, ma petite?"

"Nothing. I am not well, I am going home."

"Shall I get you a taxi? Shall I come with you?"

Anna shakes her head. Then she stands outside in the spring sunshine, at this most unusual hour, and does not know what to do. She wanders along aim-lessly, then turns to the right at random and drags herself as far as the garden of the Musée Galliéra. Silence reigns here, the white wall of the museum reflects the sunshine, pale green, young spring foliage trembles on the trees.

It can't be kept a secret from her parents any longer, the less so because they must prepare for trouble, for great and personal trouble that may be ahead of them. That is Anna's greatest worry at the moment, her own grief can wait. And István, poor wretch, under arrest. . . . Anna walks to the street corner and buys a copy of the *Matin*, for she has only glanced at the headlines before.

István had been arrested at Chatou, near Paris, where he was trying to hide. He had very little money on him, most of it had been taken by the

accomplice who got away . . . the ex-headwaiter
of Hallay's night club, the one about whom István
had always been so enthusiastic. The headwaiter
had thought of the whole plan and carried it out;
István's role had been merely to dress up as the
telegraph boy. As soon as the check was cashed, the
man had made a getaway. He had not even turned
up at the meeting place previously arranged with
István, merely sent him a few thousand francs by
a commissionnaire—that was all.

Anna nods; she quite believes István's confession.
Not even the idea had been his own, he had lied
even when he had told them about it. Now he is in
prison. He is a mountebank, and a stupid one at
that. Perhaps one could help him somehow, send
him a lawyer, take him food . . . For the present,
they must wait. Suppose they are deported—it's
so good for the children to be here. They can study
for a profession. At home, at the most, Jani might
be a workman and Klári a factory girl, and her
father and she could never earn as much as they do
here.

She watches the clock and goes to fetch Jani from
school. This time it is she who shows him the paper.
Jani looks into it; he is not particularly surprised.

"Which of us had better tell?" is his only question.

"We'll tell together." Anna sighs.

Again three days pass like a nightmare, with the
only difference that, this time, Father and Mother
share in it. Barabás also pretends to be ill and does
not go to the shop. Sometimes he looks at Anna with
disapproval. He forgets that it was he who brought

István to the house. Sometimes he shakes his head—whoever would have thought it?

Mrs. Barabás often has tears in her eyes.

One evening when the two girls are alone in their room, Klári says:

"I don't advise you to go and see that scoundrel. In the first place, you'll howl; in the second, you'll throw suspicion upon yourself. If you want to send him any food, give it to me. I'll pretend to be the daughter of his landlady, or something of the sort."

The three days pass undisturbed. No one asks for them. They find out later that Hallay has been repeatedly questioned by the police.

Anna returns to the workshop with some anxiety. Suppose they don't take her back? However, they receive her calmly, and Mlle. Rose embraces her with ardent sympathy. When most of the salesgirls have gone to lunch, Anna slips across the salesroom and knocks on the door of the mannequins' room. She must speak to Gretl, she hasn't thanked her yet . . . for what?

Gretl is not in the room. Pia Monica rises, blushing, and advances toward Anna.

"Mlle. Anne . . . I meant to call on you . . . I did not dare . . ."

"Oh, Mlle. Pia, it doesn't matter. Where is Gretl?"

"Comtesse Marguerite?" The flush on Pia's face deepens. "She . . . is not here any more. She went away immediately after you left."

"Was she sent away?" Anna asks with a catch in her voice.

Pia nods.

"I . . . I'm very sorry . . . I . . ."

Anna turns on her heel and leaves the room. After work, she runs across to Gretl's hotel.

"Comtesse Marguerite?" The patron shakes his head. "She doesn't live here any more. She moved out two days ago. Where? I don't know. She left no address. I believe she left Paris."

Anna stands on the pavement in perplexity, and the tears are streaming down her face. Gretl, dear, savage, bitter Gretl . . . perhaps the best friend that ever lived. What is she to do now? Leave the workshop? Of what use would it be to Gretl, to herself, to her broken, trembling little family? Gretl . . . Next day she goes to the workshop again, and she never mentions Gretl's name, just as she has never mentioned Vassja's.

XIV

Sᴏᴍᴇ ɢᴇɴᴛʟᴇᴍᴇɴ in Hungary have counterfeited French francs.

Anna timidly knocks at Mme. Lucienne's door, from behind which agitated noises always issue forth, dictation, calculation, bargaining and argument.

"What is it, my girl? What do you want? What's this?"

Anna places the diploma of the tailoring course in front of Mme. Lucienne.

"And I've also learned designing, if you please, Mme. Lucienne."

"Have you? That is very nice and very useful. Mme. Andrée will be able to make use of you. Well, we shall see. Business is growing. Thank you, Mlle. Anne."

Anna backs out. Two weeks later, the first tailoring task is confided to her. Only a skirt to start with, a plain tailor-made skirt, but if Mme. Lucienne likes it, then she will be a cutter, Mme. Andrée's assistant, almost as great a power as the forelady herself.

She takes a long time and the greatest pains over

the cutting out of the skirt. At the last clip of her scissors, Mme. Lucienne sends for her.

"So soon?"

Anna does not quite understand. At all events she takes the cut-out material on her arm.

"Mlle. Anne, I am very sorry indeed . . . personally I never had any objection to you, none whatever. I am sending you away with the best possible references."

"Sending me away, Mme. Lucienne?"

"I am very sorry, but you must understand, after all, that your people have committed against France . . . I cannot employ a Hungarian girl any longer. The cashier will pay you a week's wages. Good day, Mlle. Anne."

Anna reels out of the room, reels out of the shop. By the time she gets home, Barabás is home too. At the furrier's shop they had made up their minds even earlier, they had not even permitted him to start work in the morning.

"What are we going to do, father?"

Barabás shrugs his shoulders and goes to the Hungarian tavern in the Rue François-Miron. There, all is excitement and perplexity. Some of them have lost their jobs, others have to leave the country within twenty-four hours.

Barabás listens to the confused clamor and it doesn't make him any wiser. He does not know why he came here, what kind of advice or help he had expected. His blind instinct led him to his compatriots. Of course, they can't do anything for him.

He wanders homeward, deep in thought. He and

Anna have been the breadwinners even though he
made four times as much money as she did. The
little family can't cope with the unemployment of
them both. Their modest bank account won't hold
out long. He must find another job, and that will
not be easy. The atmosphere of Paris is anti-
Hungarian.

For a fortnight they both study the want ads
zealously, and offer themselves for every conceiv-
able job. Dinners and suppers grow more and more
taciturn. During the third week, Barabás says:

"South America! I've long been planning to go.
I've been talking about it a good deal with Alvarez.
He knows a lot about the Argentine. It's a young
rising country; they need every willing worker. You
could follow me after two or three months."

Mrs. Barabás grows pale.

"I'm going too," Anna says. István was sentenced
to a term of eighteen months yesterday. The headwaiter escaped without leaving a trace. István was
able to put all the blame on him, so he got off rather
easily.

For weeks they discuss the question and argue
about it. They are feverishly intent upon learning
Spanish from Alvarez. Then, on a windy, stormy
evening, the family stands on the station platform of
the P.L.M. Bardichinov, Liiv and Alvarez are there
too. Barabás and Anna board the train for Marseilles.

They have divided the little money that was in the
bank equally. Barabás takes half of it with him and
leaves half of it for his wife. They feel now what a
waste it was not to have saved more from the time

when István appeared on the scene, but a strange sense of shame prevents their speaking of it. Mrs. Barabás will not need much money. The two children are practically kept by their schools, and Jani even gets a scholarship. And maybe it is only a question of weeks. South America is very rich and, according to Alvarez, is much more the land of unlimited possibilities than the United States. Maybe the family will soon be reunited in Buenos Aires. The engine whistles, Jani runs beside the train, handkerchiefs flutter, Mrs. Barabás weeps—it is over. They have lost each other from sight.

Marseilles and going on board are very exciting, so exciting that they can hardly realize the sea. The boat sails at midnight; until then everything is in wild confusion. Luggage disappears, tickets get lost, berth reservations get mixed up. But next morning Anna leans on the railing, looks around and takes a deep breath. She is overwhelmed by the radiant charm of the voyage, by the sense of irresponsibility and the freedom from all care, the adjournment that Fate, on these occasions, accords in the petty lawsuits of human life. The ship glides along, and the sea is iridescent like an opal . . .

"Father," says Anna. "I'm glad we've come. Everything will be better, easier there, you'll see."

"M'm," Barabás says dryly. "Wages weren't so bad in Paris either."

Anna makes an impatient gesture. That isn't quite what she had meant, or is it? Work and money, a job and wages, are such important, fundamental things, and yet . . . one may be happy or unhappy with it all. One may even want to die. There is the sea, there are the mountains of Switzerland. Yes, this is the strangest thing of all, the sea, the calm, infinite sea, with its indifferent, murmuring lullaby. Who can understand the songs of the sea? An eternal monologue, to which the human voice can make no reply, to which the seventy-thousand-ton ships have nothing to say. The song of the sea is sweet, indifferent, inhuman. The human ear listens and the human heart throbs to its rhythm—that is all. Work and money, a job and wages. And love. And meanwhile the sea continues its eternal monologue, and man, just a little beyond, is unhappy.

Then the short vacation is over. The boat arrives. Going on land is again colorful, agitated confusion. Barabás and Anna lose each other. When they finally meet again, Barabás scratches his leg nervously.

"I've been bitten by some sort of big fly, confound it!"

They find lodgings in La Boca, the sailors' quarter, because it is cheapest. They found that out from fellow passengers on the way. There are many taverns in the neighborhood, from which sounds of carousing and sometimes quarrels are heard, but no matter. After all, Anna need not go home alone. She will come home with her father in the evenings. The lodgings, a sort of sailors' boardinghouse, seem peaceful enough, and the landlady is friendly.

By the time they have moved in, it is late afternoon. Anna would like to take a look at the city, but Barabás hesitates. The insect bite on his leg is rather painful.

"Very well," he then decides. "Let's go along. This bite will be all right by tomorrow, and it would be a pity to waste this fine evening."

The night is glorious. There are more stars in the sky than could be seen anywhere in Europe. The wind is different too, hot and strangely scented. The streets are wide, perhaps even more brilliant than the boulevards in Paris, and flooded by crowds of people. Father and daughter walk arm in arm, and, after many months, perhaps years, Anna again feels that life is a gay adventure, worth living and taking risks for.

Barabás feels the same, and his memories instinctively return to the time when life was an undertaking free of daily cares, risky, exciting and exhilarating. Barabás talks of the war.

Do you know, peace-loving or sanely calculating, humane and benevolent Reader, that in Europe lives a whole generation of men who, every time they must pay rent, and sometimes much oftener, yearn for wartime again? No rents had to be paid in the trenches. It sounds strange,—but the war suspended the struggle for life, relieved men of the strain of earning their daily bread. That's how it was. And it provided unparalleled, ardent, heartrending excitement, splendid intoxication, the delirium of fear and courage, self-oblivion. A whole generation of men, millions of men are struggling all around us, who achieved the completeness of life in the war, and their eyes still sparkle at the word.

This does not speak for war, but against life.

So Barabás recalls wartime memories, and Anna

listens kindly and absent-mindedly. The sky is full
of stars, the night is glorious, they are on a new
continent where anything might happen, a thousand
unexpected, radiant miracles.

They sit on the crowded terrace of a café and
order some sort of drink that is cold and sweet and
burns. Perhaps father and daughter have never
talked so intimately, although neither pays much
attention to the other. Both have their say, and each
gazes straight ahead with a pensive smile while the
other speaks. Perhaps such conversations are the
most satisfactory, because they are without contra-
diction, and there is no need to be coherent. The
subjects are simple. Barabás remembers, Anna
makes plans. People here will consider her a distinguished Paris dressmaker. She will be worth her
weight in gold. Barabás tells the story of how he got
his first silver medal. They pay no attention to each
other, and they are very devoted to each other.

Barabás suddenly grasps his leg.

"This damn bite hurts!"

"It is quite possible that I shall be able to start an
independent establishment quite soon. Perhaps the
best plan would be to go into partnership with
someone. I'll give you a compress for the night. It
will be gone by tomorrow."

But by next morning it has not gone. It has
spread, the leg is swollen and inflamed, and it hurts.

Both shake their heads over it, but they never
think of going to a doctor instead of looking for
work. They walk into town, buy a paper, search the
want-ad columns with their scant knowledge of

Spanish. Barabás finds something that might be worth applying for, but he discovers that he has misunderstood the advertisement; they want a currier.

By next morning, his leg is blue and burning; Anna is determined not to let him go out. She persuades him to stay at home. She pushes a chair to the window, puts a basin with cold water on another chair so that he can change his compresses. Barabás says that one day here or there does not matter, Anna needn't start off to the city alone, but Anna feels tempted toward solitary wandering.

"Suppose I happen to miss a good chance," she protests, and goes off.

She would not have missed any chance. It seems to be the dead season for dressmakers just now. Barabás's leg swells and grows black. Next morning Anna, relentless, calls in a doctor.

The doctor talks much and very fast. He mentions the names of various insects; all are unknown to the Hungarian man and girl and, to judge by his hesitation, also to the doctor. Yes, such things happen sometimes. The savage heart of the continent sends a winged herald to the civilized skyscraper-covered coast as a reminder of the steaming swamps and jungle wilderness, as a reminder that, over there, life and death have other laws.

From the doctor's voluble gush of Spanish, it is only clear that he is more interested in the insect than in the man. Has Barabás killed it, and, if so, where is it? Not kept it? What a pity! But perhaps he can at least tell what it was like? Not looked at it?

Well, well! (In such awe does man stand of nature.)
Still, had it one pair of wings or two? Doesn't he
know? What a pity! Certainly the best thing for him
to do would be to go to the hospital with his bad leg.

Barabás doesn't want to go to a hospital. By the
next day, his leg is black, he has a temperature and
is in great pain. The boarders of the pension come
to see him. They all feel the burning, swollen flesh,
express their opinions and give advice. When the
landlady advises powdered mustard seed with
onion, Anna revolts. She throws everyone out of the
room, runs downstairs, calls a taxi, and tells the
chauffeur to take them to the nearest hospital.
Barabás obediently allows himself to be treated like
a child.

What follows is a bad dream that lasts five months.
On every second day the doctors say that they will
amputate Barabás's leg, on the days between they
say they will make a blood transfusion. In the end
they do neither. Anna must find work because all
their money is gone, there is no time to wait for a
dressmaker's job. First she works as a servant, but
she and her mistress, Señora Asunción, can put
up with each other for only a fortnight. Asunción
is furious because Anna runs to the hospital every
day, and Anna can't get used to the funny-tasting
dishes, and she doesn't earn enough money. Day by
day, she and her mistress quarrel with increasing
irritation—Asunción is the wife of a lawyer, but
that doesn't seem to count—they fight like fishwives.
The lawyer is a little man with a protuberant
stomach, with remnants of food sticking between

his teeth after dinner, and he likes to pinch the servant girl. After two weeks Anna escapes and returns to La Boca, to the old boardinghouse land-lady and the search for a job, no matter what, if it only leaves her an hour or two free in the afternoon. Her father is lying alone in the long hospital ward, and the doctors sometimes say that they must cut his leg off.

Anna washes dishes in the steamy, vapory, cabbage-smelling kitchen of a restaurant. She gets two hours off in the afternoon, and can take her father some food. She is sweating and unkempt, as she has never been in her life. At night she rushes along the streets of La Boca, filled with drunken revelers. Her breath comes in panting, wheezing gasps by the time she reaches the narrow doorway of the boardinghouse. Easter approaches, perhaps she could find work as a dressmaker now, but no matter. She has no time to look for a job; besides, she could not accept a post which leaves her no time to go to the hospital in the afternoon.

Barabás is feverish and suffers infernal torture, but he never loses consciousness for a moment. He keeps his sane and cool judgment: a furrier remains a furrier even with one leg, he says. If only he does not die. If he does, what would Anna and the other three in Paris do? Once a week they write to Paris. Anna writes at Barabás's dictation, that they have both got jobs, but that the wages are small, they can't save much. Mrs. Barabás knows how things go in a foreign country—they must wait. Then, with great difficulty, he signs the letter so that Boriska shall not guess that he is ill. Anna rushes back wearily to the ill-smelling kitchen. Barabás sinks back upon his pillows and torments his nurse. If they must cut off his leg, why don't they hurry up and have done with it? The nurse has given up answering him; she gently gives him a drink and hurries away.

After five months, Barabás can leave the hospital. He is cured, and he has kept his leg.

He is cured, but he has become an old man, quarrelsome and weak. Anna supports him until they get to the tram, then to the boardinghouse, and she places a chair for him near the window again. At this time in the afternoon, the sailors' quarter grows lively. Seafaring men, who have only a few days in harbor, have slept off their drunkenness of the night before, and start upon their rounds at the taverns again.

Two days later, they write another letter home, and this time they tell the truth. That is why they could not send money for the passage, and have the family out to the Argentine. It takes a month for the answer to come, but it brings good news. They are all doing well in Paris, there is no need to spend a centime on the children. Mrs. Barabás is working in the laundry again—they don't seem to hate the Hungarians any more. Mrs. Barabás therefore sends the money that was still left in the bank. She does not need it. Liiv adds a hundred francs. Liiv has had a stroke of good luck. When he was well enough to sit in the garden of the hospital after his suicide attempt, he made the acquaintance of the clerk of an insurance company, and through him he got employment with the same firm as an insurance mathematician.

For the first time in his life, Barabás cries when he reads this letter.

The money is not sufficient for their passage home, but enough for Anna to leave the kitchen. This time she finds work as a Paris dressmaker—Mme. Lucienne's reference is full of praise. But it is not so easy as she thought. What she has learned in Paris—the simplicity, the secret harmony of line and color—is not gay enough for this place. Besides, pay is not good. Barabás is paid badly too, when at last he finds work. Barabás is no more what he was. He cannot fight, he cannot protest against oppression and tyranny, he cannot make his way among foreigners. Every month finds them in a different place. After the sixth or eighth change, Anna sits down and tries to write a letter:

"Chère Mme. Lucienne," she begins, and then she tears up the sheet. Perhaps, after all, she had better write to Mme. Jacqueline, or to Mme. Andrée, or maybe to Rose?

She suddenly smiles a quiet and rather bitter smile, and writes to Pia Monica.

Pia Monica is, as you might say, indebted to her. Pia Monica has taken something away from her, no matter whether it was good or bad, valuable or worthless. And Pia Monica is a foreigner too. She can understand their trouble better, and perhaps she is more ready to help than those who are at home and know only troubles that are simple and familiar, troubles that can be shared and need not be borne in loneliness.

She tells Pia Monica that the excursion to South America has not been a success. They would like to return. It would be kind of her to find out whether the antagonism against the Hungarians has abated, whether Mme. Lucienne would take her on again. They have accepted her mother again at the laundry where she used to work, perhaps the situation has taken a turn for the better. Here she does not feel happy, her work is not sufficiently appreciated; besides—here she allows a suggestion of a boast to creep in between the lines—the attentions of Spaniards are obnoxious and unpleasant. They all try to make love. . . . Foreign girls in South America hardly know how to protect themselves from their advances. And will Pia Monica please give her the news of the shop, also concerning other acquaintances?

Maybe Anna thought of István when she wrote this, maybe she did not. She certainly often thinks of the prisoner who was always gay and bragging, and had warm, dark eyes. He must be unhappy in his narrow prison cell . . . more unhappy than Anna in the restaurant kitchen? Anna shrugs; it doesn't matter. Life is not particularly fair. István has nothing to complain of. He will soon have served his term. If he begs to be taken back, will Anna welcome him again? She knows that István never cared for her. Could he have changed in prison? . . . Of course not. Still, Anna prefers not to think of what would happen if she were to meet István again.

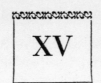

XV

ABOUT THE SAME TIME as Anna's letter reaches Pia Monica, Klári receives a letter too. Clumsy big characters form straggling lines across the page, there are many mistakes and corrections; the letter comes from Uncle Papadakis. He has addressed it to the little hotel in the Rue de la Huchette, M. Gaston gave it to Uncle Bardichinov, who brought it to the Street of the Fishing Cat.

"My dear little Klári—" this is the gist of the letter—"I am writing to you because I have no one else in the world to write to. I have been cruelly punished, dear Klári, for being unfaithful to my poor dead wife and marrying a Frenchwoman; that is why I have no children—God has sorely punished me. My wife is a bad woman, a very wicked woman; she does nothing but drive me to work and take away my money, and therefore God gives her no children. All this has happened, Klári dear, because I was unfaithful and came away and married a Frenchwoman. I shan't live long, Klári dear, I shall soon follow my children, the Frenchwoman drives me to my grave." And then an unexpectedly polite passage: "My best regards to your father and mother, to Mr. Bardichinov, Mr. Liiv and Mr. Alvarez, and to dear Annuska and Jani."

Klári reads the letter which does not bear the address of the sender. She reflects for a moment, then she folds it, puts it away, and puts on her hat. She has made up her mind to find Uncle Papadakis and liberate him from the wicked Frenchwoman.

Klári is prompt and thorough as usual. She goes to the cap-pressing workshop where Uncle Papadakis worked more than four years ago. Of course, she no longer finds him there, but one of the workmen has a dim recollection of the place to which he went when he left here. Klári follows his tracks. After the next workshop, she finds another, then a fourth. Here the trace is lost, but she gets a home address instead. Of course, the address is obsolete too, but here again she finds someone who can tell her where to go next. A few more experiments of the same kind, eager questionings, methodical inquiry, and on the third day Klári knocks at the door of a modest apartment in the Rue Lapérouse.

A worn, thin woman opens the door.

"Who are you looking for?"

"M. Papadakis. My name is Claire Barabas and I wish to see M. Papadakis," she answers in a hostile tone.

"Come in." The thin woman leads the way. "He is not at home, but he may come at any moment."

The woman and the girl sit facing each other in the humble room. Klári takes in the weary, shabby creature with a critical glance. Obviously the woman is afraid of her—afraid, because an unexpected

visitor always means trouble and complications.
Klári, however, is all for direct attack.

"I hear you're making Uncle Papadakis unhappy," she says relentlessly.

"I?" The woman's deep-set, hollow eyes are suddenly filled with tears. She starts upon a flood of
lamentation, so eloquent and fluent that it makes
Klári almost giddy. "You don't know what it means
to marry a foreigner, Mlle. Barabas—that was the
name, wasn't it? We don't know what a foreigner
really is until we live with him. Foreigners are funny,
Mlle. Barabas, they are consumed by strange griefs,
one can't get at them. Christos, too . . . if I'd let
him, he'd just sit all day and stare and never do
any work at all . . . well, tell me yourself, Mlle.
Barabas, can one stand for that? If I tell him to go
to work, he hates me. But, after all, we can't starve,
can we? And he hates me because I have no children.
Can I help that, Mlle. Barabas? He hates me and
keeps ruminating about all sorts of funny things that
he doesn't want to tell, stares ahead of him and
mutters as if he were talking to someone. Tell me
yourself, Mlle. Barabas, what can I do?"

Klári listens, confused. This is the first time she is
taken for a grown-up person, and at another time
she would acknowledge this with an air of calm and
proud assurance. But this time she expected something different. She came like an avenging angel,
she meant to drive out the wicked wife and save
Papadakis. And now the wicked wife weeps and
laments.

Then there are heavy footsteps at the door, and

the sleepy, soft-eyed, dark Greek enters, fat, flabby and indifferent. He has to take a good look at Klári before he recognizes her, and he hardly seems glad to see her.

"Nice of you to come and see me," he says in a colorless voice.

Klári is taken aback.

"You've written me a letter, Uncle Papadakis."

"Have I?" The Greek stares numbly ahead of him. "I suppose I have. How are your father and mother?"

Klári answers absent-mindedly and with no great show of accuracy; she does not even mention her father's trip to South America. She is impatient to get away. The Frenchwoman insists on offering her a glass of wine, Klári drinks it off, then she rises to go.

When she says good-bye she can't help asking:

"Uncle Papadakis, isn't there anything I can do? Aren't you in trouble, is everything all right?"

"Quite all right," replies Papadakis, and the Frenchwoman asks her to come again.

In the street, Klári shakes herself like a wet puppy. The affairs of grownups are senseless and difficult to understand for a person who is in her right mind. Klári sets off to Aline, whose official and paid tutor she has now become, and with whom one can talk sense even if she does forget things. She tries not to think of her funny, confused and unsatisfactory visit to Papadakis. But it has taught her something that she will remember without being quite conscious of it: things are hard not only for the foreigner, but also for her who binds her fate to his storm-driven destiny. This secret and silent knowledge may someday be very helpful—at present it merely takes its place among the treasures of her awakening perceptions of the world.

This knowledge would stand Jani in good stead very soon. For one day, Camille, his classmate, gives Jani a ticket to a violin recital, and Jani sees Albertine for the first time.

Jani has still no ear, and still adores music. He takes his seat with a feeling of sacred joy and shuts his eyes in advance. But he quickly opens them again when the audience welcomes the artist stepping onto the platform with great applause. The audience consists chiefly of friends and relatives. This is Albertine's first recital.

The first notes of the piano accompaniment are struck softly. Albertine, with the violin under her chin, with bow raised gracefully, is calmly waiting. Jani does not close his eyes again during the recital, he gazes at Albertine, whose thin, frightened little face with its big nose bends over the violin, gazes at her, and is entranced. He applauds more and louder than ten relatives.

In the interval, Camille prods him in the ribs.

"Do you want to come into the artist's room?" Camille is Albertine's cousin.

Jani is overwhelmed by a strange, sweet sense of fear and ardent joy. In the artist's room, the whole family is dancing around Albertine. All that Jani gets is a brief, tremulous handshake, but the handshake, and the singing violin, and the slender unforgettable figure of the girl, and the thin little face with its big nose, together make up inexpressible beauty and ecstasy. After the recital, Jani dashes to the artists' entrance to see, if only for a moment, the little girl in her white evening dress and carrying her bouquet, as she gets into the taxi.

Next day, he thanks Camille falteringly and gratefully for having let him see her.

"Do you like her?" Camille asks with cousinly indifference. "If you care to meet her, come and see us on Sunday. Her figure's good, but her face is plain."

Jani fights down the temptation to strangle Camille. He probably refrains only because, if he did strangle him, he could not call on him on Sunday.

Albertine is sixteen, a year younger than Jani, so it's simply ideal. She is a hard-driven and nervous little girl, there are no limits to her parents' ambition. Albertine must practice eight hours a day, study composition and school subjects too; she, herself, believes in her talent and her vocation, but longs for an easier life. She is good-natured and conceited, arrogant and shy. In a word, a child who has the worries of an adult.

Jani has thought out in advance the highflown oration by which he means to praise her art, and he manages to get it off his chest with some slight omissions.

Albertine listens, her plain little face beaming with pleasure.

"Oh, M. Barabas! I am really delighted that you

liked it. I was a trifle indisposed; you know"—she adds in a sudden burst of confidence—"I had terrific stage fright."

"No one could notice that," Jani reassures her.

"It is kind of you to say so. I played two wrong notes in the César Franck sonata—you noticed, didn't you?"

Jani had not noticed.

"You must be mistaken," he says decisively.

"Yes, I did." Albertine shakes her head sadly. "Camille has told me such a lot about you, M. Barabas. Would you care to come and call on us someday? Mother would be very pleased to see you, and then I could play for you, for you alone . . . without stage fright and without false notes." Albertine laughs.

Jani calculates that he will have adhered to all the rules of good behavior and etiquette if he waits three days before telephoning to ask when he may call. He makes up his mind about this before he goes to bed—and next day he telephones.

Albertine is glad to see him. Albertine has not been spoilt by boys. She has no time, and she is not pretty, but Jani is glad to sit there and listen when Albertine practices, even her scales put him into a trance. Her parents do not mind his frequent visits, they do not inquire into his origin. They are children still, they think. There is no question of love or marriage.

Albertine and Jani, however, are in love. Strangely enough, it is Albertine whose passion is more flaming. She is the more ardent, the more jealous of the two. Jani has little time. He is in his last year at college, and means to go to the Ecole Polytechnique next year. His professors have promised him a scholarship. Jani is going to be an engineer, and not a pilot. That dream has crumbled with many other childhood dreams of conquering the world. He is going to be an engineer, he is interested in the profession, and his professors are all for it, especially M. Lamy. Besides, Jani must earn money. He has again taken over some of Bardichinov's lessons; the old gentleman can no longer climb so many flights of stairs and the Barabás family needs money, every centime they can get; Barabás and Anna must be brought home from South America. No one knows what diplomatic tactics Klári had to employ to get her job as a coach for Aline. Jani did not have as many difficulties, but he has to work harder.

Therefore he cannot spend as much time with Albertine as he would like to, and Albertine is jealous.

"I can understand that you must study. I've got to study too. Bring your books with you, and I'll practice while you do your lessons. But all this giving of lessons and hanging around with a herd of foreigners . . ."

"I'm a foreigner too, Albertine."

"That's not true. You're French. Don't let me hear you talk such nonsense again."

"And my father and sister want to return to France. They are starving and they are saving every centime they can on their food, to get money enough for the passage back. I've got to help too."

"Why did they leave France? Serves them right. Let them stay where they are. I don't want you to bother about anyone else, Jean."

"Still, it's my father and my sister," Jani says stubbornly.

Albertine suddenly repents of her anger, her violent words, and runs up to Jani.

"Jean, I love you. If you were a nigger, if you were a toad, if you would break my violin, I should still love you."

"I love you too. Even if you could not play the violin, you would be music itself to me, Albertine."

It goes on like this all the time. They quarrel sometimes and often make it up. A childish affair, Albertine's parents say, and smile. Mrs. Barabás says nothing; she hardly knows anything about the matter, she merely suspects that her boy is gradually growing up, slipping from her hands, growing into a man, a gentleman. Mrs. Barabás stands by the trough in the laundry all day. At night she washes for her children at home. Sometimes she does not see Jani for days on end. Klári is studying in her own room, but then Klári never was a real, proper child, she never needed anyone. Her third child and her husband are far away on another continent. The little family is scattered as by a storm.

Yet they love and stand by each other. The children bring home every centime they earn. They work for the speedy return of Anna and Barabás; they are good children, and they stick together in all that really counts, and yet are far from each other and constantly drifting apart.

"You're lucky with your children, Boriska," says Cathrina, who sometimes sits in the kitchen of an evening, her sticks leaning beside her, and watches Mrs. Barabás's deft hands.

"They're good children," sighs Mrs. Barabás. "Only someone ought to invent a way of keeping them small. My boy Jani is in love," she adds, and sighs again.

"Is he really?" Cathrina's eyes sparkle, and with the help of her hands, she raises herself on her stool. "Tell me all about it."

XVI

Aᴎɴᴀ ᴀɢᴀɪɴ sᴛᴀɴᴅs at the ship's railing, and watches the widening banks of the Rio de la Plata. They will soon be out at sea. Such a sunset is a wicked thing. It casts a shower of ruddy gold over the city, that is beautiful and bad, and is desperately lovely in this golden flamboyance.

István always used to laugh at Anna, saying she did not know Paris. And Anna always used to smile in melancholy superiority. She felt that she had got closer to the heart of real Paris, to the poor, industrious and hard-working Paris. The Place Blanche is the hunting ground of American tourists. In this respect Anna always identified herself entirely with the spoilt city; she hated the foreigners who came to spend their money there, and whenever anyone inquired about the whereabouts of Notre-Dame, she invariably directed the noisy inmates of Cook's sightseeing cars toward the Panthéon instead. Those are the people that belong to the Place Blanche, and to the artificially specialized places of amusement to which the French never think of going.

But now, looking at Buenos Aires disappearing in the distance, she does not feel so superior. The city grows more distant, flaming and golden, and she has never known it as poor people never get to know near-by and expensive beauty. In Paris she sometimes had gone to a museum with Alvarez and Bardichinov. She mounted the Eiffel Tower and looked around, went rowing on the Marne, and visited Versailles. Here, she had had a single beautiful evening, the very first, the starry night of their arrival, when life seemed an adventure and happy excitement—and from this she was suddenly flung into eighteen months of desperate misery.

What a thin crust of ice their prosperity in Paris had been, and how deep beneath it was the gulf of poverty. In Paris they had been the aristocrats of the Hungarian colony, because they could always give a hungry visitor a cup of coffee and a slice of bread and butter. That was the extent of their prosperity. A single turn of the wheel—a few gentlemen forge francs in Hungary—a strange fly comes out of the jungle—and it was all at an end. They will have to start all over again, and be thankful for being able to do so.

Pia Monica had replied promptly—promptly and eagerly. Mme. Lucienne would gladly welcome Anna back; Mme. Andrée wasn't feeling very well these days, and it was difficult to find a good substitute. They were all conceited and pretended to know better. She would prefer one whom she had brought up herself, said Mme. Lucienne, and Mme. Andrée, who still sometimes comes to the shop, was very pleased about it too. She would rather have Anna than anyone else, Mme. Andrée said, probably because she could more easily take her place back from Anna when she felt better again. Pia Monica did not put this quite so plainly; she merely hinted at it, but Anna understood. She did not mind. Barabás had written to Mr. Brüll, although in Mr. Brüll's tiny workshop there was no scope for a skilled furrier. A little one-horse concern like Mr. Brüll's keeps only apprentices; he and his wife do all the work. But still, he was a furrier, and a Hungarian who had lived in Paris thirty-five years. In 1920, he had told Barabás that it was twenty-five. During the war, they had taken away his little shop and interned him. Of course, he had never thought of adopting French citizenship—he was a Jew, but a good Hungarian, and years ago he had been president of the Hungarian Society—and his wife had nearly starved. Fortunately, the French authorities took pity on her after all her entreaties and interned her in the same camp where her husband was, and where at least she was fed. It was a rather tame camp, for Mr. Brüll was close on fifty, and older men were less strictly handled.

After the war, Mr. Brüll opened his little workshop again, and in 1920 he visited his home country. That was when he had advised Barabás to come to Paris. Well, Mr. Brüll knew about things, and he, too, had replied to Barabás that he might return. As for himself, they hadn't made any trouble for him this time.

The ship is out at sea, and Anna thinks of István. He has left prison since. She and her father could not start as soon as they had the replies from Paris. It needed three more months of hard work and little food; and for those at home too, hard work and little food.

The city is out of sight. A man lived in it, Vicente Leiva, lived in the same little boardinghouse, and he seemed to be gentler and more kind than the others. Anna scarcely took any notice of him, although Vicente Leiva had pleasant eyes and tried to be nice to her. He asked Anna to go for walks with him, and sometimes brought her flowers, and brought ice cream for Barabás when they let him come out of hospital.

And at the dressmaker's—La Aurora—there was a little girl called Pilar, who always tried to be friendly. Once or twice she had walked home with Anna and shyly, tentatively, tried to tell her about her own, modest, little life. Anna listened absent-mindedly, and her thoughts were occupied with financial manipulations.

The city, whose beauty she had never known, has disappeared, and perhaps love and friendship have disappeared with it too.

And perhaps all this was merely idle speculation, vain reverie on the gliding boat.

Halfway across the ocean, the ship changes its mind, and no longer glides with smooth dignity, but starts to pitch and toss. A sore trial for Anna, and for Barabás in his weak state of health. When the family is once more reunited at the P.L.M. station, Mrs. Barabás cries out in dismay:

"You're skin and bone! My darling husband! Annuska dear! What has become of you?"

Gradually they soothe her, they promise her to put on flesh again. The children are calmer, but their eyes are sparkling. Jani has grown tremendously. He is as tall as his father. Barabás need no longer bend down to embrace. He merely puts his arms around his shoulders.

"My boy!"

Klári has grown too, and has become very shapely, with long feet and hands, round arms, soft shoulders; not even Klári is cool and aloof this time, but hugs her sister so hard that Anna loses her breath. She bends low over her father's hand, and won't raise her tearful little face from it. The family is happy now, if only for a few moments, simply, primitively, transcendentally happy.

On the métro, they gaze at each other in silence. Anna decides that Klári is going to be beautiful. She is not really beautiful now, but her stubborn, childish face has grown softer, so has her unruly brown hair. Her large gray eyes are intelligent, and sometimes gently luminous. She will soon be beautiful, Anna thinks, especially if she keeps this softness and warmth.

But Klári does not keep it. By the time they get home to the Street of the Fishing Cat, she is mocking and wicked, and teases everyone. Jani listens to her oration with flaming cheeks.

"The lady's name is Albertine. She is a tall and slender beauty, with raven locks . . . although malicious people might call her a beanpole. Her features are regular, her nose is regularly four times as large as that of an ordinary human being. A female Cyrano. Don't you believe that I know her because she has honored our humble abode with a visit. She has not. I watched her wandering arm in arm with my beloved brother along the banks of the Seine. They were coming from a concert—music is showered upon our poor Jani nowadays in Niagara-like torrents. He sits and suffers. What would a knight not do for the lady of his heart?"

Jani furiously tries to interrupt her several times, but it is not easy to curb Klári's sharp tongue, and she makes Barabás laugh. Even Mrs. Barabás smiles. Albertine has really not been here yet . . . Jani has asked her to come several times, a little timidly, and Albertine has promised to come, then, somehow, the visit was always postponed. Klári has finished with Jani and turns to Anna.

"And you, incomparable Anna? How many wild Argentine hearts have you smashed to smithereens? I want statistics please. How many suicides, murders, and vitriol tragedies lie at your door, knowing how hardhearted you are?"

Anna blushes too, not because of the hints concerning South America—they don't touch her to the quick, but that last ironical sentence.

She dares not ask what has become of István.

Klári finishes off her impudences with a song, a little French song about love, that is a terrible, inevitable and sweet danger. Jani and Anna turn their backs upon her simultaneously.

At night, however, when the two girls are undressing again in their room, Klári says quietly and practically:

"I often took parcels to István, and I saw him several times. And when he was conveyed out of the country by the police . . ."

"By the police?"

"Of course, Anna. Any country would do the same. Foreign citizens are deported after having served their term."

"Yes, of course . . ."

"Well, I only meant to say that I gave him some food for the journey, and a little money too."

"Thank you, Klári."

"Don't mention it. He said he was going home to Hungary and would write. He sent his regards to you."

"Thank you, Klári."

Klári does not answer. She gets into bed and pulls the blankets over her ears. During the whole conversation, they never looked at each other. Anna goes up to her.

"May I kiss you, Klári?"

"Well, if you must."

Barabás goes down to the little bistro of the Rue Saint-Jacques. The company have sent word that they are waiting for him. They did not meet him at the train, not wishing to disturb the family reunion.

The eternal raspberry juice no longer stands in front of Alvarez's place. There is a little glass of port instead. On his chair sits a tall old gentleman, with a slight stoop, white hair, black mustache and blacker eyes. Primo de Rivera has been defeated, Alvarez has returned home, his seat is now occupied by

Prince Maura, who belongs to Rivera's party and is
a monarchist.

"There, you see. Some people can go home,"
Bardichinov had said with eyes grown dim.

"Don't believe in examples," Liiv had warned
him. "Circumstances are different in every country,
and in yours . . . h'm . . . they seem to be pretty
consolidated. So they are in mine."

Bardichinov nodded. He knew this as well as Liiv
did, but for a few days he was depressed, stayed away
from the bistro, went among his Russian friends
again and conspired. Anyhow, there were only the
two of them left now, and it all seemed so dreary, so
hopeless.

Then Prince Maura arrived and took up his quarters in the hotel of the Rue de la Huchette, in the old
room occupied by Alvarez before Vassja's death. Of
course Bardichinov made his acquaintance. Since
that time, Prince Maura joins them at the bistro
every night.

Maura is still a novice. He keeps repeating the
classic phrases:

"It cannot last longer than a few months . . . A
year hence, in my palace in Madrid . . ."

Liiv knows these phrases well, and smiles com-
passionately. Bardichinov, who has not achieved
calm resignation to this day, at first feels some envy,
but later tactfully gives a different turn to the conversation.

They welcome Barabás with great pleasure.
Maura is cordial too; although he is a novice, he has
already learned that there is no difference of caste

between emigrants. Emigration acts like a mangle, heavily, mercilessly.

Besides, everyone is a democrat abroad.

They question Barabás about South America, especially Liiv, who wants to hear about labor conditions. He calls this a study of sociography, but since he is careful not to mention the word, Barabás gives useful and unbiased replies. Prince Maura speaks of the Jockey Club in Buenos Aires, of which he has been a member since his last visit to the Argentine. Barabás has not seen the Jockey Club, but his information is more useful from the point of view of sociography.

He does not stay long tonight. His wife is surely sitting up waiting for him. And early tomorrow he wants to set out to look for work. The good old days when there was a shortage of workmen in Paris are past. But conditions are far from being anything like the unemployment in Germany or in England—so Mr. Brüll had written, so Liiv says. An expert skilled worker can still find a job.

When he enters their room, Boriska puts her arms around him.

"Gyula, Gyula, how I've missed you!"

They are no longer young. Barabás has aged, his broad chest is sunken; Boriska's face is wrinkled, there are many gray hairs among the dark. But tonight they are as fond of each other as in the old Mezötur days.

"Have you been thinking of me, Boriska?"

"From morning till night, Gyula, and in my dreams."

They stand with their arms around each other; neither of them wants to move. It is good to remain in this close embrace. Distance has done away with the indifference, with the weary habit of twenty-four years. They have not achieved much, their life today is as full of worry and anxiety as it ever was, but they are together—the whole family of five—and there is a better fate in store for their children than their own has been. Barabás holds his wife in his arms and would not exchange her worn body for that of any passionate Spanish beauty or of any gadabout French dame with arched lips.

Of course, he has sometimes turned with glowing eyes to look after them in the streets. He is a man like any other. But this is where he belongs, and he does not long to be elsewhere. They cross the dining room on tiptoe because Jani sleeps on the couch, Jani who is as tall as his father and almost broader now. A chair has to be placed at the end of the couch to support the mattress on which he sleeps, otherwise his feet would stick out.

"He's going to be an engineer," Mrs. Barabás whispers, and they exchange an intimate and happy smile.

XVII

NEXT MORNING Anna goes to the shop. Everyone receives her kindly and Mme. Lucienne even shakes hands with her.

"I am sorry you came so late. I thought you would be here sooner. Well, no matter. Of course, we had to take on someone in the meantime. She is a good worker, but her manners are atrocious. Well, we shall see. Anyway, you have had no occasion to prove yet what you can do. Theory is not everything. For the present you will work with Mlle. Nicole, and your wages will remain the same as they used to be." Mme. Lucienne suddenly realizes that Anna has practically grown up here under her wing, and that she has not seen her for eighteen months. "Oh, and, of course, Mlle. Anne,—welcome back!"

Mlle. Nicole is Mme. Andrée's successor, a commandeering, hysterical and blatant slave driver. The workshop hates her, especially Mlle. Rose, who, under the rule of the feeble Mme. Andrée, had been a regular autocrat herself. When she embraces Anna, Rose whispers:

"We'll get rid of that awful person, never fear! You're going to be the new forelady!"

Anna has no objection, but for the present she thinks it wiser to pick no quarrel with Mlle. Nicole. There is plenty of time to do that when she sees that Mme. Lucienne is pleased with her tailoring. They did not like it in Buenos Aires, but that was different: what they call Paris fashions over there is much too showy and eccentric; it would send Mme. Lucienne into fits. Anna has confidence in herself, and quietly, unassumingly goes back to her old place.

What chiefly matters now is that she should provoke no antagonism in the workshop. Every inflection of her voice, every gesture implies that if she were made forelady she would still remain one of them, no boss, but a friend. No one sees through her policy except Mlle. Rose, the shrunken, shrewd, Polish Jewess. She sometimes winks at her; for instance, when Anna says:

"This certainly is not the way to speak to serious, skilled dressmakers working in a distinguished maison de couture. Funny that anyone should be lacking in manners to such an extent . . ."

The others nod. Anna is determined to stay where she is, not even an earthquake could move her from the shop now. She has had enough of knocking about. Anna is tired, and the only thing that holds any interest for her now is her work—and even that to no great extent. But she does not want to start a new life in a world that, to her, has grown cold and sordid. That is why she has no scruples against using shrewd tricks and intrigue to assert herself. South America, a servant's work and the cabbage-smelling kitchen are still fresh in her memory. "J'y suis, j'y reste," she says to herself. She is not yet aware that this does not depend on her alone.

On the first day, during the lunch hour, she looks into the mannequins' room. She must thank Pia Monica for her intervention. The two girls look at each other; they are as embarrassed as ever.

"Oh, Anne, don't mention it."

Pia Monica has not changed. Her heart-shaped little face is prettier than ever, her skin still has its golden bloom, her teeth flash when she smiles. And the strange captivating contrast between the radiant fair hair and the dark eyes . . . Anna again discovers that she envies her.

"How is everything with you, Pia?" she asks quickly, with feigned interest.

"With me? As usual. I keep busy, I've tried to get into night fashion revues sometimes too. We need the money rather badly, you know. My mother is far from well."

"Is she? I am very sorry."

"There is nothing particular the matter with her, she's just weak, and she loses weight . . . She seems to be almost wasting away. The doctors say she's perfectly healthy. I suppose she's homesick."

"Strange." Anna shakes her head, although she does not really think it strange at all. "And your father?"

"He works very hard, poor man. And there is so much running about to do. It is difficult to place articles in newspapers nowadays. He often speaks of you. He has seen you only once, but he has taken a great liking to you."

"And I to him," says Anna, warming up at the recollection of the mobile face and flashing wit of the small dark man.

"You don't like me," Pia states quietly. "Why not? I have never done you any harm, Anne. At least, not voluntarily. And when I got your letter, I thought you had forgotten all about that old affair. But you haven't. You still dislike me."

"Oh no, I don't," Anna protests weakly, and would like to avoid this embarrassing conversation.

"Oh yes. You don't care for me as you did for Marguerite."

No, Anna certainly does not care for her as she did for Gretl. Gretl was different, exceptional, one in a million. Anna cannot answer. The two girls look at each other for another moment, then, with a common instinct, they turn their heads away. At the door, Anna turns back once more to say:

"Thank you again, Pia."

Sometimes they don't meet for weeks, sometimes they see each other every day, just as their work demands. But they never again mention the personal contact between them. Pia would have been glad of Anna's friendship—she knows no one her own age. She can't get really friendly with the three French mannequins. They are nice and companionable, but their lives are so apart, so different; they belong to families and have ties with which one cannot get acquainted. One of them lives at Suresnes, and is not interested in anything except the social and personal complications of that small town; the other is constantly involved in breath-taking, thrilling and

conflicting flirtations; the third is intent on making
a career promptly, on sexual lines exclusively: she
watches the men at the fashion shows and is constantly on the lookout for a chance, like a well-
trained scout.

Pia is bored with them and feels lonely among
them. She merely shrugs her shoulders when she
thinks of these girls—anyway, their companionship
is better than Gretl's open contempt or Anna's cool
reticence.

Anna obviously has no interest in anything except
her own advancement at the workshop. She works
hard, and increasingly difficult cutting-out problems
are entrusted to her. Mlle. Nicole watches these
goings-on ungraciously, but cannot do anything to
stop them. Then comes the day when Anna enters
into Mme. Andrée's heritage and is appointed to the
post of forelady, with all the power and duties at-
tendant upon it. On that day she walks home on air
and forgets all her worries.

Barabás has a job too, although he could not return to his old one. However, there seems to be no
great difference between the two. He has much fault
to find with it, but the family listens to his complaints
with a sense of relief: if Barabás complains, he is his
old self again. He was very quiet when he returned
from South America.

"They've saddled me with a sable coat . . . I swear
it's all rags and tatters. There isn't a square inch that
hasn't a hole in it. And they want me to patch it
up!"

"You'll mend it all right, Gyula!"

"I'll mend it, of course I will. But why do they shove all the nasty work on me?"

The question is so much beside the point that no one troubles to answer. Besides, they are now pretty well content on the whole. The joy of being together again lasts; the family finances gradually recover their balance. Anna's wages are good, a little money finds its way to the bank again; Mrs. Barabás leaves the laundry, and, egged on by her younger children, meditates on the possibilities of passing the necessary examination and taking up midwifery in Paris.

Jani is at the Ecole Polytechnique now. "My son pursues his studies at the University," Barabás sometimes remarks casually at the shop or at the restaurant in the Rue François-Miron. Of Jani's old friends, only Félicien goes on with him. They mean to build bridges and railroads and dams together; great, epoch-making undertakings. And in the evenings—that is Jani's own, private daydream—he will go home and Albertine will play for him.

At last Albertine comes to the Street of the Fishing Cat. On the following day she is to start on a concert tour along the Riviera, but first she wants to grant Jani's wish and calls on his family.

She enters with a feeling of malaise and is at great pains to be charming. Anna suddenly realizes with a pang that Albertine is the first French person who has ever crossed their threshold. They have been living here for more than ten years, and Albertine is the very first! Not even a neighbor has ever looked in to borrow a couple of eggs. What a remote, secluded, strange world is theirs, that of the foreigners in Paris, or perhaps in any city in the world . . . here they are, living among the French, have been for a decade, yet they will never merge with them, never, never! Whose fault is it? Anna ponders while she absent-mindedly tries to chat with Albertine. Is it theirs, the foreigners', because they do not knock on the door loud enough, do not crave admission? She suddenly remembers the girls at the shop . . . some of them are very fond of her, yet not one has ever asked her to come to her home, to see her family. Not even Rose, although she is not really French, but a Polish Jewess, but then, she has been living here for forty-odd years. And she, Anna, has she ever asked one of them to call? No, she has not. She suddenly realizes this with surprise. It has not been done deliberately. It has just happened.

An alien body within a body—that is how they have been living here for the last ten years. Bardichi-nov sometimes comes to see them, and Liiv and Cathrina; Pia Monica has been, and Gretl. But never anyone French. Anna looks out the window; above the rooftops she can see the two blunt towers of Notre-Dame, and, beyond, a bit of blue sky. . . . Anna feels that she loves the city. Why has she not been able to merge into it, to be absorbed by it entirely, to have made it her home? She thinks of István, who used to tease her because she did not know Paris, and of her own superior smile that meant that night clubs and music halls were not Paris. Yes, she thought she knew the city, the real city, thrifty, hard-working and virtuous; the market of the Saint-Antoine quarter, the early morning passengers

on the métro, the busy modest girls hurrying to their
workshops. She thought she knew the city—but did
she? Homes were all around them, closed and impenetrable homes, the intimate hidden life of a city,
of a whole country. Albertine is the first French girl
to cross their threshold. Yes, love could perhaps de-
molish the barrier—love, and nothing else.

Anna, too, is at great pains to be charming to Albertine.

As a result, their conversation consists of flattering
and empty platitudes.

Albertine feels uncomfortable, there is no denying
the fact. The furnishings of the flat are of the type
which the Bon Marché turns out by the thousands,
yet they are differently placed and adjusted, their
whole character is somehow changed. The chocolate
that is set before her is Meunier's brand, the cup in
which Mrs. Barabás serves it comes from the Sama-
ritaine, yet the food tastes different and the atmosphere is strange.

The reason for this is not that Albertine comes
from an upper middle-class home and is now sitting
in a workman's lodgings. No, Albertine has been
brought up in the atmosphere of French democracy,
and democracy may be snobbish when it looks upward, but it is magnanimous toward those who stand
below. Besides, the little three-room flat is clean and
tidy, the young people in it are well dressed and
smart. Albertine would be unable to explain why
the gesture with which a chair is pushed toward her
is so very peculiar—Mrs. Barabás has instinctively
dusted it with her apron because it is meant for the

visitor of her boy, her own pet, to sit on; she does not know why the way Barabás clicks his heels when he bows to her seems so awkward, yet he does it with the smart precision that he learned during the war. Also, the old people do not speak really good French yet, neither Barabás nor his wife; Albertine winces at some of their barbarisms, and Jani instantly reacts to this. He corrects his parents with a slight show of irritation, a thing he has never done before.

Klári is the only one with whom Albertine really gets on well, because Klári speaks the careless and amusing jargon of the schoolgirl. She is far better educated than Albertine, who, besides her studies at the Conservatoire, has just been able to get through school somehow—and she now throws herself into the breach, determined to make the best of the halting stereotype conversation, and to amuse their visitor. At the same time there is a gleam of quiet compassion in her gray eyes—poor Jani!

Jani is scared and uncomfortable and terribly anxious to make Albertine feel at home among them. A man in love suffers tortures if he and his people do not appear in the most enchanting, most seductive light to the woman he cares for.

"Will you come again?" Anna asks when Albertine says good-bye.

"Certainly," Albertine replies with scant conviction.

"Do come." Klári slips her arm through Albertine's. "You'll see we aren't as alarming as we look. When people know us better, they all fall in love with us. Remember that we, too, have had to grow accustomed to you French people—we've grown accustomed and we've learned to love you. My brother Jean has specialized upon a single Frenchwoman . . . but then, boys are like that!"

Two pairs of eyes light up gratefully at her banter: Jani's and Albertine's. Klári has a special aptitude for mentioning delicate subjects in a way that does not make them appear delicate at all. Anna listens, amazed; and when Jani and Albertine have disappeared in the gulf of the staircase, arm in arm, she says:

"Klári, I advise you to take up diplomacy as a career."

Klári shrugs wearily.

"Nonsense. Do you think it was worth it? Either they'll put up with each other as it is, or . . ."

"Do you think they won't?"

"How should I know? She's in love with Jani, that's all I can see."

Anna watches Klári with growing respect. This headstrong, sarcastic little girl has more brains than either she or Jani. But is that an advantage? Anna reflects. Is it good for a child of eighteen to see things so very clearly? Living abroad has done it, independence, isolation. At home she would have grown up without all these worries, she would have remained a child, more lighthearted and more credulous. Perhaps this is better—who knows?

The family can't decide what to think of Albertine. Father and Mother evidently do not like her. Her aristocratically narrow hands and long legs, her slim, small-boned, fragile figure, obviously do not tally

with their ideal of beauty; as for Albertine's face, it
is undeniably plain. Anna has formed no opinion of
her, she cannot judge by the superficial small-talk of
that afternoon. She found Albertine's embarrassment, her nervous politeness offensive rather than
otherwise. Only Klári says apologetically:

"She worships Jani, that's quite clear. Of course,
she would prefer Jani to be the son of the Prince of
Wales . . . or, better still, of some French duke. In
that case he need not even necessarily be the heir to
a throne."

When Jani returns, he anxiously tries to read the
expressions on the taciturn, reticent faces. The two
girls feel sorry for him.

"Surely she is very talented . . . you can see she
must be," Anna volunteers.

"And she's great fun . . . awfully nice girl," Klári
adds.

Jani is a bit relieved. He dared not ask Albertine
what she thought of his Hungarian family. While he
walked home with her, he hurriedly spoke of their
love, of the tremendous miracle of their belonging to
each other—for the very first time, he was a little insincere. And Albertine, as she listened to him, was a
little insincere too, replying that it was indeed a miracle, and that never had there been two people who
cared for each other quite so much as they did.

XVIII

ABOUT THIS TIME strange things are happening in Germany, and the Barabás family, who does not know the Germans, automatically accepts the French point of view. The French say that the boches are an absolutely incalculable, savage and repulsive lot, their proper place would be on the Kirghiz steppes, not in Europe.

This opinion is confirmed by Barabás's only war experience associated with Germans; his company lay near them. The Germans had less to eat than the Hungarians, so when the Hungarian wagons arrived, the Germans simply took away their food. Barabás still remembered the injury; besides, his French sojourn of twelve and a half years has also left its trace: he simply accepts common opinions.

Now, when all at once German emigrants overflow France, public opinion is no less hostile toward them than it is toward Hitler, who has driven them from their homes. That meanwhile all sorts of things have happened, that there was a Locarno, that two oddly opposed statesmen, Briand and Stresemann, used to dine together in small taverns and call each other "mon ami," that, in short, the two races, according

to politicians, have been approaching each other—
honest and skeptical Frenchmen know very little
about that, and believe it still less. Jani and Klári,
to their knowledge, have never seen a live German
—that is to say, they certainly have seen some, for
Cook's autocars evidently carry them, but who
would look twice at such rabble? A decent Parisien
certainly would not. So all that Jani and Klári have
heard about the Germans in school is that they have
heads like cubes. And Anna, in the workshop, has
heard even less.

And now, suddenly, they inundate the town. Two
of them who happen to board in Bardichinov's hotel
look quite human. Most decidedly, their heads are
not cubical. Günther Volkmar is tall, quiet, slightly
bald. Hans Hahnreiter is shorter, darker, more
square-built. It is suspicious, most suspicious indeed,
that they don't seem to be friends. Bardichinov ob-
serves on the first day that they sit down in the bar
at separate tables and merely exchange slight nods.

At night, the company has an animated discussion
on the matter in the small bistro of the Rue Saint-
Jacques, and Liiv gives an instructive lecture on the
different strata of castes in the German "Obrig-
keitsstaat." According to M. Gaston's reliable information, Volkmar is a university lecturer, while
Hahnreiter is an ironworker; the two, Liiv says, "are
wider apart than Hindu Brahmans and pariahs."

"Although," he adds pensively, "I thought that
Weimar had put a stop to this."

Of course, Liiv is mistaken. If Volkmar and Hahnreiter do not talk much, it is because the communist

workman and the humanistically-intellectual historian have little in common. But men who have
spent a long time away from their countries cannot
understand this. Prince Maura and Barabás both
shake their heads. For two people may loathe each
other—Alvarez, for instance, loathed Cathrina (not
Maura, he pays homage gallantly to the lame
woman)—two people may loathe each other, but to
live side by side, like the deaf and dumb . . .

"Peculiar race," Maura and Barabás say. And
they positively discourage Bardichinov, who wants
to make the Germans' acquaintance.

Somehow the whole city of Paris feels the same
way about it. They ardently hate Hitler, the Germans in Germany, the people dancing a war dance
in the frenzy of naziism. And just because of this
glowing hatred, they do their best to receive the
German emigrants with compassion and with sympathy. Yet to do so is extremely difficult. The emigrants wander through the country, they criticize the
casual and rather instinctive discipline, they want to
reform French life, they have all sorts of improbable
eccentricities. For instance, a group of them had an
island on the Seine given to them, and there they
established a nudist colony—the French are startled.
They used to read about German and Austrian nudist movements, yet that seemed far away. But to
have a whole group of men go crazy here, right in
the middle of their own country . . . ! The French
people by common consent are afraid of catching
cold—perhaps that is why they are the natural allies
of the English.

At last Cathrina gets to know Günther Volkmar. Cathrina drops her stick one day and Volkmar at once picks it up, clicking his heels. Cathrina thinks the tall fair man is nice to look at, and soon brings him along to the Street of the Fishing Cat,—with the object, she sincerely admits to herself, of introducing him to Anna. Cathrina is a cripple and forty, and she feels an instinctive urge toward one of the most ancient womanly professions: matchmaking. Moreover, Cathrina is the only one who does not work; the communist relief funds, though scanty, maintain her, so she has plenty of leisure.

Anna does not consider Günther nice to look at. To begin with, she does not care for people who are getting bald. A decent man turns gray, like Maura, or Pia Monica's father. Anna considers Pia Monica's father the most attractive man she knows. True, Bardichinov's hair is falling out, but then Bardichinov is old, well over seventy; besides, he is an old friend and above criticism.

Günther is undoubtedly an educated and learned man, but he is a great bore. An hour later, Anna escapes and runs down to the bistro to the old men. Perhaps, on hearing the news, they can be induced to come up and share the effort of making conversation.

"The German is sitting in our room!" she announces, and drops into an empty chair.

"Indeed!" The company takes a great interest. "Which one?"

"The historian, Volkmar."

"How did he get there?"

"Cathrina brought him. Won't you come up? I thought he would specially interest Uncle Liiv because he is a university man too, even if he is only half a professor, just a lecturer."

The party holds a short council of war. Bardichinov particularly wishes to go, he is always curious. Liiv is weary and afraid of new acquaintances, Maura dislikes learned men, Barabás does not care for Germans.

"What kind of person is he, Anna?" Bardichinov asks eagerly.

"He is a darling." Anna pronounces the lie without a tremor in order to lure the company upstairs. This fib and Cathrina's matchmaking have sealed her fate. Henceforward everybody considers them destined for each other and there is no getting away from it.

The party sets off to inspect the new acquaintance. In Liiv's opinion he is quite bearable; in Maura's, annoying; in Bardichinov's, interesting. Barabás thinks nothing of him at all. But later, on every possible occasion, they leave him alone with Anna, and watch over their being left alone like a hen watches over her chicks. Rather unpleasant!

Then Pia Monica's mother dies, and everybody forgets the Germans.

The cold, lovely, blond woman died with as much distinction as she had lived. She was not taken to a hospital, she hardly suffered doctors at her bedside. It was, in fact, a quiet and unobtrusive hunger strike on her part, she simply never had any appetite. The ambitious middle-class girl did not care for this life in emigration, in obscurity; she found no comfort in her husband's joke, that dethroned kings were living here too. For years she had been weakening gradually, then came a slight springtime influenza . . . all was over.

The shop received the news with compassionate headshakings. Pia was generally liked, the affair with Gretl had increased her popularity rather than otherwise. Anna does not know to this day why Gretl hated Pia. Perhaps because Gretl was of Dalmatian origin and Pia was Italian. (There are such queer feelings between races, and other nations cannot understand them.) At the funeral, the shop was represented by a delegation of three, among them Mlle. Rose, who was a passionate cemetery-goer.

Of course, Anna, as head of the workshop, cannot get away, so she manages to run up one night to the hotel on Montparnasse. She would like to press the hand of the little dark man. Meneghetti's hair has turned whiter, he has grown quieter, yet in his black eyes animation and intelligence sparkle with undiminished fire. He makes the visit of condolence easy for her: a mute and cordial handshake and already he talks about simple and practical topics.

They are going to move into Bardichinov's hotel. They ought to have moved long ago—the expensive apartment was beyond their modest means—but they did not want to move the invalid into more humble surroundings. But he and Pia . . .

"It will be even more convenient for me," says Pia. "I shall be nearer to the shop."

"You two can come and go together." The dark-eyed man points to them, and the two girls exchange a rather uncertain look.

The removal has taken place, and Bardichinov, at night, drags Meneghetti along with him to the bistro. It is on Klári's suggestion that Pia is occasionally invited to the Street of the Fishing Cat. Anna quickly and penitently acquiesces; she ought to have remembered the girl, sitting at home alone, her mother so recently dead. How odd that Klári should think of it—Klári, who formerly never troubled about anyone. To all appearances she does not trouble much more now . . . she seems absorbed in her work. She studies medicine, she works hard, she teaches too, she has little leisure. Still, her large gray eyes see everything.

Yet another pair of eyes faithfully follows Anna, and follows Jani and Klári faithfully too: the dim, caressing, brown eyes of their mother. If Mrs. Barabás were one day to begin to speak, if she could put into words all she knows about her children's affairs in her intuitive, quiet, melancholy way—her children would be amazed.

When Anna sits beside Günther in the dining room, those dim brown eyes sometimes look in through the open kitchen door, and beyond the open door of the next room, the large gray eyes are sometimes raised from a book. Mostly Cathrina is also sitting in the kitchen, but Jani is nowhere to be seen. Jani wanders about with his girl, he may have gone to a concert or to Albertine's flat. On the other hand,

Pia often comes, thus making up for the third child at the dinner table; upon her, too, falls the glance of the brown eyes and of the gray.

The brown and the gray eyes think the same thing: nothing will come of it. Cathrina has infected them with her matchmaking enthusiasm, but the case looks more hopeless as the time goes on. Yet Günther sits here every night, and in his deep, slow voice explains learned things to Anna and does not take his eyes off her. Günther has caught onto the bait, so far things are as they should be.

But Anna—all is not well with Anna. She no longer thinks the German lecturer a bore. Günther is the kind of man one must know well to find out what a lot he knows and how reliable he is. Anna realizes this, and almost likes Günther. She feels a sort of pallid friendship for him, indifferent and remote. This is worse than aversion, Mrs. Barabás and Klári think regretfully.

Things go wrong with Pia too, though in a different way. Pia hangs on the German man's lips. She listens to him with devotion, her heart-shaped little face is rapt and eager, and, with lips half open, she drinks in the deep, manly voice. This was not what Cathrina wanted, and not what Günther wanted either. He is happy when Pia does not come, and he can be alone with Anna.

Moreover, Pia's visit is dangerous because on such occasions Anna is inclined to escape, to run down to the bistro and settle down between Bardichinov and Meneghetti:

"Don't send me away! Günther and Pia are making such clever conversation up there, I was pining for human society."

Barabás shakes his head; he has been initiated into his wife's and Cathrina's schemes. Who has not? Cathrina has let it out to all and sundry. Cathrina cannot keep her mouth shut for two minutes. Cathrina is as proud of her idea as a mother sparrow of her fledglings. So Bardichinov, too, looks at Anna pensively, wonderingly; Maura's glance, however, conveys secret approval. Liiv smiles. Here they are living, fugitives, their life but a wingless semblance of the life for which they had been born. Every year the construction of another empire collapses around them, and buries a few thousand or a few hundred thousand, buries them and condemns them to this shadowy form of death-in-life existence. . . . In the meantime their greatest concern is, whether or not Anna has taken a liking to the long-legged German. Well, she has not. Perhaps such concerns help them to keep up the semblance of life.

On the other hand, the fact that Pia Monica has taken a liking to the German is only noticed upstairs by the brown eyes and the gray. They notice it without animosity and without approval.

Mrs. Barabás just takes in the fact and does not comment on it. There is a moment, a certain boundary line in a girl's life, when she irretrievably falls in love, even if she has never done such a thing before. This petal-faced girl is twenty-four, though she does not look more than twenty. Perhaps this is the boundary line. Mrs. Barabás recalls her own youth in Mezötur; the gay, good times boys and girls used to have together, Sundays teeming with relatives, hosts of brothers and sisters . . . well, that was different. Here the girls have somehow grown savage. It was better in Mezötur. Never mind now, no good brooding over it.

"Did you speak, darling?" She turns to Cathrina, because she has paid no attention to her for a few minutes.

Klári considers the matter more from Anna's point of view. Anna loved Vassja, she loved István, but she does not care for Günther—Vassja was all life and gaiety, István was overflowing with an impudent, roguish, wicked humor and mirth. Well, Günther is not. Yet it appears that that is what Anna wants. Perhaps because she is so quiet herself. And Pia, foolish Pia . . . That is just it, Pia is not at all foolish now. Klári wonderingly recalls their first meeting, when Pia babbled no end of nonsense . . . but that is over. True, her mother died not long ago, but Klári believes that it is love more than anything that worked the change. Love makes her so sublime, such a mute, awe-stricken listener—what an impossible muddle this is, how full of suffering! The gray eyes flash impatiently, and return to the stout volume before them.

XIX

IN THE MEANTIME Jani has come of age. His twenty-first birthday was celebrated—his twenty-second too. His sisters gave him neckties, Albertine gave him a wrist watch, and not once did anyone hint that this was the time to step forward and renounce French citizenship. Barabás, himself, made no allusion to the fact. He was a little subdued at the time. He gazed ahead of him with an empty, wandering look, and at nights, instead of going to the bistro, he went to the Hungarian restaurant or stayed at home. Yes, this was defeat, the defeat of his patriotism, of his will power. Yet what could he do? Jani will be an engineer in two years' time—should he now put an impediment in the way of his career? Of course, he could have continued his studies as a Hungarian; they were able to pay the fees now if there was need of it; besides, there are scholarships for foreign students too. But what then? There are no jobs for foreign engineers. In days past there were, but those were better days. Should he go home? Nowadays Hungarian emigration has become more sporadic, yet those who do come are nearly all engineers and doctors, and they deplore the misery of professional men. The papers from home also lament about the same thing, the papers Barabás sometimes purchases ostentatiously.

Besides, what would happen if he mentioned it to the boy, and the boy would say he did not want to reclaim his Hungarian citizenship? Jani loves a French girl. He would have mentioned it himself if he had wished to become a Hungarian again. Then, perhaps it would have been the duty of his father to dissuade him.

A few weeks go by, full of care, brooding, silence. Then everybody in common, tacit consent seems to have forgotten the decisive anniversary.

The only one who really forgot it was Jani himself. He is working hard, and he is very much in love—to him his birthday meant only the wrist watch Albertine gave him.

"Aren't we a tactful, considerate family?" Klári laughs when she is alone with Anna. "Not for all the world do we talk about a matter that might not be agreeable to one of us. Yet perhaps it would be wisest to mention it to Jani."

Anna has a lot of work to do now. The autumn season is at its tempestuous height in the shop, and she hardly emerges from the mountains of sea green, black, royal blue, and especially russet brown material. Russet brown . . . this year the color of falling leaves is the rage. Anna's brain is occupied with solving the intricate drawings of their designer: this gold-threaded "mosquito" three-piece suit is simply unfeasible, no one in the world could possibly cut it out. . . . Anna starts:

"Are you thinking of the citizenship?"

"I might have thought of that too, but I was thinking of Albertine. This match is impossible, and Jani had better be told, rather today than tomorrow."

Anna reflects.

"I should not be so positive about it. Albertine loves Jani, perhaps more than Jani loves her."

"I am not saying that Jani is the more eager of the two. Albertine, poor thing, is doing her best. She tries so hard to treat us like human beings."

"Klári, you're crazy. After all, this is not the first marriage between two people from different countries, and as for foreigners . . . just think, how well we get on with Bardichinov, with Liiv, with Maura."

Klári bursts out laughing. Anna looks at her in astonishment.

"Would you mind telling me what the joke is?"

"Were you there when Jani took Albertine down to Father and Mother? I secretly suspect that the poor fellow wanted to show off Maura, our prince. And did you watch Albertine's face? She was tremendously polite, in every sentence she said 'prince' five times, and all the time you could see that she thinks he is just a prince out of a musical comedy. These foreigners bestow all sorts of titles upon themselves, and in the end believe them. Of course, an aristocrat is genuine only if he is French. And maybe if he is English. Lord and lady may impress them, but nothing else."

"But the Spanish are their neighbors. They don't live at the end of the world, farther away even than

Austria, like we do. And they are a Latin race too. They know the Spanish have princes, and . . ."

"They know, and yet they don't believe it. And as for our getting on with Bardichinov, Liiv and Maura: isn't it even a greater joke that they get on among themselves? Don't you see that nothing matters, neither party, nor politics, nor convictions, nothing except the bare fact which obliterates all boundaries—the fact of being away from home."

Anna is tired, and the gold-thread suit looms at the back of her mind.

"There have been happy matches between foreigners." Perhaps it is Vassja's memory that haunts her, perhaps she only wants to put an end to the conversation.

"You may have seen one, I certainly have not. And this is not going to be a happy one, that's a certainty. Other people may be more adaptable than Jani. Every movement of Albertine's jars on Jani."

Anna goes to bed.

"You tell him if you dare."

"I daren't." Klári ponders. "We are not bad so far as brothers and sisters go, are we, Anna? When there is real trouble we back each other up and readily help all we can. But to speak about it . . ."

"The only real trouble happened to me," Anna says gloomily.

"How silly! That's not what I meant." Klári can see that Anna's lids are drooping, she turns out the light. "Sleep well."

Klári is right. Albertine's every movement jars on Jani. He can't say what it is that annoys him.

Petty and innocent remarks call forth violent antagonism.

"Divine!" Jani exclaims enthusiastically after a violin sonatina.

"That?" Albertine purses her lips. "*Träumerei* is like sugar water; it passes as an encore because it is short. Sentimental and provincial souls love it."

They quarrel, of course. They even differ about music, the one thing that linked them together. For Jani really understands only clear, simple, sentimental melodies, while Albertine turns more and more toward modern composers, abundant in colorful cacophonies. The antagonism may not be a national one, yet Albertine is ready with repartee.

"Of course, you care only for German music because it is so nice and broad and rolling and lukewarm."

"I abhor German music," replies Jani savagely. "You always play these impossible, frantic German compositions, every piece sounds like a nervous fit!"

"That's quite true." Albertine laughs. "You've won. Let's make it up." She runs up to him, cuddles him, but Jani does not like that either. Such questions must be talked over, settled properly; one should not skip lightly from one standpoint to the other as Albertine is wont to do. Yet the slim little body is clinging to him, so he goes on more gently now:

"Look here, little girl . . ."

"No, you grouchy old bear, we will not argue. You are ugly, stupid and wicked! This hard skull of yours is full of impossible thoughts, nothing is good enough for you, but I love you. Do you love me?"

Jani does. Yet he cannot bear her nimbleness, her flutterings, her careless unscrupulousness when flirting with concert managers or artists on tour, for the sake of an appearance, and he cannot bear the strange moral intolerance which Albertine blends so well with lightheartedness. Life here has made Jani's heart charitable, while Albertine, from the austere tranquillity of her sheltered life, passes judgment on the living and the dead.

But why enumerate these sore points? Jani finds the good in Albertine just as hard to bear as the bad. His own failings are insupportable if found in her; the good he is proud of in his own character he misinterprets in Albertine's. The same flaw and the same virtue seem different when seen in her. Their tastes, their temperaments, their minds disagree. There is not one dish they both like.

And . . . about foreigners. Albertine makes an effort to disguise it, yet she looks at every foreigner as if he were the rare specimen of an exotic kind of animal. Klári is right: Albertine is rather touched by the fact that they behave almost like human beings. She listens to Bardichinov's flowing and elegant French conversation; she looks at him with the same approval she would give to a trained seal.

To her, Jani is no foreigner. Jani is—Jani. Klári she also accepts as nearly of the same rank; she takes her advice and sometimes calls on the Barabás family. She tries to get accustomed to them, with little result though. She sits among them with her big nose, like a cuckoo nestling gone astray. The elaborate Hungarian dishes cooked in her honor give her immediate indigestion, and she startles Father and Mother Barabás by the detailed and precise description of her process of digestion.

Yet the old people learned to put up with Albertine, just as Albertine's parents learned to put up with Jani. Only Jani and Albertine are not yet reconciled to each other. They don't understand each other, they are merely in love. An unfortunate business!

Each of the three Barabás children harbors a secret. Different ones, yet very much alike. The three secrets are three encounters.

One of her colleagues, the snub-nosed little French medical student, asks Klári whether she wants a good, cheap dressmaker.

"I?" Klári laughs. "I am the best-dressed woman in Paris. My dresses are not only cut out by the head cutter of a great maison de couture, but they are also sewn by her. Moreover, she does it for love. She is my sister."

"All the same"—Suzanne echoes her laughter— "do come along to my dressmaker. She lives quite near, in the Rue de Vaugirard. I am having an evening dress made. I want you to have a look at it, especially since you belong to such a learned family."

"All right." Klári consents, since she happens to have time. "I'll go with you."

"She is just a little dressmaker, you know," Suzanne explains, "but she is very clever. She is not French, she is a Russian, and very cheap."

They talk about other things, exams, clinical practice, colleagues—particularly about one called Raymond, about whom Suzanne is teasing Klári.

In a battered house of the Rue de Vaugirard, they have to climb five flights. A weary-faced, blond woman receives them; her faded hair is unkempt, her face anemic. "Bon jour, Mlle. Desvernois," she greets Suzanne.

"Bon jour, Mlle. Dinotchka."

Somehow the name strikes Klári's ear. She watches the dress being tried on, she criticizes, she suggests improvements, and all the time something is nagging at the back of her mind.

"Have you been living in Paris for a long time, Mlle. Dinotchka?" she suddenly asks.

"About ten years, mademoiselle."

"A political refugee." Klári nods her head in sympathy.

"No." The woman with the weary face looks up. "I came out to meet my fiancé. We meant to get married out here."

"Ah!" Suzanne exclaims startled. "And did the blackguard desert you? Was he a Frenchman?"

"He was a Russian, and he did not desert me." The Russian woman's voice is flat, indifferent. "For years he had been saving the money to bring me out here. It was a very expensive and difficult journey, I had to flee from Russia because I had no passport. When I got to Paris, my fiancé was dead. He was a taxi driver, and he had been killed in an accident."

The colorless voice is silent. The Russian woman is kneeling on the floor, and pinning up the hem of the frock.

"Is this long enough, Mlle. Desvernois?"

Gradually Klári's memories become clearer. She was a remote and incompletely informed spectator at the time of the tragedy. They had concealed all they could from her, because she was little; she had just managed to hear scraps now and then.

Yet she knew enough to keep the visit in the Rue de Vaugirard from Anna and from everybody.

Jani's encounter was briefer and, perhaps, of a more dramatic kind.

The students were taken to visit factories; among others they went to see the Renault automobile works in Billancourt. The group of students pressed through the gate, chattering gaily. Young men of twenty-two sometimes behave as if they were not yet twelve. In the vast courtyard a building was being erected; workmen were shoving wheelbarrows laden with gravel. Jani suddenly stopped, his face became rigid—one of the workmen in a ragged, dust-colored suit, with a dust-colored, sallow face, straightened up and turned toward the noisy group. It was Elemér Hallay. The two boys' eyes met for a second.

Then Jani quietly went up to the professor in charge and reported that he was going home, he felt giddy and feverish.

He did not go home though. He roved about in the streets, and pondered over the Kuruc-Labanc theory. Never in his life had he felt so miserable.

This was Jani's special secret, born chronologically a month earlier than Klári's, yet to be forgotten ever so much later. Perhaps never.

Anna's secret is a continuous one. It began on a winter's night, when, just for once, snow sparkled in the streets of Paris, where the winter is usually damp. Coming from the suffocating workshop, where the air was close with the smell of fresh pieces of silk and of machine oil, Anna was pining for air. For a while she trotted along the Rue Saint-Honoré, then she got tired of the clattering thoroughfare, went down to the Seine, crossed the Pont-Neuf and, on the left bank of the river, lost herself in the labyrinth of well-known little streets.

As she was quickly turning a corner, she collided with a staggering figure. For one second, they had to take hold of each other to keep from falling.

"Sorry!"

"Sorry!"

"Did I hurt you, mademoiselle?"

"No. . . . Oh, is that you, M. Fedor?"

The wobbling figure clung to the wall and gave Anna an intense look. His eyes showed stupor and astonishment.

"I am so sorry . . . I don't know you, mademoiselle, but my name is Fedor. How did you know?"

An unaccountable excitement took hold of Anna.

"I am Anna Barabás . . . Annuska, don't you remember? In the Hotel Rue-de-la-Huchette?"

The dull eyes slowly came to life. Suddenly Fedor roared:

"Annuska! Of course, I remember. How you have grown!"

"Well, M. Fedor, it is many years since you saw me."

The man's vivacity seemed strange to Anna. Fedor used to be haughty, arrogant. And now she saw with dismay that he was standing in the wintry street without an overcoat. There he stood, gesticulating and shouting:

"Indeed, many years . . . but to grow at such a rate! You were a tiny little girl then, hardly aboveground."

"Are you not mistaking me for my sister Klári? However, she is twenty now. But, M. Fedor, you ought not to go out like this, you will surely catch cold."

"Like this? What do you mean? No, I am not cold. But if you think so . . . here is a small tavern. Let us go in and drink half a liter of wine? Have you got time?"

Anna hesitated. She had no time really. Günther would be expecting her at home, he did not know that she was walking home from the shop and would be later than usual. Her family, too, would wonder. But Fedor, this new and talkative Fedor . . .

"Very well. But don't you live near here? You ought to run up and fetch your coat."

With a disdainful gesture Fedor took Anna's arm, and led her to the tavern.

"My coat . . . I don't know where I left it. But it does not matter. I am never cold. It will be nice and warm in here. They have excellent wine."

Fedor's gait was just a little unsteady, but his statements were all the more positive. From his lips a strong smell of alcohol wafted to Anna's nostrils, but even without it she knew Fedor was fairly drunk.

Now they sit in the warm and noisy tavern. Fedor orders some wine.

"Now let me take a good look at you," he says to Anna. "You look smart. Do tell me all about yourself."

"All in one breath?" laughs Anna. She notes that Fedor is not as elegant as he used to be. True, he looks smarter in this worn suit than others do in expensive dress coats. His monocle also is missing. He must have lost it.

"Yes, all in one breath," Fedor demands. Anna shakes her head and smiles. However, when half an hour has elapsed, she realizes that they have talked a tremendous lot in an excited, breathless way. Fedor puts questions, she answers them.

There is a queer familiarity between them. They do not know whence it has sprung, perhaps because they have known each other for so long. Fedor is drunk, sensibly and charmingly drunk, and his sullenness has disappeared.

"And you, Fedor?" cries Anna. "What have you been doing meanwhile? You've made me talk the whole time!"

"Nothing of interest has happened to me. I have not been in South America. I work . . . sometimes."

"Where? And why only sometimes?"

"There is an automobile repair shop not far from here." Fedor makes an uncertain gesture toward the door. "If I am in need of money, I can always find work."

"When you are in need of money. And when you get the money, what do you do with it?"

Fedor smiles.

"I spend it on drink." Hurriedly, emphatically he corrects himself. "No, I pay my rent first. Honestly. I only spend what is left on drink."

"And is that right, Fedor?"

"Why not, Anna?" Fedor looks at her provocatively.

"Need I tell you? I am not going to. I must dash now, but I can see your shirt is torn. Tell me where you live, I shall run up one day and mend your things."

"I won't tell you. Do stay a little longer, can't you? What a pity! When will you have time for me again?"

"I don't know," Anna says hesitatingly; "perhaps on Saturday afternoon."

"Splendid! I shall wait for you here on Saturday afternoon."

"What time?"

"I shall be here all afternoon," Fedor replies with a broad gesture.

Saturday afternoon is Günther's appointed time. He takes Anna out for her training, as she calls the rather strenuous long walk, after which they go to a cinema. Well, she is going to shirk one or the other, or both, as the two can hardly be separated. She might say there was extra work in the shop.

Anna feels no remorse, not even when she sees Günther's anxious face. As soon as she has gobbled her supper, she declares that she is going down to the bistro. Since Meneghetti has been coming there, she often runs down for half an hour. Anna takes her coat, Günther's beseeching eyes do not keep her back.

"Stay here if you like—perhaps Pia will come."

"No, I am coming," Günther says dolefully.

Anna does not mention Fedor to anyone. On Saturday afternoons, she sneaks away, has a few drinks with Fedor in small bars, and talks much and gaily. Not every Saturday afternoon though; Fedor sometimes rings her up in the workshop to put her off. This happens when he has no money, not even enough to pay for half a liter of wine. He will not let Anna pay, not for the world.

"Why not?" Anna asks angrily.

"Just because!" says Fedor, with a laugh.

XX

I DID NOT THINK you were as wicked as all that!"
Bardichinov looks at Anna reproachfully.

"You really are scaring that boy away!" Cathrina
adds. "You keep tormenting him."

Anna laughs aloud.

"Are you thinking of that post-office business?"

Anna has heard the story from Fedor; of course,
she takes good care to keep that a secret. After the
revolution, Fedor escaped first to Germany; there he
wandered about for several years. He had come to
Paris from Hamburg with Vassja. He had witnessed
the post-office scene in Munich.

"Günther," Anna asks innocently, "is it true, that
when the mail has been distributed to the postmen
at the general post office in Munich, they form in
twos and march out of the building with a clattering
goose step? With stiff knees? Like this? Is that true?"

Günther's face darkens, he knows Anna wants to
hurt him.

"It may be true. I've never seen them."

"And don't the people of Munich stand around the
post office and explode with laughter?"

"Why should they, Anna? Is discipline such a bad thing?"

"You don't know what a jolly thing it is to be a postman. I wish you knew my friend from the Boulevard de Sébastopol, who pins the letters for the old vagabond on the back of the bench on which he sleeps!"

"Don't you think it is a much jollier thing if vagabonds do not have to sleep on benches?"

"No. There always have been vagabonds and there always will be, even in your country. Only there they will probably be properly trained, and march under the bridge where they sleep on the command of: 'Form twos, right about face!' And they may go to bed only when the head vagabond shouts 'Lie down!' Do they get up at the sound of a bugle?"

"I don't know why you are laughing at me, Anna."

"And is it true that when two Germans meet they found a society?"

"It is wrong to hold societies in contempt. It is a good thing for people who have similar views to associate. We are just discussing the plan of forming an association for emigrant university men here."

He is interrupted by Anna's outburst of convulsive laughter. Günther turns away. He is hurt.

This is why Bardichinov and Cathrina are reproving Anna.

"You will never find a better husband," Cathrina says reproachfully. "He even has a job with the *Pariser Tageblatt*. Not much salary, but still . . ."

Cathrina is a communist and a revolutionary, she has been in Siberia and in jail, but her notions of the foundations of matrimony are as strict and old-fashioned as the notions of any scrupulous Finnish mother can be.

"One must be either a Byzanthologue or a reformer," Anna replies firmly. "I don't say I don't like Günther. When he talks about Byzantium he is quite bearable, and he is an honest boy. But don't let him try to reform France. These Germans are simply awful."

"You have been educated in France, and you have imbibed French prejudices," says Bardichinov, shaking his head.

"I have not been educated at all," says Anna earnestly. "You have taught me all I know, Uncle Bardichinov. You taught me to be patient, you taught me that life is about equally good and equally bad everywhere, and every human being and every country is different, and that is how it must be. But the Germans stalk about in this country, find fault with everything and constantly boast about things at home."

"Isn't it natural for them to love their own country best? Don't you wish you were going home? I do."

"Uncle Bardichinov," Anna argues earnestly, insistently. "That is different. How can I explain? Of course, we all long to go home, although most of us would be worse off at home—at any rate, we should be. At home my sister would be a factory girl or a typist at the most. Here she will be a doctor. Jani would have been a workman, maybe a mechanic.

Here he will be an engineer. Yet we are longing to go home. You would go home if your life were not at stake; Cathrina would go if she did not have to fear jail. But Günther and his fellow emigrants keep lamenting about Hitler doing this and Hitler doing that, yet they can't bear anyone being happy in any other way than the patent German one."

"Günther is an idealist . . ." Cathrina begins. Anna shrugs.

"They are all alike. I came to see you the other day, Uncle Bardichinov, and you were out. I was leaning against the bar, talking to Mme. Germaine. This other German, Hahnreiter, came up to me; he is more human than Günther, he can laugh. But he, too, kept on criticizing all the time, and explaining how marvelously Germans organize everything."

"They have not been here very long. It is just homesickness, that's what it is, Anna."

"They have been here two years. Uncle Bardichinov, do you remember when Primo de Rivera died? He could not survive his defeat. We were afraid then that Maura would go insane with melancholy. He didn't. He is still here, even if somewhat subdued, his spirit somewhat broken. He has realized now that he is living abroad, he knows we are fish out of water, all of us."

"And he is trying to develop lungs." Bardichinov nods. "Yes, Anna, I know what you mean. He may not succeed, but even then, he will not preach that it is possible to breathe only through gills."

They are silent. Then Cathrina remarks with a sigh:

"However, he would have made you a very good husband."

On Saturday afternoon Anna sits with Fedor, tells him all about Günther. She is rather malicious, and they both laugh a good deal. Anna has no scruples in thus delivering up her faithful servant and suitor.

"There is one thing I cannot understand, Fedor. There is Pia—you don't know her—she is very beautiful. And she adores Günther and gapes at him like a swooning calf. Why doesn't Günther care for her?"

"Because you are very much more charming, more intelligent and amusing, Anna. I know all about it, so you may believe me."

"That's nonsense. Life is a crazy thing, Fedor. But since we are inquiring into each other's characters, I should like to ask you something."

"Do!"

"Fedor, you used to be so taciturn, so morose, so disagreeable. Now you are different. What has happened?"

Fedor gives her an astonished look.

"But that is quite simple, Anna. Formerly my old grievances rankled in my heart. I made desperate plans which were to get me home. But now I know I shall never get home, and if old sorrows well up in my heart . . . that's quite clear, isn't it? . . . I get drunk."

Fedor laughs; a cold chill creeps over Anna's heart.

"Another question, Fedor. Why don't you let me come to your lodgings? Surely your things need tidying? I suppose you live in some horrible place."

"Just wait," Fedor begs, laughing. "Just wait another two weeks. For two weeks I am going to work, I shan't touch a drop of drink, I will be loathsome, sullen and wicked, but we shan't meet during that time, so it won't matter. Then I shall ask you to come into my palatial residence."

So he really lives in some horrible place. Well, no matter now, since he is going to move.

One morning, when they are squeezed side by side in the crammed métro, Pia Monica asks Anna:

"Say, Anne, don't you think I had better learn dressmaking?"

"Dressmaking?" Anna asks wonderingly. "Why should you?"

"Tell me, how long can I go on with my job? My hair is getting darker, my hips broaden. We are twenty-six, Anne."

"Have your hair dyed; everybody does. Your figure is perfect."

"Why don't you give a minute of serious consideration to my troubles, Anne? You are on top now; you know it, don't you?"

Anna blushes slightly. She did not expect such straightforwardness from Pia. She faces her:

"I have never thought of these things in that way: superiority . . . or defeat. I was not at all surprised when István chose you. I am surprised *now* that Günther does not. You are worth so much more than I."

"That's not true, Anne."

"It is true. I always knew it, although I never

mentioned it. Not only because you are prettier. You are also better, more affectionate, more womanly. And you had much more charm and you were much more vivacious. Perhaps that's gone . . . we are almost on a level now . . . you have come down to mine."

"I don't want to contradict you. I am glad you did not think so badly of me as I thought. Your way of putting it is different, but your meaning is the same. I *am* worn."

"It's the profession. Well, to learn dressmaking takes a long time, and meanwhile you couldn't go on with your job."

"It won't do then. My father works hard and earns very little. His name has lost its glamour too. The newspapers don't take his articles so gladly now."

"Is there no job you could learn in less time?"

"I don't know. At first I thought of becoming an actress or a dancer. Not that I thought I was gifted, only because I was pretty. Of course, it's too late now. You know, Anne, deep down in my heart I think I was born to be a wife, a good and handsome married woman. I could, for instance, very well have smoothed the way for some politician . . ."

"Or for some professor." Anna smiles.

"Or for some professor, for that matter. I could have talked agreeably, been a hostess, cultivated valuable friendships. A scientific or political salon . . . something of that kind. I should also have taken an interest in my husband's work. I would have been the one to encourage, to stimulate him . . . a sort of muse, shall we say? Not a good job nowadays."

Anna's mind is of a more practical turn.

"After all, you know the fashion business well. You could become a saleswoman. . . . We get out here."

"This was our first real talk, Anne," says Pia, as they hurry toward the shop.

Anna laughs outright.

"We are getting old, Pia. However, you needn't take up another profession yet. For the present you had better stay where you are. Mannequins earn most."

When she is alone, she ponders over Pia's fate, for the first time since she became acquainted with her. The Italian girl's life has been more secluded than hers, first of all because the hotel on Montparnasse where she had lived was a smarter one, there were hardly any other foreigners staying there; only transitory travelers and sightseeing tourists, and those do not count. They seem even more remote than the French, much more so because of their unconcern, because of the imperturbable rigidity of their program of diversions.

Perhaps their countrymen, the young Italians, did visit the Meneghettis occasionally. Human lives have perhaps swarmed around Pia too, and she has as numerous recollections as Anna. Yet this is not quite probable. That lovely cool creature, her mother, surely cared for a few people only; however, Anna reflects, there was her father, all intellect and rich vitality. No one could be quite lonely near such a man.

Anna is absolutely convinced that there is no one

in the world superior to Meneghetti. She is in love
with him in a kind of abstract way: it is a convenient
and exclusively intellectual love, valid only when she
sees him. Otherwise she forgets about him for weeks.
Whenever she meets him, Anna tells Meneghetti
that she adores him, that he is the best-looking man
in Paris, whereat the plain little dark man laughs
heartily, and, profiting by the difference of age,
she hugs him and kisses him on his forehead.
Meneghetti enjoys the kiss; yet, two minutes later,
he has forgotten it just as Anna has. Only Bardichinov grumbles, and says it will all end in a
vitriol murder, and Liiv looks on mildly curious and
speculative.

When the two weeks have passed, Fedor turns up.
They meet in a small bar, slowly drink their half
liter, and solemnly set out toward the new lodgings.
Fedor explains:

"I have given in to your arguments about ruining
my health, so I looked out for mountain air, harden-
ing exercise combined with a sub-Alpine situation,
and I chose the sixth floor in a house which has no
elevator."

A small hotel in the Rue Monsieur-le-Prince,
precisely like a thousand or five thousand others.
The patron is bustling about in the bar, just like all
patrons do, only this one is a particularly robust,
chubby-faced butcherlike patron. In due time they
reach the sixth floor. Anna is panting; Fedor calls
her attention to the view from the staircase window.
Then he takes the lead, jingling triumphantly with
his keys.

He opens the door wide, and says with a deep bow:

"Fedor Jarossev-Pelczinski devoutly begs the duchess to enter his humble abode."

Anna throws back her head, and walks in with mincing steps. The room is minute and unutterably shabby. It is no cleaner and no dirtier than other little cheapest hotel rooms on top floors. Tidy the wardrobe? There is none. But Fedor pulls out an ancient traveling bag from under the bed.

"My queen! On the day before yesterday, with my very own hands, I washed every garment which has touched my unworthy body. Yesterday I ironed them, and this procedure had only a single victim: one collar."

"A person who is all thumbs shouldn't iron," Anna reproves him. She takes out a small sewing case. "I knew you had no needle and thread, so I brought some."

"Haven't I?" groans Fedor. "Here you are: needles, thread, thimble. I bought everything for the purpose yesterday."

"Fedor," Anna says, unaccountably moved, "you are really not such a monster as one might think." But the emotion does not last. Anna's attention is riveted on her task.

"My boy, your most tattered shirt must be sacrificed to mend the others."

Henceforth, after every meeting, they climb to the little room on the sixth floor. Anna sews, Fedor amuses her, makes tea, sometimes produces a hidden bottle of wine. Then, one day, when the mending is done, Anna stays. Not because she has had too much wine—no, she remains there in full possession of her mental faculties. Often her senses have troubled Anna, particularly in the days of István's stormy love-making. Then came a heavy, weary silence; body and soul were numb, but of late her body has again been clamoring for its rights. Anna is twenty-six. No great power of persuasion is wanted: a single beseeching look, Fedor's slow pressure on her arm.

"What is it, Fedor?"

"Won't you . . . stay?"

Anna is silent. She looks at the man's face. Light brown hair, slightly misty gray eyes, his smile just a little constrained, but there is a lovable irregularity in the sweet and boyish face.

"Do you think it will be well, Fedor?"

"It will."

Anna nods and stays. She resisted István whom she loved; she does not resist now. Why not?

The two are not in love, no irresistible passion drives them toward each other. But they have a homely feeling when they are together. They can talk without restraint, and without mental reservations. They are friends.

The first embrace is not exactly enjoyable. It seldom is. Anna walks down the stairs; she is crushed and weary, but she feels no remorse; on the whole, she is contented.

Somewhat stunned, she does not notice the

agitated uproar of the street, the mad galloping of the newsboys. At last, when a shrill voice yells into her ears, she is startled and listens:

"The King of Jugoslavia and the French Foreign Secretary have been killed in Marseilles."

XXI

NOTHING HAPPENS during the next few days. A king and a foreign secretary have been killed, certainly a great event. Yet, after all, in Anna's childhood recollections there is the assassination of a crown prince and his wife; the killing of the prime minister in neighboring Austria; the murder of her own country's most prominent statesman during a revolution; as for the story of the massacre of the Czar and his family—she has heard it from Bardichinov two thousand times, to say the least; in France a president of the Republic has been shot since she lives here. In a word, Anna and her family are slightly indignant, but otherwise not personally perturbed by the occurrence. At the bistro it is discussed every night. Liiv and Meneghetti throw an authoritative light on the causes of the Serbo-Croatian conflagration, and its presumable political effects. Bardichinov, being conservative, sides by inclination with the oppressed Croatians; Maura, being Latin, abuses the whole Balkan set and recalls the assassination of the Obrenovitch; Liiv, being a socialist, strongly condemns violence.

Then comes a day when Anna, returning from the shop, finds the family in a riot. It appears that her father has been home since ten o'clock: he has been fired.

None of them can quite understand why, although Barabás has been to see Meneghetti who reads every paper, so he knows more. Meneghetti did say something, but Barabás could not grasp it. He will wait until Liiv comes home from the insurance office. Liiv can explain things lucidly, and make them intelligible to simpler minds. Liiv used to deliver lectures to workmen, Meneghetti spoke in prominent liberal clubs—that makes all the difference. To the Barabás family, for the present, everything seems confused. If the Croats have killed their own king, why should the French harbor a grudge against the Hungarians?

At night, Liiv explains the matter in the bistro, Günther in the flat.

"I wonder what will happen." Anna sighs. "They haven't said anything to me yet."

For a whole week she goes to the shop anxiously, and prepared for the worst. She is almost relieved when, at the beginning of the following week, Mme. Lucienne sends for her.

"I am really very sorry, Mlle. Anne . . . I will not say you never made mistakes, but, on the whole, I was satisfied with your work, and we have grown accustomed to each other. I am sorry, but it cannot be helped. Two customers have spoken to me about it. I would never have thought of it, but today the old Duchesse Maillard said again, 'Do you still keep that Hungarian woman here? Is she to fit me? Never!' She said something else too, but that I would rather not tell you. And she went away."

"Oh! Did she?"

"I am so glad you have my interests at heart, Mlle. Anne. She is coming back tomorrow. She said she hoped by then I will have realized my duty as a patriot. She must be fitted by someone else—it will be all wrong, I suppose."

"I am sorry, Mme. Lucienne."

"You are a good girl, Mlle. Anne." Lucienne gives her an absent-minded look, yet somehow she is not so offhand as usual. "I should suggest you try to find another job for a few months. Meanwhile the thing may be forgotten. I really can't understand why your countrymen are so quarrelsome!"

When Anna gets home, her people are just having dinner; Barabás too, as he is out of work. He has not even tried to find anything else: he waved aside the idea, saying it was hopeless while the present atmosphere prevailed. Anna has not reached the end of her tale, when her father suddenly thumps violently on the table:

"We are going home!"

This declaration is unexpected, yet no one is really surprised. There is just one minute's silence while each estimates his own weight and position within this little community, the family. Then, quietly and objectively, with a special guardedness in tone and manner, they set about discussing the plan.

"Let's see how we could bring it about," says Klári. "All of us couldn't go at once, not even if we wanted to. And as for myself, and I believe Jani too, I don't want to go—yet."

Jani will be an engineer in four or five months. Barabás looks at his son.

"Will you get married?"

Jani nods sullenly, without looking up. This anti-Hungarian atmosphere, this press campaign . . . again many misunderstandings have arisen between him and Albertine.

"And I have to study for another year and a half," says Klári. "But you need not worry about me, I can put up at one of the homes for girl students."

They deliberate on the problem for a little while, then come to an agreement. Again it is Barabás and Anna who will set out, as they did once before for the Argentine. Mrs. Barabás will stay on for the moment with the two younger children: she will wait for news from Hungary. Anyhow she would love to stay for her son's wedding if they would let her. Jani is sure to get work at once, Albertine's family have excellent connections. Jani mutters between his teeth that his fiancée's uncle has an interest in some sort of communication's undertaking. Then perhaps Klári could live with Jani and his wife, or maybe in a students' home after all. And Mrs. Barabás will sell the furniture piece by piece—not precipitately, because if you do that, you get simply nothing. Then she will go home too. Klári will follow when she has become a doctor. Jani—maybe Jani will never go home.

The atmosphere is depressed. Jani feels the tearful eyes of his mother upon him and turns away awkwardly. Klári, deep in thought, beats a tattoo on the table and glances now at Jani, now at her mother. Barabás, too, is twisting his neck uncomfortably . . . it seems as though he were scattering the family. Yet what can he do? And they did want to go home sometime anyhow, neither of them intended to live here always. Of course, it is a pity that the boy has fallen in love with a French girl, but it may be to his advantage. A distinguished family, a job in view . . . And Klári, at least, will come home . . . yet will she? Barabás suddenly looks at the girl with suspicion. Again she is saying, for the second time now, and most emphatically:

"I won't go home on any account until I have my diploma."

Until then. And after that? The girl does not say a word about afterward. She does not say she will go home then. Barabás knows his daughter well, nothing can be wrenched from her if she will not say so of her own accord; besides, it is better not to tackle the question. Mother is very much distressed about the boy.

I can't help it, Barabás justifies himself in his thoughts. It's not my doing. If the boy had a job, if he were married already, the separation would be easier. However, we can't wait, we must go now. Politics have no special regard for simple folks.

Anna gets up and goes to the window. Barabás's eyes follow her. A good thing that Anna at least goes willingly, lightheartedly, that she leaves no one behind. How lucky she did not fall in love with this German, Günther, yet they all seem to have done

their best to bring them together. Up till now Barabás had had nothing to say against the match either;
he had heard no end of praise about Günther, and
Anna is no longer sixteen . . . but now he is glad it
did not come off.

Anna stands at the window, she is taking leave of
Paris. She, too, is thinking that she has no one to
regret. Fedor, perhaps, in these last weeks—a little.
Before him, no one. Vassja and Gretl—they have
vanished. Bardichinov and Meneghetti—it will be
pleasant to remember these two. Poor old Bardichinov, he will miss her. Fedor, perhaps, too. Fedor
will start drinking again, and his shirts will go to
rags.

"I am going," Anna had replied without a moment's consideration when her father asked her.
But now her heart aches a little. She looks out upon
the Seine and beyond the Seine upon that narrow
strip that shows from the Cité—just the back view of
the Préfecture—and in this moment she loves the
city very much.

They are going in a week's time. During this last
week Anna rambles about, sometimes with Fedor,
often alone. She makes no plans, she does not revisit
the places linked with her memories. She roams
about, strolling idly, saying farewell to the atmosphere, to the refractions of light on the Seine, to the
climate that is more misty than the climate in
Budapest. She could never leave any underwear or
stockings lying out at night with the window open,
because they became quite damp by morning. The
sea is near. Winters are rainy, snow is a rare thing;

though when she met Fedor that day it was snowing hard. These were the things Anna was bidding farewell to: things like the hawker heralding his coming with a horn. Such trifles were without significance; yet to her they outlined the city much more acutely than did Napoleon's grave. She wanders among the ancient houses of the Ile Saint-Louis, stands still at the narrowing end of the island, thinks of the snails and mussels for sale in open sacks in front of the food stores. To this day she has not tasted them. Once, when she was little, she would have loved to. Later, she went to work and her mother did the marketing. Anna forgot all about mussels and snails. But now her childhood curiosity haunts her. She thinks of buying a handful, then with a shrug and a smile she walks on. . . .

Anna had two honorable offers, one on the very night of the great resolution. Günther heard the news of the journey from Cathrina because Mrs. Barabás ran across to Cathrina immediately after the council and poured forth her sorrow. So Günther dons his black suit—as a sign of mourning, Klári remarks afterward—and proposes to Anna.

"Of course, I don't mean to take advantage of this turn of events," he explains; his face is red, and he is stammering. "My request naturally is founded upon deep and sincere feeling . . . however, if you marry me, you need not leave Paris. As the wife of an emigrant you partake of the same rights of hospitality . . ."

"No." Anna shakes her head. "Thank you, Mr. Günther, no. To begin with, I don't know that I should like to stay in Paris at all. And then, too . . ."

"Very well," says Günther and bows stiffly. His face is red and his eyes are hazy.

"Don't look so unhappy," Anna says with a laugh. "You are such a decent fellow, Günther. Why don't you look out for a sensible girl who likes respectability and things in order? Probably I am not quite right in my mind, I don't know what I want myself."

"Very well," Günther repeats, and his bow is stiffer still.

Anna glances toward the adjacent room whose door, for once, is closed. Klári is studying, but Bardichinov and Cathrina are hiding in there too. They know why Günther is wearing his best suit, and they are awaiting the result. Quite a musical comedy, Anna thinks; the family at any rate will be pleased she said no.

The other suitor is Fedor. This offer sounds rather different, but the argument is amusingly identical.

They are in Fedor's room, on the bed, leaning on their elbows, side by side.

"Do you know what I am thinking of, little girl? You needn't go to Hungary if you don't want to. You can have your job again too. I will marry you, if you like."

"Have you gone crazy, Fedor?"

"All right. You needn't rub it in. I know I am a rather shady individual. I didn't mean we should live together, I couldn't very well make up my mind to do that myself. I merely offered you my name, the only thing that is distinguished about me. Jarossev-Pelczinski is an ancient Russian-Polish name—it has patina. I must call your attention to the fact that from the distance I would be a husband you could boast of: 'My husband, the ex-officer of the Czar's Guards.' Of course, I must be properly stowed away, or they might find me out, a drunken vagabond."

"Fedor, you are an angel. And that isn't what I meant. But look here, you could still make a good match, marry someone with money and family."

Fedor bursts out laughing.

"Are you in earnest? Your intellectual faculties are rather undeveloped, my girl."

"American women positively hunt for Russian emigrants."

"Princes, my dear. The Pelczinskis were Polish princes once, but the title got lost in one of the many hurricanes. I could not possibly unearth it any more. But let us suppose they would hunt for me too, and succeed in capturing me—do you think I could bear it? I should run away from any good, distinguished and rich marriage and come back to my small bars."

"But why? One can drink just as well in a palace."

"You are mistaken. One cannot. Not in a palace. If a man has been thrown out by the door, he should not try to climb back through the window. Into good living, I mean. That is not the right way. It can't be done."

"So many people start a new life . . ."

"A new business, you mean? Of course, bankrupt stockbrokers do it. But to start a new life . . . my dear, you are duller than I believed. Do you know how old I am? Forty-five. In nineteen-seventeen, when the crash came, I was twenty-eight."

"All right, Fedor. I don't want to convert you. I did not even try to cure you of drinking, did I?"

"No, you were a good comrade. That's why I would like to help you. My queen, I am pining away for your answer: may I keep that tiny hand forever?"

"No, Fedor. I am going home. Father would be lonely without me."

"Is that your only reason for going?"

"There is even less reason for staying."

She is right there, and Fedor stops arguing.

"At least you are going home," he says pensively.

"Shall I write to you, Fedor?"

"Don't write, darling. I wouldn't answer, but I shall think of you more often than you suppose."

"Vassja—" Anna unexpectedly pronounces the name—"do you remember him, Fedor?"

The Russian looks at her gravely for a long time.

"He was the only friend I ever had," he says slowly.

"He was the only man I ever loved," nods Anna and believes that she is speaking the truth.

On the day before Anna's departure, they meet once more in a bar. Later they go to Fedor's room.

"Try to keep your balance," Anna begs him as she says farewell. "Don't drink more than you work."

"Don't make your last will and testament!" Fedor retorts. Then they stand on the threshold in a long, silent embrace. Anna runs down the stairs.

Again the entire company sees them off at the

station. They are starting from the Gare de l'Est, where they had arrived fourteen years ago. Bardichinov comes waddling along, Cathrina arrives, briskly setting her sticks in front of her. The night train leaves at ten, at this hour they are all free. Pia Monica is standing next to her father, Günther is at her left. They all withdraw a little, Mrs. Barabás and the two children are in front, directly under the window. Albertine had run up to say good-bye in the afternoon.

The train starts. Pia Monica mutely gazes at Anna. Anna feels the look and returns it with a hardly perceptible smile. She steps out of the picture in which, till now, their lives had run side by side.

A great number of Hungarians are traveling by this train, but the Barabás family knows no one. The travelers are mostly of the kind that sits about the terraces of the Dôme and the Rotonde: young would-be artists, correspondents of unknown newspapers. The Barabás family never got near their hunting grounds. Günther once took Anna to the Dôme, but it was not a success. In the ten modest rooms of the hotel in the Rue de la Huchette, she had already met the multicolored conglomeration of peoples and races, and the only one she was amazed at in the Dôme was an Annamese with rather improbably protruding teeth.

They reach Bâle in the morning; the train wakes up. They exchange courtesies with fellow travelers. Now the Swiss mountains are approaching, but it rains, and fog is drifting. The snowy peaks that once told a tale of majesty to a crouching little girl are invisible. They reach Buchs in the afternoon, and at the station where once upon a time a little fairy queen passed three small children holding their milk jugs tightly Anna and her father do not alight at all.

Trains run quicker now than at the time they came out. Then they traveled for two whole days, now it will take them only a day and a half. It is night when they reach the Hungarian frontier. Father and daughter feel like crying, but in come the frontier police and energetically ask for passports; then the customs official, who bids them open their boxes. If the exiles wish to kiss the sacred soil of their fatherland when crossing the frontier, they cannot do it: no one may leave the train before the examination is finished. Liiv, if he were here, would certainly explain the role of frontiers in the economic and political life of countries; then he would smile and say that politics have abolished the ancient human right to sentimentality.

XXII

IN BUDAPEST they take up their abode in Bethlen
Street, because they know this part of town best.
They set out to look up some old acquaintances—
are fourteen years such a long time?—but Mrs.
Koppány is the only one they find in the old house
in Nefelejts Street. The thin woman has shriveled
down to the bone, her eyes are weak, her memory
lapses, it takes her a long time to realize who her
visitors are. Then she breaks out in joyous and
excited shrieks. She cannot believe Anna is really
Anna; then, again, she forgets them, ponders and
broods, starts to tell a long and mumbling story
about some mysterious injury that has befallen her.
Barabás gazes at her and is shaken: the woman is
scarcely older than he—is it possible? Is he also
threatened by this collapse, this suffocation, this
torpor?

He gives Anna a sign, and Anna jumps up gladly.
The woman, in her lucid moments, looks with un-
disguised suspicion at Anna's clothes and ladylike
manner. Father and daughter hurry down the
almost entirely forgotten stairs of the old house, and
they know they will never come back.

Then begins job-hunting, which is a more or less similar procedure in all countries of the world. Anna has excellent references from Mme. Lucienne. In Barabás's pocketbook are similar documents referring to shorter periods; these they produce several times every day.

It is not all smooth sailing. They set out upon their daily rounds, more and more wearily, concealing their growing depression from each other. But by the end of the second week Anna has found work.

"Not what we expected," she tells her father; "perhaps I ought not to have accepted it. I ought to have waited for something better. However, I can change later on."

Barabás nods. Being very much together, and very much alone, they sense each other's thoughts as if they were uttered aloud. Barabás knows that Anna accepted this first job offered to her because she did not want him to be discouraged. He can tell himself now: "Anna has succeeded, it is my turn now." And he can write to Paris: "Anna has got a job, I shall soon get one too."

A good girl, she is, Barabás thinks. And Anna says to herself:

"I am not being good. One must begin somewhere. It encourages me too if I can get a footing. If it cheers the others, all the better."

Anna certainly expected that her Paris references and her rank of forelady would call for more respect. Here they say "directrice"—queer that she has never heard the French word in Paris, and the applicant must be able to refer to a large circle of acquaintances and personal customers. Anna's position in her new place is somewhat uncertain: she has to cut, but she has to sew too. She has no definite title, but is often referred to as "our Parisian cutter"; her sphere of action is wide, but in surprisingly trifling matters she is not allowed to decide for herself. Her salary is comparatively small.

She often remembers Günther's criticism of the lack of order and organization in Paris. Now Anna misses the incoherent, yet balanced, instinctive and spontaneous discipline of the Paris shop. Here discipline is artificial, the air is full of tension, they all do their work more or less well, but they do not take it as a matter of course, and they are proud of their achievement beyond measure.

"Everybody here is a separate individual," she tells her father. "If something has to be done, it is not enough to say: this is necessary. Everyone must be personally handled, persuaded. In Paris girls are *women workers*, the ones here are like artists or dilettantes. The directrice rises above us to sublime heights, and it is inconceivable that one dare knock at the boss's door, as I did at Mme. Lucienne's."

"Democracy," Barabás grumbles, recalling Paris night debates. He is ill-humored because he has not found work. If only he could have got as far as Anna. He would not mind if the system were different, even if it were worse. Perhaps, after all, it isn't worse, only different. Anna in time will get drilled into it.

Anna is doing her best. What she has to learn is strange. Abroad—certainly at first—they held her in contempt, they looked down on her, because she was an alien, but the dignity of her profession and her pride as a worker were never involved. At home they do not despise her at all; on the contrary, she has some personal authority because she has lived in Paris. But her social position, her value within the human community, has suffered a loss. The esteem due her trade has decreased. In Paris she was Mlle. Anne from the start, Mlle. Anne to boss and customer alike. Here it is: "Look here, my girl." Anna does not feel hurt, she only thinks it strange.

She has lunch in a small restaurant near by. It is not worth her while to run home to Bethlen Street from the city, particularly because Barabás eats wherever he happens to be at noon. Anna glances into the newspapers during lunch, as she is alone. The other girls bring their lunch with them, and those who live only a short distance go home. Thus it happens, between the soup and meat courses, that István's name catches her eye. For half a second she feels a queer sort of apprehension: what has the wretch been up to again? Then she reads the article with growing amazement.

István has done nothing; István gives an interview. István is a producer, that means that István is making a picture, a Hungarian picture, and now declares himself unto the papers in enthusiastic phrases: he sings the praises of the scenario, the music, the director, and, above all, the actors. He also praises himself, which makes it likely that the interviewed István Weygand and Anna's István are identical.

"I shall prove that Hungarian films can compete with the world film production," István declares.

Anna reads the article again. Then she finishes her lunch rather absent-mindedly and goes out of the restaurant deep in thought. Suddenly she stops in front of a telephone booth. The great producer surely has a telephone. Anna turns the leaves of the book. How strange that she cannot handle it as deftly as the Paris directory . . . Here it is: István Weygand, Nürnberg Street. She will know in a minute whether it is the right one.

Five times the dial falls back into its place. Anna listens.

"Hallo!" says István's voice at the other end of the wire. It is unmistakably his. Anna's heart gives a throb.

"Hallo—this is Anna speaking . . . Anna Barabás from Paris."

"Who?" For half a second the voice is gruffly indifferent, then suddenly becomes all jubilation: "This is a wonderful surprise! Splendid! When did you come?"

"Two months ago."

"And you only tell me now? What a disgrace!"

"I just found out by chance . . ." Anna begins to explain.

István interrupts her:

"Of course, I want to see you . . . an old friend from Paris." He lowers his voice. There must be someone in the room, Anna thinks. "Wait a minute. I am engaged today, also tomorrow. Day after tomorrow I have a conference in a café. It will take about half an hour, and after that we can have a talk. Are you disengaged?"

"Certainly. Which café?"

István mentions a name. Anna has never heard of it. "Where is it?"

"You have been here two months and you don't know?" says István, horrified. "On the Körút of course, on the corner of Wesselényi Street. About half past nine or ten, will that do?"

"All right." Anna sighs. Half past nine or ten is a bit late. She does not want her father to know about the meeting with István, he probably still resents all the anxiety he had had on account of him. Never mind, she will explain it away.

She sets out before nine, this being a more plausible time for meeting a girl friend. In the café she does not see István, so she sits down, sips her coffee; she does not pick up a paper, and keeps looking toward the door. No, she is not specially excited as she waits for him. Those days are past. But she expects him kindly, almost with friendship, and she smiles at her own mood. When she loved him, she used to wait for him with hatred and apprehension.

At a quarter to ten, István arrives. He nods toward three tables, at the fourth he stops while his eyes search the room. He notices Anna, waves to her, and signals that he is coming at once. Anna feels she is blushing.

How long is it since she saw him last? Six years, or is it seven? István has not changed. Probably I have, all the more, Anna thinks with slight bitterness. She has done her best to look pretty. She has put on a trifle more make-up than usual, and has taken ages over her hair. But under my eyes, there are many wrinkles, she thinks. At that time, I had none.

"Here I am!" István sinks into the chair next to hers. "How do you do, Anna?"

"And the conference?" the old, severe Anna involuntarily asks.

"The conference?" István is at a loss for one second. Then he replies with all the more animation. "I put it off. I put it off for your sake, to be able to talk to you undisturbed. Well, let me have a look at you!"

Anna smiles. The conference must have been a fib. István only mentioned it because it sounded well.

"You are tired," István says, shaking his head. "I don't like your looks. Your eyes look tired, yet your eyes are the most beautiful thing about you."

"It's age, István," Anna laughs. Yes, the wrinkles, she says to herself. "Do tell me about yourself. I see you are a great man now."

István makes a modest gesture of denial.

"I am making my second picture. Of course, I do not finance it all by myself—not at present. In time I shall. An important group of capitalists back me. And I am married. Did you know?"

"I didn't, István."

"Four years." István takes out his pocketbook and shows the photographs with a young father's usual gesture. "My two little girls."

Anna looks at the photograph, but she cannot see it. Unaccountably her eyes grow dim.

"And this is their mother." István shows her the

other photograph. Incoherently yet with irrepressible pride, he adds:

"My father-in-law has a title."

"She is very pretty," says Anna.

"And you?" István leans toward her. "Are you married? No? How stubbornly you resisted that time . . . I wish I knew why? And since? I hope you have been faithful to me."

"Like a dog," smiles Anna.

"You are telling a lie, you cat. But we will make up for it, shall we?"

"We shall not, István."

"So you are still the same stubborn witch. What a pity. And yet you loved me, you horrid creature."

"I loved you. Now tell me how you come to be in pictures."

István stares at her in amazement.

"Don't you remember? I took up pictures in Paris, I was trained for the profession."

Anna reddens. Twice István acted in Joinville as an extra, yet his amazement sounds sincere and natural.

"Well then, tell me how you went about it at home."

István gladly tells his story; the rebuff does not affect him in the least. Perhaps he had not meant it seriously himself, had just made the offer because he did not want to hurt her feelings. Undoubtedly the story of his own career has more fascination for him. The words simply pour forth, figures flash up, large figures and big names. István is well acquainted with both.

"I do an enormous amount of work. Sometimes

sixteen hours a day. A tremendous responsibility, you know. Not only materially toward my financiers . . . but also morally. And in this business there are so many mountebanks! And to deal with actors! If you want to do honest work, you must spend your heart's blood. Good thing I can manage it. I am simply indefatigable. They all think I'm marvelous."

It amuses Anna that all he says might be true. There have been men who after a "youthful blunder" have never again departed from the proverbially "rugged" path of virtue. There have even been men who have really learnt to work afterward, though this has seldom happened.

István concludes his autobiography, and now he questions Anna about her doings.

"Have you all come home for good?"

"Only Father and I." Anna reports on family matters.

"Do you know," István says pensively when she has finished, "I think it would be better for you to stay abroad. In this country, you need imagination. Abroad you can make a living if you work; here you must have ideas."

They speak about the children. It obviously impresses István that Jani will be an engineer, Klári a doctor. He particularly praises Klári: "Mark my words! That child will get on in life!" More and more István's statements resemble the revelations of a prophet. It is now the turn of their Paris acquaintances.

"Is old Bardichinov still alive? Have you heard from the Hallays? And Cathrina? I liked her, silly old communistic parrot that she was, yet she had a wonderful disposition. And that sour Lithuanian, what was his name?"

Anna answers faithfully. The Parisian friends march past them—there is only one name they have not mentioned yet.

"You know," István begins quietly, as if in answer to Anna's thoughts, "I am very fond of my wife. She is a darling, warmhearted and affectionate. You have no idea what a serious, decent person she is. But there is only one woman I really loved . . . really and truly . . . you know what I mean . . . and that was the little Italian girl."

Anna's heart contracts, not much, only a little as if for an instant a human hand had pressed upon it.

"I think she never even noticed me," István continues slowly. "We may speak about it now. You are an old chum of mine, and you just told me you don't want me. I loved her. Is she still as beautiful?"

Anna nods slowly.

"Very beautiful."

"Tell me all about her, or, God knows, perhaps you had better not. I don't want to hear about it if she cared for someone else."

They have finished with the Paris acquaintances. The two have told each other the little about themselves which they deemed fit for communication. Now they sit mute, talk a little in jerks, without animation, then István gallantly pays for Anna's coffee, and hails a taxi. In Bethlen Street he takes leave with a brotherly kiss, and promises to ring her up at the shop soon. But he never turns up again.

XXIII

ANNA and her father have spent three months in Budapest. It is a Sunday afternoon, but they don't stir from the little room in Bethlen Street because early summer showers sweep the pavement outside. The weather is not fit for walking, and they have no other amusement. Barabás, it is true, might go to a wineshop in Nefelejts Street where he can always find some distant acquaintance, someone he used to know by sight, or one who heard his name from mutual friends (generally linked with some fantastic story of having made a large fortune in Paris, and therefore they look at him with some disappointment), but with these he does not find the true rest of conversation. Yet Barabás is a real Hungarian, politically-minded by tradition, and there was a time when he abused government and taxes with relish. Now he cannot merge into the atmosphere of the Budapest tavern. He has been torn away from the continual and eternal flow of public criticism, and he has nothing to say about state labor for the unemployed. Besides, his language and his mode of expression are transformed, his countrymen do not understand him, so he sits at home in the darkening

277

room and is gloomily bored. From the kitchen next door he hears the intensified Sunday clatter of his landlady. In Budapest people do not live in hotels, they live in furnished rooms. It is not easy to put up with this sort of life for one who has been used to greater independence.

Anna stands at the window and looks down upon the shower-scoured street. Then slowly she turns back toward the dark room. She cannot see her father's face, but his stoop betrays him.

"Father, I am going back to Paris."

Barabás starts. He cannot see his daughter's face either. Her figure is silhouetted against the lighter square of the window. It is motionless.

"You, Anna . . . you? But you have got a job . . ."

"Still, father . . ."

For my sake? Barabás ponders. Because I can't find work? Is she uttering the words I have been afraid to speak for months? Or is it on account of "Look here, my girl?" Evidently the girl cannot adapt herself to life here.

Strange nostalgia, this stubborn subterranean rumble, has not stopped, although they have come home. Perhaps it did, in the first three days, when they were strolling along the streets and said: "Look, this is Andrássy Street! And look at the buses! There were none when we left. Do you remember?"

Then, unaccountably, the rumble started again. What is it, for God's sake? They have come back; why does not the peace of home-coming enter their hearts? What are they missing still? Is it Mezötur?

Barabás reflects. Or something more remote, something out of the depths of childhood Kenderes?

Anna's thoughts do not brood on the names of places. Everybody here speaks Hungarian, that is very pleasant. It was strange at first. Anna turned around every minute to look at the passers-by, as she did in Paris, when she heard Hungarian conversation. Her name here is pronounced properly and not metamorphosed into French, and that's all right. Yet what else is there? They are cheerless, homeless, as though hemmed in by the dense loneliness of the Argentine.

"I am going back too," says Barabás. Anna foresaw this answer.

"We will get on somehow," she says comfortingly.

On the same day they write a letter. If Mrs. Barabás is disappointed, her answer does not betray it. She only asks them to visit relatives before leaving. This they do. The two days in Mezötur are a pleasant diversion, and Barabás again is tempted to stay. But at the bottom of his heart he knows that he cannot do it, he can't make a living here. It is only because the blossoming trees have seduced his heart.

"If I had brought plenty of money and opened a workshop of my own . . ." he begins to tell Anna, but he does not finish the sentence. "Even in that case . . ."

The train rolls along with them, the Swiss mountains are clear this time and haughtily brilliant. The snow sparkles, fir trees look up to the sky, the old, confused ache of her longing is reduced to a feeling that is little more than regret, a feeling that, though crippled, may yet be molded into words: to live as mountain peaks and trees live . . .

They have passed the French frontier. The train is rumbling through the night.

"It is not so bad for you," Barabás says. "You may come back. But I shall die out here."

"Nonsense, father."

"I know I am not old yet. Fifty-four is not old, not here. But at home, you see, I was considered old. When I thought I'd found a job, they were looking out for a younger man, even if he had not been to Paris, and, after all . . . fifty-four. How long will I be able to work? Let us reckon lavishly: fifteen years? Can I save enough to go home, buy a cottage and live without care?"

"Surely."

"Well . . . maybe. For that would be the only way to go home. Abroad, old people need not starve. They get a pension from their trade union . . ."

"And we, father? The three of us? Jani will have earned millions by then."

"May God grant it. You are good children, Anna, all of you, even that chit, Klári."

"I am not sure, father, whether she is not the best of the lot."

"I have thought so myself sometimes, but I cannot complain of any of you. I am not like other parents, I am not at all afraid of living on the charity of my children. We need each other abroad. But . . . only abroad, Anna!"

Anna meditates on this, for a little while. Barabás now ends the conversation.

"And that is why I believe I shall die out here."

In Paris, a few minor surprises await them. For example, Maura has disappeared. When they came back from South America, they found him here, and now, when they have arrived from Hungary, he is nowhere. Well, it appears that the conservatives were victorious in the Spanish elections, so Maura went home, but Alvarez did not come back to take his place. Incredible! Is there a country in the world where every citizen may reside at home at the same time?

They are inclined to forget France, where they live and where this is possible. They forget France because, although they live here, they compare everything with life at home, and at home such things cannot happen.

In short, Maura went home, and in all probability got his fortune back untouched, since he sent three thousand francs to Bardichinov and five thousand to Cathrina, and wrote them both touching letters about how good they had been to him. (Of course, no one as yet foresees that Maura will reappear in two years' time. Some countries are more assiduous, others less so. Spain is an extremely assiduous country. Maura, for that matter, is not going to reappear in the actual sense of the word, because he will have money, and will settle down in Biarritz.)

The other, more unpleasant surprise, is that Meneghetti is ill, not so seriously that he needs to go to a hospital, but he has such bad rheumatic pains that he can hardly walk. When he goes down to the bistro betweenwhiles, he takes two sticks and hobbles along like Cathrina.

As soon as Anna hears the news, she rushes across to Meneghetti. If Pia Monica were dying, she would not hurry like this.

"We arrived this morning, and here I am, M. Meneghetti. Does it hurt? What could we do to make it hurt less?"

The eyes in the thin, brown face are still smiling eloquently, but strange wrinkles have gathered round them.

"You take an interest in my illness, dear little friend. I am very grateful, you know that, don't you? Tell me all about your adventures at home, and, if possible, do tell me that life there is ugly and dismal, and that you could not find your way back . . . because that is our only consolation here."

Anna laughs confusedly.

"Well, M. Meneghetti, that is nearly . . . nearly true."

"Splendid! Tell me all about it! You see, you have already eased my sufferings."

"Well . . . I don't know whether that is so. Gradually I am getting to know us, M. Meneghetti. You will listen to my story, you will even nod assent and you will be shocked, and all the time you will think there isn't a word of truth in it and life is worth living only at home."

"How clever you little girls are. It's alarming! My own little girl too. She says: home is continuity. Therefore, it is indifferent, for the moment, whether she is here or there: no country really means home to her, but if we go on living here, perseveringly, then maybe, in time . . . the whole thing is a question of perseverance, she says."

Meneghetti groans, because he happened to move; then he smiles again. "I think we ought to have left you behind when we came abroad. Orphanages are not so bad. Many children of the same age and of the same kind . . . Can we make up for this, Mlle. Anne?"

Anna forgets time, and realizes it only when Pia comes. Is it possible that she and Meneghetti have been talking for two hours? No matter though, because she wanted to hear from Pia what was going on at the shop.

There is not much work now, because it is the dead season, but Anna knows that. About the new forelady? Pia has the impression that Mme. Lucienne is satisfied with her work, and that she is liked in the workshop. Still, Anna had better see madame, or should she, Pia, put in a word?

"Thank you, I shall go myself one day," Anna replies. God knows why she is so full of asperity again.

When she leaves, Pia accompanies her. They stop in the passage.

"Anne, I want to tell you something. You were leaving for good. I did not expect you to come back again. I deliberately tried to take your place this time. Will you take it as an excuse that I failed?"

Anna hesitates with her answer, only because she is examining her feelings and trying to decide how the news affects her.

"You need not apologize," she says slowly. "It is odd, Pia, but I somehow feel your debtor and I don't like the feeling . . . I am sorry you failed, and, as usual, I cannot understand it. It somehow goes against all rules."

"Well, life on the whole does, doesn't it?" says Pia with a shrug. "Perhaps, if I had had more time . . . well, I only wanted to confess my sin."

"You have full absolution." Anna laughs and hurries home. She would be insincere if she did not admit her pleasure at Günther's fidelity, yet she knows it is vanity more than anything. All the same in the end. She would be more pleased if Fedor had been faithful, but in the long run that does not matter either.

At night there is a festive dinner in honor of the home-comers. Bardichinov, Liiv, Cathrina and Günther are the guests. Liiv brings two bottles of champagne. Liiv thrives more from year to year; his salary increases: he would have moved into a flat or to a better hotel long ago, but he stays on for Bardichinov's sake. This, too, goes against all rules. Liiv used to be the clumsiest, the most incompetent of them all. As a bookbinder he was always covered with wounds and bruises. Once, realizing the aimlessness of life, he opened his veins. Then, in the hospital grounds, he chanced upon a man, not an all-powerful manager or a business potentate: the man Liiv got acquainted with was just a small official. He gave Liiv a recommendation as an insurance mathematician. This, to Anna, seemed a profession as unlikely as mallow gathering, and Liiv had already sent some money to Buenos Aires, he maintains Bardichinov almost entirely, and now provides champagne for dinner. Talk about rules!

As for the dinner, it is a great success. Everybody is cheerful and confident. The family is happy to be reunited. Klári moves about with the perfect grace of the French hostess and is full of attention; her intelligent, candid, slightly cold gray eyes sometimes shine with emotion. Jani also discards the moroseness that has descended upon him in recent years. He is the old, lovable Jani again. After dinner he lights his very first cigar from Bardichinov's case, and pleasantly suffers himself to be teased about the possible results. Anna lazily joins in the conversation, and dimly remembers there having been no gala dinner on their return from South America. True, they were without a sou then, had spent their little capital; they had just managed to get home by dint of starvation and by the children's feeble assistance. However, Anna thinks the gala dinner is a reward Mother grants them because they were well behaved this time, and none of them fell ill. Suddenly she laughs aloud, kisses her mother, no one guesses why, but Bardichinov rises tremblingly and proposes a toast to Mrs. Barabás. Penelope and Solveig are mentioned in the toast. Although these ladies are unknown to Mrs. Barabás, she blushes and a few tears trickle down her cheek.

Cathrina keeps maneuvering until Anna and Günther find themselves alone in a corner of the room.

"I could not forget you." The slow, virile voice, which Anna considers Günther's only asset, strikes a deep note.

Anna now commits the sexual treason even the best of women commits once in her life—if only once, she deserves a medal. She delivers up Pia Monica without a moment's hesitation.

"I hear Pia did her best to comfort you," she says wickedly.

The man's face closes hermetically.

"Pia Monica is a very nice girl," he replies stiffly, queerly.

"She is in love with you."

"I know."

"You know, do you?" Anna is genuinely astonished.

"I know, because she told me. Certainly I should never have noticed it, I am so stupid about such things. She begged me to try, perhaps I could care for her too."

So this is what Pia meant when she said she had tried to take Anna's place.

"Well, Günther?"

"I still love you."

"The whole thing is incomprehensible to me. I don't understand why you love me since Pia is so much more beautiful and entertaining, and then . . . May I speak candidly, Günther? I don't understand why Pia loves you."

"I can tell you. You, Anna, estimate superficial values: wit, glibness, spirited conversation; Pia Monica despises these cheap treasures."

Anna is silent. What she values is sparkling life and humor. Meneghetti has it and perhaps—she admits it grudgingly, perhaps Pia too. With Günther it is difficult even to talk about it.

"And why do you care for me? I seem to be on the lookout for the man who is my opposite . . . while you are satisfied with me, although I am much more of a bore than you."

"Are you? I must confess I never thought of either of us as a bore."

"Don't be angry, Günther. And don't answer. It was a stupid question, there are no regulations in these matters. I promise you one thing: I shall do my best. I have come back now, I shall stay here. I know how decent, serious and honest you are; I suppose it would be best for me."

Conversation ends thus encouragingly, and on the next day Anna sets out to find Fedor. She does not find him in his hotel, he is not staying there any more. He has returned to the place from which I lured him, Anna thinks, because it was cheaper and left him more money for drink. She goes to Fedor's favorite tavern; he is not there either. She asks the patron whether they are expecting him today.

"I couldn't tell you, mademoiselle. He seldom comes here now, he haunts Duclerq's bistro across the street."

"Thank you," Anna says and starts toward the door. Let us try Duclerq's bistro.

"Isn't mademoiselle Hungarian?" Someone suddenly stops in front of her. He wears a white apron, and is the new waiter of the tavern. He has grayish hair, his well-marked features seem vaguely familiar to Anna.

"Yes, I am."

"A Mlle. Barabas, aren't you? I called at your flat once, but I have seen you several times with . . . my manager."

"M. Hallay?" Anna cries out and then blushes, because he mentioned the István episode. But Hallay already speaks about something else.

"You recognized me, after all!" He smiles contentedly. "How are you all getting on?"

With half an eye he looks back at the patron. But the tavern is empty during early afternoon hours, there is nothing to do, the patron can scarcely object if the waiter exchanges a few words with an old acquaintance.

Anna sees the look and quickly comes to a decision. She has not seen Hallay since the short and memorable period of glory of the Hungarian night club, and she wants to hear what has happened to him since.

"I am thirsty," she says. "I want a glass of wine. We can talk between sips."

Hallay gratefully goes behind the counter, Anna leans upon the "zinc," the tin-plated bar.

"We have just come from Hungary," she tells him, "my father and I." Strange how she is able to speak lightly and naturally about everything, even about her meeting with István. Hallay is flabbergasted.

"Well, bless my heart! You don't say so! Who would ever have thought it!"

"He is married and has two children. His father-in-law has a title. He specially mentioned that." She can speak about István in this way now, so calmly and in a tone of slight mockery.

Hallay shakes his head.

"I had awful trouble at the time on account of him. When that check fraud business came out and he was arrested . . . they very nearly deported me with my son. Although I don't know, it might have been for the best. The night club has ruined me and maybe we should have got on better somewhere else."

Hallay is decidedly what you would call an interesting man. Even in his waiter's apron he looks well groomed and impressive. There is a certain assurance and elegance in his manner, even when he runs the kitchen towel along the zinc-plate. This is his alibi, meant to blind the patron.

"Of course, it is nonsense, I might have fared worse in another country, and yet Paris, I adore this city." Anna starts. This, to her, is an unusual declaration. "I love its inventive genius, its rough-and-ready truthfulness, its irreverence, its fraternizing with life and death. There is only one other city in the world: Budapest." (Anna smiles. This is more familiar, she thinks.) "One other city in the world that is as instinctively, as profoundly philosophic and has its tongue ever in its cheek."

"Do you really like living here, M. Hallay?"

"I do. In spite of everything, I love it. This is what I should like to teach my son, but youth is so bitter nowadays."

"What is your son doing?"

"He is a workman, poor fellow, doing any odd jobs. At home they would call him a 'hand.' He used to work at Renault's, now he has a job out on the Avenue Gourgaud, on some building. It is my fault. I did not make him study, but I had no money and took the matter easily. This is Paris, I said, here you learn as you live."

A proud, foolish, handsome man. A little depraved —Anna can very well imagine him playing vile conjuring tricks with the bills of drunken customers, yet he is very attractive. Anna gladly promises to return.

"I used to come here often with a friend of mine. I will bring him again."

From the door she smiles back at the waiter, who returns her a warm, chummy smile. That was a good talk.

Anna goes across to the bistro and luckily chances upon Fedor. Of course, his shirt is torn, but at Anna's appearance he breaks out in such jubilant yells that she is really moved.

"My lodgings?" he says later when he has calmed down. "At present I haven't got any. Just wait for two weeks, no, three, because I pawned my things too; by then I shall have regained our palatial apartment."

XXIV

JANI GETS HIS DEGREE. The family at lunch duly celebrates the occasion. In the afternoon he calls on Albertine.

"Well, that's that. Now for a job. Perhaps I shall get one without much difficulty. I could go to the colonies at once."

"Uncle Roger says he will take you on in his business any time."

"I know. We can get married now, if you like, Albertine."

The girl watches him attentively. Jani's eyes rove about, his face is indifferent.

"Is this the way they propose in your country, Jean?"

"In my country? We happen to be here now, in your house, in your country! Aren't you fed up with these eternal comparisons?"

"Don't be so irritable, Jean. I only wanted to mention that your voice rather lacked enthusiasm. Tell me, Jean, truthfully . . . if I did not exist, what would you do now?"

"I don't know."

"Would you go home to Hungary?"

"I don't know." Jani is reflecting. "I don't think so. My father and my sister have come back. The state of affairs over there is rather unfavorable. Why did you ask?"

Albertine answers slowly:

"My impresario is negotiating for a South American tour."

"Oh!"

"If it can be settled, I shall start in two or three weeks' time."

"That means no, Albertine?"

"No, Jean. You know deep down in your heart that it is better so."

"I know, perhaps. Yet it hurts."

"It hurts me more. . . . I love you, Jean."

They embrace and have a good cry. Jani asks halfheartedly:

"Shall we not try?"

"Since we could not become compatible in these five years . . . and yet, I never loved anyone else."

"Nor I, Albertine."

They sit about for a little while, very unhappy.

"I shall put in a word with Uncle Roger in any case," says Albertine.

"Don't. I shall find something else. Shall I see you again, Albertine?"

"If I go to South America, I will let you know. And you tell me if anything happens."

At the door they cling to each other for a last kiss. Then, finally, the door is closed.

Jani, at home, does not breathe a word. For a few

days he goes out on mysterious errands. One night he announces:

"Father, mother . . . I am going away. I have a position, but—it is far away, in French Congo."

In the terror-stricken silence you might have heard the wild beating of Mrs. Barabás's heart. Everybody stares at Jani, who, hurriedly and as though in torment, pours forth:

"Road building having been started on a large scale there, they are on the lookout for young engineers. It was posted up at the Ecole a month or two ago. Very good salary, double what one gets here. I have a three-year contract. . . . Félicien is coming too," he adds hopefully, as a mitigating circumstance.

Félicien has been Jani's fellow student all through college, and he had always meant to go to the colonies. Félicien knows how to blend the love of adventure and sober material calculation into perfect harmony. Exotic scenery and naked, singing negro girls allure him, but he is also allured by the large salary.

The Barabás family is not consoled by Félicien's companionship. They stare at Jani, petrified, and Barabás slowly, heavily, begins to question him:

"And . . . what about your marriage?"

Jani shakes his head.

"It won't come off."

"An engineer is a lucky fellow," Klári babbles dreamily. "He can go to strange continents, where even trees and animals are fantastic. His job is really international."

Jani clutches the life belt, but clumsily.

"Why? A doctor's profession is international too. You can go to the colonies when you are ready."

Klári silences him with flashing eyes.

"A feeble woman . . ." she says, prim and facetious.

But the joke comes too late. Mrs. Barabás has already burst into tears. She turns her face to the wall, sobs and abuses poor Albertine, who does not deserve it. Jani would like to explain, but he cannot get beyond a few inarticulate, choking sounds. Klári feels she can't be of any help here, and sneaks out of the room. Anna thinks the example worth following. She escapes to Meneghetti. Barabás stays a little while, tries to soothe his wife, and then realizes that it is best to leave mother and son alone. Perhaps Jani will be able to pour out his sorrow in peace and solitude, and they will comfort each other as best they can.

The few weeks left before Jani's departure are mournfully quiet. The family does not know that he sees Albertine nearly every day. The South American tour has been postponed. Becalmed and without hope, they love each other more than ever. Sometimes they are on the verge of upsetting everything and remaining in Paris. Yet all the time they know, at the bottom of their hearts, that they will not do it, that they will upset nothing.

The Barabás family see comparatively little of each other. Anna and her father are working—not quite in the manner and in the place they would have wished, but they are working. Barabás is employed in a suburban furrier's workshop, whose owner is a Pole. He does cheap work and uses cheap labor. Never mind, so long as it is a job.

Anna's situation is not much better. When she calls on Mme. Lucienne, the woman's nervous bird-face brightens:

"Tiens, Mlle. Anne! In Paris again? Have you come for models?"

Anna's face falls at the first sentence.

"It is very difficult, Mlle. Anne, very difficult. Your successor, Mme. Jeanne, works very reliably. And there are no complications. She is French. Not that I mind, but you know what customers are . . . I could not let you go near the fitting rooms. Wait a minute. Let me see what we can do. Perhaps I could let you have your old post, I mean the former one . . . as a seamstress. Not as if I needed anyone just now, but the season may soon revive; you were a good worker. At present I can't make a better offer—even that is rather above my capacity. Let us say the first of next month."

Anna accepts with thanks. She thinks she will work her way up again. She did it once before. But when she sees Mme. Jeanne's smiling face, her ever-lasting cheerfulness and imperturbable calm, doubts assail her. This is a different enemy from the hysterical Nicole. Never mind, so long as it is a job. Anna repeats to herself the words of her father.

Jani's train rolls out into the gloomy, sultry dust of a late summer evening. Although the family has had a remarkable amount of training in seeing each other off, yet never has such melancholy sadness descended upon them. Perhaps because never before has one of them gone away by himself.

Mutely they wander home, and after dinner they all vanish as if hunted. Lunch on the following day starts in dumb silence too, but between soup and meat Klári suddenly declares in a casual tone:

"I am engaged to be married. My fiancé is Raymond Mérel, a fellow student. He is coming tonight. I have asked him to dinner."

For one second everybody is struck dumb, then suddenly Klári is inundated by a babel of voices. For once even Anna loudly and impatiently clamors for details. Mrs. Barabás shrieks and gasps for breath. Barabás bangs on the table for silence.

"I have known him for a long time," Klári calmly informs them, "and we decided to marry long ago too . . . about six months ago. But I did not want to speak about it till Jani's affairs were settled in one way or the other."

Jani's name brings tears into Mrs. Barabás's eyes, but curiosity prevails.

"How old is he? What is he like?"

"He is two years older than I am, and just got his degree. You will see tonight what he is like."

Nothing more can be got out of Klári, although Barabás uses paternal authority.

"And if I won't let you marry such a youngster?"

"Alas, through the shortsightedness of French law, I am of age. But, father, I thought you would be glad to get rid of me?"

"When do you want to get married?"

"As soon as I have my degree. But if you don't

give me anything to eat, I shall be a desiccated mummy before then."

"Heavens!" Mrs. Barabás runs to fetch a dish.

All afternoon she is busy getting dinner ready. Cathrina helps with zeal to peel potatoes and shell peas. Anna, on her way from the shop, runs up to Günther and begs him not to come tonight.

"Dinner strictly en famille," she explains.

Günther mumbles something unintelligible and looks at Anna queerly.

Klári does not come home in the afternoon, so she cannot take part in the feverish preparations, though very likely she would not have done so even if she had been there. At seven she appears on the scene with a tall, broad-shouldered, sun-tanned boy, plain rather than handsome, one of his eyebrows wrily drawn up, which gives him a funny, sophisticated look. However, with his flashing, white, wolf's teeth, he is rather good to look at. Naturally he is confused, and therefore grins ecstatically.

"This is my family, Raymond," Klári says gravely. "Good, intelligent and honest people, and I want you to love them. It won't be easy, for they are of a different kind. Many things will occur which will affect you strangely; I can't tell you what, because they don't affect *me* strangely. You must always tell us, because we have to explain and you have to understand and get accustomed."

The family listens with surprise. They have never heard such a long speech from Klári—not such a serious one, at any rate. Raymond has long since stopped grinning. With calm and simple interest, he contemplates the old workman and his weary wife, who have drifted to his country from so far away.

Then in an amiable, harum-scarum way, yet self-consciously, in the conquering manner of the French, he goes up to them, kisses the old people and kisses Anna.

"We shall love each other," he declares with a winning smile, rather moved.

"Be good to my little girl," says Mrs. Barabás anxiously, thinking of her son.

"Welcome, my boy." Barabás squeezes his hand.

Klári stands unmoved amid the torrent of these mutual votes of confidence. Her face is grave.

"There is one more thing I want to say, Raymond," she continues when silence is re-established. "We have suffered no end of humiliation since we came out here . . . petty humiliations and grievous ones . . . like all foreigners. In a way you must make up for these too. I beg you to be patient. Never forget that we are homeless, and often have been very miserable here. You must be something like a liaison officer between us and your country."

Raymond is sincerely moved and solemnly promises to obey. Like most of his countrymen, he also has the gift of touching hearts with simple words. Mrs. Barabás is duly moved to tears, but Klári laughs at last.

"The end of my oration is a warning to you, Raymond," she says, sitting down. "I begged you before to be patient. Now I ask you not to overdo it. We often had quarrels in the past. We shall have quarrels in the future. That is the way two people get adjusted to each other. Fight with my family if you disapprove of things. That is the best way to become one of us. Deal with them as you would deal with your own people. Grumble if something doesn't suit you, but condone petty failings."

"Entendu!" cries Raymond. "Agreed! I shall be glad to fight if that is the price of being accepted. I am quarrelsome anyhow, unsociable," he declares, turning to the family. "A Corsican, you know. I draw a knife if she so much as dares to look at another man."

"That's Claire's concern," says Anna, smiling. "She has been intriguing against love; she looked down with contempt at everybody who fell in love, and now she has fallen for such a bloodthirsty fellow. With us, Raymond, you may fight to your heart's content. There Claire is right. It is the quickest way to get used to one another."

As for getting used to each other, Klári sees to that as thoroughly as she does all things. Raymond is bound in duty to dine at the Street of the Fishing Cat every other night. At first he tries to protest on the plea of lovely summer nights, but soon he discovers that kissing opportunities are ever so much more favorable in the Barabás home than on the Seine embankment. They cruelly leave Anna and Günther alone, and, on the pretext of study, they settle in the adjacent room. Besides, all things considered, the people he meets there, the family and their friends, are quite amusing. Raymond enjoys Cathrina as if she were some cabaret performer. He makes her talk, not a great feat in Cathrina's case, he chaffs her, and incites her to deliver one blaring propaganda lecture after the other. Sometimes Raymond visits the bistro with Klári, sits discreetly at the table and listens to Liiv's and Meneghetti's discussions. Bardichinov seldom puts in a word now; Bardichinov is old and slightly asthmatic, talking wearies him, and he often forgets what he was going to say. Raymond even tolerates Günther—he is an educated man, he says, only a little crazy.

Klári smiles, she knows that that is what Raymond thinks of them all at the back of his mind. Never mind, she tells herself. Far better than to be taken for a strange species of animal.

XXV

GÜNTHER HAS GONE. His departure is not un-expected; last summer he used to talk rather vaguely about an American offer. But now he has become a regularly appointed professor of a United States university; his ticket has come and some money also, and Günther once more proposes to Anna.

"You promised me, Anna, that you would try to care for me. I don't know whether you have suc-ceeded. I can offer you more now than I could a year ago. A more secure material basis, a more advantageous social position. I don't think it counts with you, I don't use it as an argument. I just men-tion it."

Anna reflects. Incidentally, material security and a solid social position do count, particularly if the earth is wont to quake under your feet and several times has hurled you out of your home, out of your position, from every place where you have been able to find a footing. It does count. On the other hand, she cannot see herself steering her course on into the new world at Günther's side, sharing his work and his life with him as his faithful wife. Günther is a good man, a sensible man, but a man

without a sense of humor. Life beside him would be
restful, but rather tiring.

"Can't I have my answer, Anna?"

"I don't know what to say, Günther. There are
so few things in life I cling to . . . only my family and
a few friends who have drifted here too, a frightened
little community . . . none of us can ever belong to
any other. I cannot abandon them, Günther."

"You would find new friends over there."

Anna slowly shakes her head.

"And you have been away twice, Anna, once in
South America and once in Hungary. You left
them then."

"I did. I can't account for it." She does not speak
the words that are on her lips: perhaps because I
went with my father. She does not say it, for now
she would be going with her husband. Anyhow,
what one says matters so little. It wouldn't be an
explanation. There is no explanation.

"I loved you very much, Anna. God bless you."

Günther is gone.

Months have passed, and now it is spring again.
Anna goes to the shop, she is one of the girls, subordi-
nate to the forelady and also to Mlle. Rose, the
head seamstress. Sometimes with the ghost of a
smile she remembers that she might be a professor's
wife in America. Once she speaks to Fedor about
it, but to her astonishment he is not at all indignant
at such levity.

"You were right," he says pensively. "You could
not have borne it anyway. We do not belong among
decent people any more." Suddenly he strikes an

attitude and shouts angrily: "And to make a marriage of convention! What a disgrace!"

"I had no moral scruples," Anna avows. "If I had
married him, I would have made him a good wife.
I did not refuse him because of my lofty ideals, only
because . . ."

"I know." It is good to be with Fedor, because
such things need not be explained, and it is good to
be with Meneghetti for the same reason.

"Yet America is said to be the great melting pot
which amalgamates all foreigners."

"It's said to be, but we know nothing about those
who were burnt to death."

Fedor orders another half liter, offers some to
Hallay, then they stroll across to the hotel. Hallay
takes away the glasses, and wipes the table. America is settled for good.

A mild spring rain is falling. Anna and Pia Monica
step out of the shop doorway at the same time.

"Shall we walk together?" Anna says civilly. Pia
Monica nods.

"If you have time, do; let's have a cup of coffee or
a vermouth somewhere. I should like to talk to you."

Anna draws up her eyebrows wonderingly. They
find a small café.

"I wanted to say good-bye to you," says Pia
Monica, when they sit down at the table.

"To say good-bye?"

"I am going away. I haven't told you . . . I have
been studying dancing these last months, not much,
just what is wanted in cheap variétés. A few numbers."

"But why, Pia?"

"I read in the Nansen report that there are ten thousand Russian girls employed in cabarets in South America. Emigrants, of course. Well, let there be an Italian girl too. They ought to have a bit of competition."

"Won't you tell me the reason, Pia?"

"I cannot go on living here. My post . . . how long can I keep it? Of late they let me show only mourning frocks. My beauty is still effective against a dark background. South America is less fastidious."

"And do you think it will be better to live there than here?"

"It won't be worse. I don't want to remain here, Anne. I am nervous, or call it what you like . . ."

"Günther?"

"Maybe. Also too many things have happened here, and too few. Our lives have pretty nearly run side by side, Anne. So I duly let you know that I'm stepping out of the row. I had an idea you, too, might feel relieved. I want to go to another continent where even the atmosphere is different. I would like to go away to another planet if I could."

"I hoped you would comfort Günther."

"Thank you. I have comforted him."

"What do you mean?" Anna starts.

"That is what happened. When you went to Hungary, I offered myself to him. Didn't I confess it to you when you came back?"

"You didn't tell me *that*."

"Maybe. But that is what happened."

"What happened is of no consequence. And what

you said isn't either. I have no rights whatever over Günther, only . . . I am surprised. Somehow I thought he was so honest."

"Among men, such things have nothing to do with honor."

"I was not thinking of your affair. That's all right. You said you offered yourself to him, and . . . I only wonder he didn't marry you before going to America. I wonder he did not take you along."

"He took an emotional farewell instead. For the last time . . . and he poured out his grief over your great cruelty."

"Aren't men funny, Pia? You remember István, don't you? Well, he always dreams of you. I met him when I was at home last year, and he wept on my shoulder. . . . I don't know why I didn't tell you before."

Pia smiles.

"I know. But we are not going to argue about that now. Thank you, at any rate, for the feeling that prompted you to tell me now."

"I am against your emigrating, and I particularly dislike South America."

"Don't look at me so severely, Anne. I know your virtuous mind now fears I shall become a 'bad woman.' That's not quite certain. Not so compulsory in my new profession as many people assume. Very likely I shall live all alone over there too. I am used to it. And if not, it would not matter either."

"My virtuous mind, you say. Well, this is what *I* won't argue about. But what about your father?"

"That is the second problem I wanted to talk over

with you. Curious, how fond you two are of each other—curious only because you and I were never able to warm up. You will stand by my father, won't you?"

"Don't you think it is rather heartless, leaving him behind?"

"Do I make him happy? And he has no idea that we are probably saying good-bye forever."

"Forever."

"Perhaps, Anne. Let us pay and go now."

In the métro they mutely cling to the straps, side by side. Then mutely they walk along the Rue de la Huchette. Before the hotel Pia stretches out her hand. Anna holds it fast.

"Pia, if I thought that my love, my friendship, might have made life easier for you . . ."

"Probably not much. Au revoir, Anne. I am not going until a week from today."

Anna does not turn into the Street of the Fishing Cat, she goes for a walk in the lazy, lukewarm rain. She is not thinking of Pia. She is thinking of them all. Here they are, living side by side, a lot of useless lives . . . sometimes one of them gets torn away. Jani, too, has fled to a strange continent. Klári—perhaps with Klári things will be different; saplings can be transplanted only at a certain age, later they do not take root. Maybe Klári was lucky, maybe it was the right moment for her. Klári was seven then, Jani nine. Maybe two years make a difference, maybe even two weeks. Who knows? These are intricate problems. István went home; he found his way home. His sojourn here was shorter, four or five years in all. Who can say how long is the span of time that is past retrieving?

A lot of useless lives, Anna thinks: Liiv's, too, is useless in spite of his good situation, and so is poor old Bardichinov's. When he was ill and in a delirium, he presided at a meeting in his bank. Useless lives.

Good thing they have no continuity, Anna thinks with a smile. In emigration no children are born. Her mind quickly runs along the string of more distant acquaintances: no, the homeless do not give birth to children. Pia might have had children, and she, Anna, too. Pia is going to South America, and she, Anna, will become an old maid, or maybe not. She might find a comrade. But Günther could never have been her comrade—because Günther has never really surrendered to homelessness. Now she understands. That is why Günther could not be a brother, but Fedor is one. Or Meneghetti, who will be very lonely now, or Hallay. Meneghetti and Hallay are much older, but they need a woman more than Fedor does. And what does age matter? She will be a companion to one of them, and help him bear loneliness.

Klári? Several times she has broken her engagement with Raymond and then made it up again. Every time they start anew, they are wiser and more resigned. Klári is shrewd and, for her, astonishingly, unbelievably yielding. She divines how difficult it is to link your fate with that of a foreigner.

Klári may have children. She came abroad at the right time.

And the others? Jani in the Congo jungles; Pia

Monica in South American dives; they, the others, in the Street of the Fishing Cat, and in little hotels in Paris and all over the world. Very likely this is always the proportion. Very likely this always was the proportion among those who were cast adrift; the exiles, the emigrants. And so it will remain forever. One or two put up their tents on foreign soil; the others? They slowly vanish and leave no trace.